A Well Full of Leaves

of Leaves

A story of happiness

BY ELIZABETH MYERS

"... ready to be anything, in the ecstasy of being ever ..."
"URN-BURIAL" (Sir Thomas Browne)

Aspal Classics

Published in Great Britain in 2022 by Aspal Classics

an imprint of Aspal Press Limited

1 Quality Court, Chancery Lane, London WC2A 1HR

Originally published in Great Britain in 1943

A catalogue record for this book is available from the British Library

ISBN 978-1-9162895-9-8

Printed in Great Britain by Clays Ltd, Elcograf S.p.A

www.aspalpress.uk

Introduction

ELIZABETH MYERS died in 1947 at the tragically early age of thirty-four. By the time of her death she had three successful novels to her name. This book, her first, was published during the war in 1943 to considerable acclaim.

The Well Full of Leaves begins with the childhood of the heroine Laura and her three siblings in a dysfunctional family somewhere in the North of England. In spite of the dire circumstances in which she is brought up, Laura's enthusiasm for life enable her to experience the 'singing and the gold' not only in nature but in the most mundane of her surroundings. At the heart of the novel is the relationship between Laura and her brother Steve which evokes that between Cathy and Heathcliff in Wuthering Heights and even the 'dybbuk' of Jewish folklore as so powerfully portrayed in the 1930s play of that name by Semyon Ansky.

Myers' second book, *The Basilisk of St James*, which came out in 1945, demonstrates an astonishing depth of knowledge of its subject, Jonathan Swift, and both his literary and political significance. The third, *Mrs Christopher*, was published after the war in 1946 and inter alia ponders the nature of good and evil. While the author's Christian faith and depth of literary knowledge shines through the text, they are applied with a light touch and never to the detriment of the narrative flow. In 1951 *Mrs Christopher* was made into a film called *Blackmailed,* starring Dirk Bogarde.

Chapter I

"The childhood shews the man, as morning shews the day."
JOHN MILTON

ONE afternoon in the summer holidays of 1920, four children were standing in a northern park—arguing.

It was like this: visits to the park were not easily come by, and we were trying to hit off a way of getting the most out of the precious afternoon.

The park must have been a shabby little place; it had lost all its springtime freshness, and the grass and trees looked as though they had been steeped in lemonade; as for the flower-beds, anxious not to seem bold, they had limited themselves to little events of sparse antirrhinums—the colour of liver. For all that, we thought the park a wonderful place.

Anda, who was the eldest, nearly sixteen, wished instantly to go to the refreshment place where the boys, as well she knew, would stare their hearts out at her personal glory. For she was absolutely unforgettable. She had only to appear anywhere and she stopped thought and conversation. She had that kind of beauty which gives some people a pang of sorrow, sorrow biting deep that they could not take this

1

perfection into their keeping. Her tawny hair was shoulder length, straight and heavy. Her skin was palest brown with a faint rose-stain in her cheeks; from this face her violet-coloured eyes beamed back on the world, humorous and starry. So there she was, lovely, exacting, and frowning now with her wishes for the afternoon.

Anda (her proper name was Miranda) meant to have her own way. Not only this afternoon, but always. Perhaps she would have to do something spectacular to achieve it: very well, then, she would be spectacular. Perhaps she would have to commit a crime or make a sacrifice to get what she really wanted. But in that case her wants could wilt. She never desired anything so badly that she would suffer for it. Ambitious she was, but indolent and cautious, too.

Our brother Robert wanted us to go and look at the Roman pots and coins in the pocket-handkerchief of a museum which stood slap in the middle of the park. This preference was in keeping with his deep affection for all old things—the weapons of prehistoric men, rocks, old battle-grounds, wych-elms, old books, old musical instruments, old prints. He also had a strong attachment to things typically English—Queen Anne houses, Chaucer and Shakespeare, the quads of Oxford and Cambridge. He would have given half his life to be a scholar at Oxford or Cambridge. He had, besides, a powerful loyalty to English institutions fast disappearing such as blacksmiths, Morris dancing, millers, beaver hats, chop-houses, skittles, milkmaids, and street-cries. Robert was fourteen, and the only one among us who went to work each day.

My little brother Steve indicated that it would give him the most pleasure if he could just go and see what it was like in the girls' lavatory before which we were standing.

"What a stunt!" I said. But Anda did not see this so lightly.

"Oh," she screamed, affrighted and disgusted at the little boy's candid choice, "how *can* you, you little monster! Oh, what a revolting disclosure!"

"Take it easy," I said. "He means nothing. It's just his idea of the unknown, so it fascinates him. What about you and I last year peeping into the 'Gentlemen Only' in High Street for the very same reason. Simply to see what was hidden from us! Monster nothing!"

I turned to him.

"Well, just the same, you can't go in the girls' place. You'll get us locked up! Nothing special there, anyway. Choose somewhere else."

"But," he grumbled, "I'm old enough to go and see inside there, I'm eleven! Well, I know where I want to go, instead. It's where the park joins the cemetery. We can climb up the steep bank there and maybe we shall find a coffin sticking out, or an old bone or two bursting from the soil."

"That boy is mad!" said Anda.

"Where he wants to go is no more idiotic than where you want to go," said Robert. He turned to me.

"What's your idea, Laura? Where do you want to go?"

I wanted to go where no one ever went, which was a wild and weedy tract behind the lavatories.

Robert, who was always fair, who loved his family and wished to dictate to them for their own good, then said we should go and spend a short time at every person's favourite spot, beginning with mine since we were arguing right in front of it, and ending with the refreshment-place where he, Robert, being on his one week's summer holiday with extra pay, intended to treat us with lemonade.

3

Now the immediate charm of that dank wild glade of my choice was that, apart from the joining of park and buryingground where Steve had decided to go, it was the only *lonely* place in the park.

There was a mysterious emerald haze under the immense close-growing trees, a twilight pierced at intervals by thick shafts of dusty sunlight, silver and strange. Elms grew there to make you think of witches, and alders, and perhaps a stream flowed underground for some willows stood in a meandering line—willows love water. Their branches poured with greygreen leaves descending in a herring-bone design that made the trees look like poles covered with down-falling tweed. And that year, a little oak tree was making a fluttering debut in the glade with three tiers of branches!

Many of the trees were stuck about with brilliant eddies of fungus, and little companies of large flat toadstools on thick sturdy stalks marched exuberantly in the shade, the colour of brimstone and iodine. In places where the rain never penetrated, fallen leaves, acorns and beech nuts appeared to have gone through a process of dry-curing.

There was every variety of grass, cocksfoot and rye and totter grass, lovely and pleasant, and sown thick with shellaced buttercups.

Dim red butterflies hurried to and fro, and you could see a wild bee or two emerging tipsily from the blossom of one tousled little lime tree, late in flowering.

It was very silent. The sparrows did not care for the dark green exclusiveness of this glade, and had gone to make a commotion beside the pond. Only an occasional blackbird ripped the silence with piercing sweet notes loitering on like bells in a person's hair.

I stood entranced before all these riches, unable to do anything but look about and listen.

Occult sighs and air came from the stalks below and the boughs above, and sometimes the grass, for no accountable reason at all, would be taken with a quiet slow-attacking ague.

"Isn't it eerie!" broke from Anda. "Oh, I hate it here! What can you see to like here, Laura? Why is this your favourite spot?"

"There is more to be seen here than you can see," I answered.

"Pshaw!" she exclaimed. "But it's easy to see that you're only thirteen, choosing an awful place like this!"

"Thirteen is not a bad age to be!" I said.

Thirteen is *not* a bad age to be. You have got over the shock of hearing about sex. You have even come to see the decent fittingness of it, the dignity, the sublime outlet for tenderness. And yet, and yet, you know that nothing will ever quite take the place of the world that has gone, the world that suddenly receded when you got knowledge and so lost wisdom.

And if you are lucky-young as I was, you grasp then the shape of the battle to come. You see that the fight will not be for power or riches, beauty or learning, or a long procession of lovers. You see that it is *to find the way back* to being a little child again.

Aye! You've got to grow up to become as a child again. You've got to learn by unlearning: you've got to imagine, not to *know!*

But now I moved forward into my little paradise of a dell, and began touching the leathery mounds of leaves, and rocking the buttercups. I held my breath to see jolly crimson beetles rollicking wildly among the damp roots, winged seeds floating on the wind, pigeons' dropped feathers, and the bizarre small skeletons of mice and birds.

A kind of cosmic shorthand was written everywhere for those to decipher who would, resplendent in forgotten dew-drops, in sunstarts and wing-gleamings; in the tapestry of the rhododendrons with their strong reek; in the rustlings of rats and worms and an estrayent toad from the pond; in rain stains and drippings; in the lawless grass; in the withered bluebells that had flowed in sapphire thousands under the trees in the springtime; in the crimped and fluted leaves; in the aromatic smell of the tansies; in queer blights on tree-trunks; in cobwebs swinging between branches; in a lone fleshy marigold; in twigs and dust and moss and stones. All these things gave off messages going deeper than life.

Anda stood with her back to a tree, steadfastly refusing the spirit of the place. Robert said he couldn't make up his mind whether he got from it the atmosphere of the fen, the spinney, or the country cave, but he finally allowed that it spoke to him of all three.

Steve said nothing, but followed me about where I peered and pried and with inhuman joy *became* whatever I looked at. I was a blob of cuckoo-spit; a writhing spray of ivy; a very pungent smell of dockweed; a willow-leaf frizzling in the wind. I burrowed, I flew. I was beside myself. I could have stayed there for ever.

What has been broken lies in pieces. The pieces fly everywhere. The kingdom that has been shattered can be picked up, piece by piece, everywhere. The success of a life lies in the number of recaptured fragments. A few lucky people go on looking for pieces till they have found them— every one. Just how long it shall take is a matter not for the parson or the philosopher to determine, but depends upon a person's own inclination and the porousness of a person's heart.

In that glade I never failed to find something of the stormed citadel, something of the Absolute, though I didn't call it so then, and it all wasn't so clearly aware to my mind. All I knew was my own joyful affection for the *livingness* both of sentient and inanimate things. Every clump of grass, every chirper on the wing replied to my heart. The personality of a stick and a stone were more thrilling to me than the personality of a man or a woman.

"Oh, do let us get on," wailed Anda, clasping her hands in despairing boredom.

"Wait, can't you?" bawled Steve, who hated her.

Robert, who was busy trying to light his first Woodbine, was too engrossed to add his weight to either side. Steve stood enthralled, watching his elder brother's attempts at manliness.

"Does our mother know?" Steve asked.

"No, she doesn't. And don't you go and blab," said Robert, lifting his absorbed face to glare down at the little boy.

"I might, and I might not," replied Steve, moving out of Robert's reach.

Anda stepped forward, and gazed at Robert in a way to wither him.

"Draw in, silly," she said at last, "don't blow!" Anda was not famous for her tact.

Robert tried anew, but he seemed to be unable to grasp the simple principle of smoking.

"Here, give it to me," cried Anda, impatiently. She snatched the cigarette out of his mouth, took the matches from him, and in a second had the cigarette going.

"See what you do?" she said, contemptuously, handing the glowing cigarette back to him.

"Have you been smoking all the time, then?" Robert asked interestedly between laborious puffs—but now he had got the trick.

"How much longer are we going to stay here?" she fairly screamed at him by way of answer.

"We're going in a minute," said Robert, determined to continue this new delight for a few minutes longer. "I say," he continued, "you do get up to some tricks at that school of yours!"

Since she was eleven, Anda had been going to the town's art school, where she was learning textile designing. She was there on a scholarship, of course; it was the only way our family ever got beyond the Board School. For two years I had been at a High School myself through the same avenue.

"Yes," replied Anda, complacently; "we get education there, all right."

Steve strolled nearer to them.

"Education," he drawled. "You don't need education, you were born knowing! You don't go to school for education, you go there like you go everywhere else, to prance and patter to an audience!"

She dealt him a stinging slap across the head which, coming unexpectedly and he being small, knocked him off his feet.

At the sight of him struck down, I was so violently agitated I couldn't collect my wits sufficiently even to go and help him to his feet. He scrambled up instantly, without the least attempt at retaliation. He stood, arms straight at his sides, kicking at a tuft of grass with his shoe, and looking down with rigid eyes.

To escape the angry pitying thoughts that had come to me, I felt the need to do something so, sitting back on my heels, I began to pick up handfuls of a mysterious deposit of silver sand at the bole of a tree, letting the glittering stuff speed through my fingers, and trying in the touch and the look of it to forget what I had seen—and forgetting in that heavenly diffused sensation that comes when you allow yourself to pour into the element you are contemplating. And the exquisite feel of the sliding sand linked up with many another memory—the particular look of some dandelions I had had in an empty potted-meat jar—their private gold—the moss creeping between the cracks of the paving stones in the backyard at home: these things were ever so many little admittances to a plane where sorrow and anger melted right away.

I was recalled by the hollow notes of a bird. I looked up into the tree-tops and I went off on a little spree of imagining how this glade would be in the grey stillness of a Christmas afternoon, in that hour just before tea when friends and relations are hurrying to the houses of their kin, their faces flushed with the cold and the prospect of gay warm rooms out of the quiet icy streets. I was picturing my glade when *all that* was going on, my glade shut out from *all that*, given over to the iron frost and the oncoming sparkling stars. I saw something sinister about its disposition, about those lonely trees carbonized against a grey sky, in comparison with the lighted gold globes in cheerful rooms and the especial jollity going on in homes. I shuddered to think of the glade's unseen *tenants* at that time, its utter desertion, its implacable continuity.

It was then that my little brother crept up to me, nudging me sharply with his elbow and whispering bitterly:

"She hit me, she hit me—I fell down—and all *you* can do is to run your fingers through this sand!"

"Are you hurt?" I asked, searching his intent face to try and find out what was going on in his mind.

"Yes, I am," he replied at once. "But not where you think!"

"Where, then?"

"If you don't know and can't guess, I shall not tell you," he retorted proudly.

I was looking down: on his shapeless shoe was a lump of ochre-coloured clay and caught up in its glistening moistness was a single bright green chip of grass. This gave me extra ordinary pleasure to see; and somehow, I don't know why, seemed packed with the hint that beyond these hurts and grievances and all that we did in our days, there was *something else* besides, close, unknown, exciting, and surely nothing could be more of an achievement than to respond to this something whenever we became aware of it, as I did now in the lump of clay.

Steve's clothes, like all our clothes, were poor and graceless but he, like Anda, was a glory to see. His fine narrow head was covered with cool gold hair, and his black eyebrows almost met at the top of his nose in two wonderfully correct and slender lines. The structure of his face went sharply back from the top of his cheeks to his startlingly light blue eyes fringed with heavy dark lashes, and looking out so strangely and insolently under those imperious brows. His nose, which was long and straight with delicate up-flaring nostrils, could insinuate anything. The skin of his hands and face was like a silver ribbon drawn over his bones—all this, and a moist furled mouth, darkly red, like a halved carnation, made up a beauty of a rare, thrilling, and sophisticated order; it had nothing childlike about it. In fact, right from the start, there was little that was childlike in my brother Steve.

From his and Anda's outrageous beauty, I have seen people turn with positive relief to Robert's pleasant homely mug and my own nondescript face. One of Robert's eyes was fixed in a shining parrot stare: it seemed to be ringed with quicksilver and gave his face an odd searching awareness. He now having had enough of his cigarette made a move towards the museum, our next place of call.

A museum is as good as anywhere else for excitement. When we arrived the sun was streaming through the windows like a wry clear wine, turning the glass of the cases into sheets of blinding crystal. The waxed floors stretched endlessly on like gold ice. The disciplined enamel and glass and polished oak seemed to expand and rejoice in the light, becoming twice their normal selves. It was all a shining decorum, like an undertaker's office. I began to have a feeling of unease. It seemed that the centuries'-dead people from whose dwellingplaces and tombs had been lifted these coins. and vases and shards and gems, these broad Tudor shoes, daggers from the bronze age, and Renaissance rings, were hovering and bridling beside their goods, goods made so dear by the familiarity of use, and so subject to outrage and misunderstanding under our askance eyes.

For my part, I did not care to be long under the scrutiny of the anxious dead, while Anda was restive because there was no one whom she could strike lunatic with the wonder of herself except two busts of the worst of the Roman emperors in blinding white stone.

Steve was amusing himself by trying to rap out a toccata on the pipes of the radiator with a twig, till pounced on by the janitor who angrily asked him where his respect was.

"Respect for what?" asked Steve mildly, looking up unaffrighted into the working red face with its marmalade whiskers.

As this rather cornered the janitor he did the only thing left to him in his defeat he turned us all out of the museum, to Robert's great chagrin, for he had been engrossed before a collection of musical instruments popular in the time of Henry IV.

"That's the worst of bringing infants out!" said Robert disgustedly as we emerged into the park again.

"So you brought some out, did you?" asked Steve, interestedly.

"Would you like me to throw you into the pond?" Robert said to him. "You're out for mischief—you always are. You'll come to no good—you impudent brat!"

On the whole Robert was a tenderhearted boy, only given to moments of asperity when things went a-cross with him.

As soon as Robert began to get really angry, Steve hurried to my side, grinning sardonically while his brother scolded on and on, turning every once in a while to send a heartbroken look back to the museum and its collection of Henry IV musical instruments.

"Never mind, Robbie," I said at last, for I felt that we had had quite enough about it; "when we get home I promise I'll read you the whole, well, three-quarters anyway, of Shakespeare's 'Henry IV'—you'll get a marvellous atmosphere of the period from that."

"Yes, yes," said Steve, dreamily, "and don't forget the bit about the carriers and 'They will allow us ne'er a jordan ...' That's good, that is. That's atmosphere!"

We arrived then at Steve's place. The little boy rushed

towards his chosen spot and, having squeezed himself through a gap in the railings, began to hoist himself feverishly up the steep grassy slope which was topped by an unarguable thicket of hawthorn and holly, beyond which could be seen the sandy paths of the cemetery winding into the shade.

We followed more slowly and presently joined our youngest brother in the snail-crawling gloom under the thicket.

But Steve had chosen a bad picketing that day. He had selected a place and time when the occult was ready for battle with the living. We hadn't been there so long before extreme unease settled upon every one of us. Some passionate and criminal imagination seemed to be standing off on the upper air, emanating from the graves of the malevolent dead.

Even Robert's honest face grew troubled.

"You girls," he shouted suddenly, "*come on!*"

And we turned and fled downwards, crashing between the sprawling roots and tussocks of coarse grass, landing breathlessly at the bottom of the slope, with Steve behind us shrieking:

"We've not had enough time in my place, you cheats, you mean beggars!"

"Right," panted Robert," Will you go back again—alone—and shall we wait for you here?"

"No, I won't," answered Steve promptly, "though I will if Laura comes with me."

"Laura isn't going to go with you, nor anyone else," said Robert. "We just got away in time."

"Got away from what?" stammered Anda, who was trembling with terror.

"I—don't—know," said Robert, wiping his face on his handkerchief. "But it was—something: something awful!"

We were glad to move off at a brisk walk to the refreshment-place, while Steve, in the happy prospect of being treated with lemonade, forgot his sense of being ill-used.

Anda also recovered in the thought of undoubted forthcoming admiration, and Robert said he thought of attempting a second Woodbine over the drinks.

The refreshment-place was like an aquarium; it was a bulging rondure built of glass, and everywhere you looked trembling leaves were to be seen nodding against the glass. The light that filtered into the place through the tall shrubs and evergreens planted round it, was like the shifting, wavering light under the calm sea on a sunny day when you swim under the waves with your eyes open. All this, with the glass vats holding the sea-green gallons of lemonade completed the illusion of sitting at the bottom of an underwater retreat.

Anda, Steve and I thumped ourselves down at an irontopped table, gazing with pride and gratitude at our benefactor who was bargaining at the counter for our glasses of refreshment. The nymph of the place, a somewhat battered-looking but very independent cross-eyed young woman, filled four glasses to the brim so that it would be impossible to carry one of them without spilling some of the precious contents. We three took this as a personal affront to the Valley family, but Robert hadn't noticed it yet. He was standing staring into his purse in that faintly anxious way where money was concerned; his expression seemed to say: God, perhaps there will not be enough to pay for what has been ordered!

I have seen Robert, when a well-to-do man with twenty pounds in his pocket, sitting in a taxi with a look of guilt and anxiety watching with despairing eyes. the meter moving to a maximum two-shillings fare.

But probably in that fourteenth year of his the fact that his first job was a junior clerk's and he was in charge of a fivepounds-a-week float of petty cash, added to his feelings of responsibility where money was concerned.

Besides, he was not a very good or a very accurate clerk, and complete honesty made him an easy victim not only to a brutally competitive world but also to his own scruples. His marble-faced, warm-hearted young Jew of an employer had twice written to our father suggesting that a little more application to the rudiments of arithmetic at home in the evenings and a little less conning of "The Decline and Fall of the Roman Empire," would greatly facilitate the lad's climb to the top of the commercial ladder.

But Robert had no heart for the commercial ladder. He only wanted to sit and read and write about the Athens of Herodotus, the jurisprudence of Justinian, and Alexander mingling Greek and Persian blood. Robert had a terrible grudge against figures because when he was ten he had failed in a scholarship chiefly on the arithmetic paper, so he had had to continue at the Board School till the age of fourteen without the chance. of pursuing his heart's interests further, except within his own limited means.

Now he came to our table carrying two of the drinks and spilling only a few drops which rolled the dust up into beads that went racing like discoloured mercury about the dirty floor.

Having deposited the drinks on the table, his next action was to slap Steve across the face for presuming to lay his hands on a glass before either of his sisters were served.

"Where are your manners, you young dog?" asked Robert, scandalized.

"He hasn't got any," said Anda. She sat and spread her hair to the sun—it became her mightily. She was accepting complacently the looks of passionate interest sent across to her by a solitary young man at a neighbouring table. All the time she queened it; if people, and they were in the majority, of course, refused to treat her like a queen, she so vehemently saw herself in this role in her thoughts, that she was able to turn even insults into the semblance of dark twisted homage.

"Oh, leave Steve alone," I said to her. "You never leave that boy alone. No wonder he's such an imp to deal with—he never gets a chance!"

"His sort shouldn't get chances," said Anda, calmly. "They should be kept down and down. You heard what our mother said—if he doesn't improve he's going to be sent to a Reform School."

Steve grinned at her in pure hate, but the eyes he turned to me were stretched wide with anxiety.

"But he isn't going to a Reform School," I said. "Can't you tell yet when our mother means a thing and when she is only threatening! Steve is not going to a Reform School, but I should say that you would be packed off to one tomorrow if our mother were to see that old-world way of yours right now in full exhibition!" And I turned to have a look at the excited face of the young man she was coolly ogling.

"What do you mean by that?" she asked me, angrily.

"You know you needn't ask," I said. Steve grimaced at me with joy.

Robert now sat down with us, and we drank his health in lemonade.

I couldn't help shuddering with pleasure as the greeny drink went down. It was like taking in all the park, swallowing the landscape, the bottle-green shrubs nid-nodding at the glass walls, the dell. I drank into myself the magic dell. I had given myself up to the full private glee of this pursuit when I became aware that my brother Steve had begun to give a little account of his last day at school before the summer holidays. He had now left this elementary school for good, having won a scholarship into the town's grammar school where his first term would be beginning in the coming September. Steve was bragging dreamily:

"The Headmaster said: 'Stephen Valley, I've never had in my school such a boy as you! You ought to go far—*if* folk handle you properly.' That's what he said—'*if* folk handle you properly! Go in for foreign languages, my boy, for you're a wizard at them. Look at the progress you've made here with your French!'"

"Isn't that rather nonsense" Robert broke in with weary superiority. "Elementary schoolboys don't do French."

"Yes, that's well known," allowed Steve with calm importance, "but, you see, clever, I and the other four best boys in the school were doing French with the Headmaster—private!"

"And, no doubt," sneered Anda, "the Headmaster was also coaching you in his own little jobs so that you could take charge of the entire school within the next few months—private, of course!"

Robert yawned loudly.

"Anyway," remarked Anda to Steve, "we've heard quite enough about you and your dazzling cleverness. Shut up!"

"No, go on with what you were saying," I invited him.

"Take no notice. You should let him have his say," I told Anda.

"But he's always boasting," she cried, angrily.

"Well, so are you," I retorted. "We all do our share."

"I don't boast," she said, indignantly.

"You never do anything else," I said. "Look at you now, sitting there and boasting of your good looks for all you are worth to that young man opposite."

She crimsoned.

"I've never said a word," she cried.

"You don't have to," put in Robert, coming over to my side. "You know damn' well what Laura meant. I'm just wondering how far you intend going with those nasty silly looks of yours! I'm just asking myself if I shouldn't get right up and go and thump that young lout on the jaw!"

"He'd make quick mincemeat of you," said Anda, near to tears of rage. "Oh, how mean you all are. Nobody tries to understand me."

"We understand you very well, we understand you too much," said Robert. "Aren't you going to finish your story, Steve?" he placatingly asked his younger brother.

But Steve would not continue. Between them they had doused him. He sat there, violent and askance, playing hunch with his shoulders. He had wished to shine. They had not let him. It is very important that people should be allowed to shine sometimes. If they are not allowed to do so in their own right, they will dare to shine as criminals or lunatics—a brief magnesium flare—instead of the good steady glow denied them—and then, the blinding dark.

Steve, somehow, was not led in any fashion to make the most of himself in his childhood, and there came a day when we would have been glad if we had let him. There came a time when we could have taken a train or a ship to the world's end, and could not have been taken to Steve. And we would have been glad to go and scratch up his bones out of the earth, crying over and over: "Here we are. Come to us. Do come to us!"

As it was, this little boy was made desperate by neglect, and the main reason for this would, perhaps, come under the heading of Economics. What happened was that Anda, Robert, and I had all been born within a year of each other. This was considered rather too exuberant of us by our parents who were very poor persons.

After three such hasty brats they decided that they had done their duty by Church and State, and having arranged all this to their satisfaction, what was their chagrin when Steve unexpectedly gave all evidence of coming to town.

This is the sort of thing to sour people who have decided vehemently on a set and altogether different course. Our parents, and our mother in particular, never forgave Steve. They could not get over what he had done to them just as, in his turn, he never got over what they did to him. Our parents resented him all the days of their lives, our father mildly, our mother ferociously. The wonderful good looks that the little boy brought with him as some kind of compensation for his innocent appearance in a world that didn't want him, were received by them with all coldness; his traits and even his qualities were decried. He went unloved, this urchin who needed so much love and was destined to have so little—so little of the right sort.

All at once the light in the lemonade room began to falter and change. The sun had gone in. The breeze died, the leaves hung limply like dead fish against the glass walls and roof. The day turned cindrous. It would rain very soon.

Robert, noticing this, said in his cautious way, that we had better get home before the shower began.

We went out into the park. The wind suddenly revived and began to hum, a low wind, no higher than our knees, and a pulsing diamond light glared down through rifts in the enormous mountains of cloud rolling solemnly across the sky. The grass cowered away into the earth; other children were streaming home. It had ceased to be a day of sunshine and frolic.

I began to think about going home. The home we were going back to was in one of the meanest streets of the town, but as I thought of the kitchen that was pell-mell with memories of all the little daily mortal events that had taken place there—preparing food (Oh, how dramatically beautiful is a colander full of sprats, slivers of aluminium with blood-ringed eyes), plunging hands in flour, pouring boiling water on tea, sitting down to steaming dishes, rising with pleasant bellies, reading, painting (the delicious smell of children's paint-boxes!), struggling with homework, throwing down on the table the bright kings and queens of playing-cards, lighting the singing gas that would throw its bright bald light on the little shabby sticks of furniture: as I thought about all these things, the kitchen suddenly caught magic and power, and its dearness overwhelmed me. It was home, the den, the nest, the place that was ours, that was us, whose spirit was easy and familiar and known, in a vast world that was uneasy, foreign, and unknown. I couldn't get back to it quickly enough.

I hoped, as we waited for the tram, that the darkening summer day would cause our mother to light the fire. There is something especially poignant about a fire in the summer. Knowing itself to be strictly unseasonable, it lights up shyly, unsure of its welcome, but as the twilight darkens and a cold wind flings the rain against the window, as eyes turn gratefully to the hearth, the little fire glows with a deep, joyful glow, its many little gold hands fly exuberantly up the chimney, and then the little summer fire comes into its own; then it demands that you shall stop what you are doing and admire it, commune with it for a little while.

Now we were on the top of the tram, careering wildly down the dreary hills of the town to the hollow where we lived.

Since we had boarded the tram the conductor, who was young and handsome, simply ignored every other passenger and remained with us till we alighted, unable to take his eyes away from Anda and Steve.

"The little boy, as well!" he muttered in amazement, as one exquisite face followed the other aboard the tram.

Poorly clothed as they were, and neither of them as clean as they might be, withal these two had a jewelled air about them. The conductor thought so very emphatically, indeed. He very willingly allowed Steve to make the most offensive personal remarks to him concerning his uniform, his row of tickets, his job, and his general prospects in life. This teasing, wicked as it was, nevertheless gave the young fellow a splendid opportunity to loll against the seats and give his eyes and heart up to a contemplation of beauty the like of which he had never seen before.

He kept looking at Anda very wistfully, as if unable to believe the evidence of his senses, and into his tired young face came an excitement and a gratification as though some face he had only known in his dreams had at last materialized before him; not for him to own, he did not aspire to that, but to remember—always. For the effect of such beauty on a cheerful unambitious person as he was, unthinkingly following his fate, asking nothing but that immediate needs should be satisfied, was stunningly to open out to him prospects of a world in which he would never have a place; to outline his poverty and insignificance, and drive home how all his poor art was to trundle up and down the stairs of a tram issuing tickets.

And then he looked at her ragged clothes. Why, his sisters were twice as well dressed! For, in truth, we were a ramshackle family. Perhaps, after all, this girl was of his world. Perhaps such prizes could come his way. Perhaps it was possible for men like him to win as much charm and grace and beauty as were gathered here. Thinking this, it was like all his lifetime in our ten minutes on the tram. Or so it seemed to me who had been steadily looking at him for clues as to what this encounter was doing to him.

Steve also had been watching him through laughing half-shut eyes. And Robert had been watching him, wondering if he should say something to restore the dignity of the family against that arrant staring.

The tram came to the place where we had to get off. Anda went down first. Steve last; as the little boy passed the entranced young man, he gave him a push in the chest.

"Don't upset yourself," said Steve, conceited and fly. "She's only going to marry an earl! Nothing less! But never mind. She will grow old, like everybody else, and ugly, and come to die like a duck in the market. I *know*! I'm an old man cut down!"

We plunged into the straggle of mean streets lying off the high road. Down past ugly small houses where people were sitting on the doorsteps looking out at the life of the streets or arguing or repeating jokes and politics; children greedily buying sweet lumps of ice-cream at a barrow; a coalman groaning at his horse; a cat playing with the gas steaming up from a manhole; little foul factories for making soap and pencils and screws; a small power-station where the dynamos were keening; pieces of waste land under layers of tin cans and brick—till we came to our own street.

It looked as though it was a street without any lyricism at all. It consisted of two long rows of dismal little houses looking at each other in varying moods according to whether they were scooped into the golden maw of the sun, metamorphosed by moonlight, had all their poverty increased in a merciless downpour of rain, or became romantic forms transmuted by an overlay of snow. The long length of the street was halved by a railway bridge. If passenger trains had had their "magic comings and goings" upon its track, this would have been something to see, for a passenger train is bearing people away to the brilliant unknown. Even a short journey from the heart of the town to the suburbs, through back-gardens where the lilac grows and beans are blowing like little red rags on their sticks, can be Homeric. But all that rumbled over our railway bridge were goods trains carrying freight, and even that was masked from view in dour covered wagons. That was our traffic—angry, clanking, unpardonable.

Under the white-tiled arch of the railway bridge some pigeons had their innocent greedy life, larky birds who had no alarm from the outrageous clamour of the freight trains, but industriously added their own contribution to the din, for their throaty squabbling was amplified by the echo into a nightmare roar.

Almost every time I turned into our street, I couldn't help thinking to myself how different it would have been if only the corporation had been happy enough to plant trees down the pavements; then all the street's complexion would have been changed. In the spring I used to picture how it would have been if the elegant hanging gold of a little laburnum, say, had been there for all to look at, and the thought of it and the longing for it were sometimes more than a person could bear. We should all have been different, we should all have been better and consoled for the sight of one little tree. "But trees are wanted, and ought to be wished for, almost everywhere, especially amidst the hard brick and mortar of towns."

Good town councillors, good dull men, at their meetings discussing gruel for paupers and grey stuff dresses for orphans in institutions, would be serving humanity a sight better if they would plant a few trees on the streets of the town. The first batch, no doubt, would be uprooted wholesale by nonunderstanding mischievous brats, but the second lot of trees wouldn't all go because the people would remember how the street had looked when trees were there. This would be a stunt worth while.

So then—ours was any big-town street, mean and grubby, in which a magpie collection of lives were uproariously lived, devoted to grog, a dim soaked idea of Our Father Who art in Heaven, or maybe somewhere else, betting slips taken on the corner, the mysteries of sex worked out in the entries between the backyards cynically overlooked by chemises pegged on the clothes-lines, the raucous ventilation of woe, and the tired flogging of lost causes.

Its decorative motif was a fleur-de-lys of fish-heads on a backcloth of dust and dung, with the Byzantine blue of the sky beyond the dirty chimney-pots. Its music was a symphony of cat-moans, enormous crashes of sound from the trains, street-brawls, and the rain on the roof. Its incense was the reek of beer, fish and chips, nasty smells from the houses, and a wind that rarely brought rumours of the hedgerow and the wild wood.

Old men in cloth caps sat on the doorsteps in the sun, mildly enjoying the curious vapours that came from their own carcasses, and they groped in their memories, thinking how once they had been Somebodies but now were brought down to rheumy eyes and uncertainties about food and shelter—fallen and lonely. Ignominious old women scratched and moped among the ruins of food on tables everlastingly spread for a meal, the jam never taken from its jar or the condensed milk from its tuppenny tin. Young women who had long ago ceased to care for anything, especially themselves, leant their arms on, the door-posts and gave the eye to passing men. Bald-headed babies in high bassinettes held forth in a nidnodding occult world of their own, a world more beautiful than all beauty, more sane than reason, having no need of words or learning or morals. And there were cross, unwanted old mothers, their out-of-work sons, urban and tough; whippets, heroic adolescents, grave drunkards, draggled little birds in cages, some lovers, corpses often—lying in state on the sitting-room table; catastrophic children full of vim; a number of drearily puritanical people, and a criminal or two for leavening.

The voices leaped, the hearts sank. The contrasts were violent—scoundrelism and saintliness—the paltry and the pied.

The street affected every member of our family in a different way. Anda and Steve detested it. Robert accepted it. Our father loved it because, wretched as it was, it was home. Our mother liked it because only in such a place could she have been looked upon as a superior type—as was the case; "a stuck-up sour bitch" the neighbours called her. As for me, I was so buoyed up by the pleasure of being alive at all that the absence of elegance and the presence only of shambling sordid circumstances, were facts I scarcely noticed. And then, knowing nothing better, there were no means of making fretful comparisons. Besides, I was beginning to see that it isn't what you get that matters—it's what you *receive*. I was beginning to see that with enough fire and insinuation, there's as much that is provoking and memorable in the mud as in the moon, no less of life's romance in the white stars of broken egg-shells in the gutter than in the stars flying about the night sky like divine white bees.

In the street we once had a chorus-girl, very thin, with a lime-white face and glossy black hair—reported to do a side-line in whoring. When the people in our street pronounced this word "whore," for sweet economy's sake they used all that was provided and sounded the "w" as well.

But our whore ever afterwards seemed quite special and set apart in her calling first by reason of being a whore against other girls being whores, and second by the drama of her death.

This girl, in time taken off from her two professions, had been a great friend of my brother, Steve. From the time of her coming to live in the street, he had found something wonderfully fascinating about her—her air of unusual contacts, her sorry beauty, her gaiety. Steve had already formed the eerie habit of thinking, and this merry, engaging prostitute provided for him a release for romance, no less because he had a subtle intuition of there being something of disorder in her ways. Her appearance, though tarnishing somewhat, was seductive as ever was. She gave off that poise coming to women who have been timelessly successful with men. She was a kindly, unfinicking person, tolerant and drowsy.

To each other, she and Steve had confided many a sordid secret in her sitting-room where there had been lots of things for lying on at your ease: spilling boxes of cachous; piles of bright magazines; cigarette-holders of tinted glass; stunning clothes flung about; a gramophone that belched stirring music at any selected moment; a stalky cat named Rosie; vases pell-mell with wax flowers. Everything slap-up and amazing—as Steve had concluded in describing to me these appointments of the lady's living-room.

She had given him presents of toys and confectionery, and he had brazenly lied about their source to our questioning parents. She had also often given him free tickets for the tenth-rate shows in which she had appeared. In this way it came about that from quite an early age he had some association with the theatre.

Her name had been Joy Considine.

"Some joy!" said the street. But she had been a character, all right, with any amount of pithy observation. I once heard her say to Steve at leave-taking:

"You're getting too much woe for a little 'un! Your time of life should be nothing but cuckoo-clocks and drinks of sarsaperilla! You keep off the telegraph wires till you know how to keep your balance, see, then you'll come home safely at the last! But, there, what's the use of talking! You're a little fire just beginning, and soon I'll be an old one burning out. What went on to my fire won't go on to yours. You'll go your own road, same as me, an' same as everybody else. Them that has to be broken will be broken. Let's hope the smash won't be a big 'un!"

And the end of it all was she was burnt to death through falling into a tired doze and setting the bed alight with the cigarette she had been smoking.

When Steve heard this appalling news he blinked and said nothing, but in the evening of that day he asked me to go for a walk in the streets with him. After a long silence, he said:

"Laura, would it … would it have hurt her?"

"No," I said instantly, hoping this was true. "The smoke, you know, the smoke would make her unconscious before … before the fire … before she would feel it."

After another interval, he brought out:

"She said once—it was the time the outdoor-beer-licence woman was getting buried—she said: 'Death isn't death unless you want it to be! It's going home—see—to those who never had a home! It only comes death to moneyed people. Naturally! Leaving all their stuff behind. Toffs like them!' Oh, Laura, she was good and nice. I loved her better than anyone but you. She used to smell of *horse!*"

Passing the next gas-lamp, I saw tears spirting from his eyes. He caught my look.

"You needn't think I'm crying," he sobbed. "I'm …I'm only *thinking!*"

He thought about it for weeks: indeed, I'm sure he thought about it all his life. That loss had been a great one for, just as our mother used to make him feel how unspeakably insignificant he was, never failed to make incandescent the staggering handicaps of his thwarted life, so had his unusual friend restored him, and her love had consoled him. But Miss Considine being dead and gone and his haven with her, his sensitivity and ignorance, his struggles to fit into a scheme of things utterly uncongenial to him, were left to our mother's mercy alone. From then on she had no obstacle in ramming home to her little boy that he was bad-minded, cruel and heartless. He began to believe this, to be troubled by it; indeed, in time, he was so haunted by our mother's suggestions that he *became them*.

Well, on that darkened summer afternoon we arrived at the door of our house (the cleanest in the street) in a sirocco of derisive hoots from some children swinging on a lamp-post. We were not admired in the street. Anda and Steve were too good-looking for the well-being of the other children. Besides, they were both considered haughty and anti-social. So they were.

As for Robert and me, they thought we were dotty because we loved reading. In the street reading books was thought to be a horrible waste of time. Both our parents thought so, too; they thought it was a sin. With the grimmest virtue our mother used to say that she had never read a book in her life. This was very painfully obvious, but from earliest times and natural inclination, Robert and I learnt to make a low bow to a book.

Of course, our father had not much time for reading because he was always "studying". This was the term our parents applied to his intense concentration on the chances of the runners in the horse-races. He was "studying" when he was reverently though usually inaccurately blue-pencilling likely winners in the sporting columns of the newspapers. It was about his "studies" that he furtively took himself into bookmakers' parlours, and spoke with the touts on the street corners. He was "studying" when he came home blind drunk as the result of himself and a rank outsider being of the same mind: we never knew anyone with such a flair for backing losers as our father.

None of us had a key to the front door. We had to thump on the knocker and wait, and while waiting I darted some affectionate looks across to a little shop on the corner. On the window in white enamel letters were these words: "Violin and Mandolin Strings Sold Here," and it was surprising how much magic those words held for me, not because of their gist, but because from earliest times I had looked at them every day, and the thoughts I had been thinking and the feelings I had had were packed away in those white enamel letters, jolting me, jogging me, prodding me, and throwing me head first back into little secret forgotten happinesses. As I had stared at "Violin and Mandolin Strings Sold Here," the words had stolen from me my sensations of that time, and they carried for me any number of wordless undertones and overtones, curious intimations of a life-feeling *that went beyond life.*

So now I savoured what they had determined to throw off for me just then, and felt sustained to meet our mother who came to open the door for us in that angry way in which she did everything. As soon as we were in the passage there came to our nostrils the whiff of frying cheese and bacon; we knew then that we had stumbled in upon one of those exceeding rare occasions when our father had been fortunate with his "studying."

We seldom had cooked eatables for tea, and not every day for midday dinner. It cannot be stated that we ever knew the out-and-out drama of sheer starvation. We hovered on its brink fortified by the dull rickety fencing of perpetual bread and butter.

But on this evening it seemed that a regular little feast was being prepared, and we hurried down the lobby that led into kitchen living-room to see what we were to have.

Apart from the exciting preparations going on in the scullery where the stove was, tomatoes had appeared on the table, and lettuce and a seed-cake; there was also a big glass bowl of sliced cucumbers and onions in vinegar.

"Good," said Steve, his eye beaming at this; "I love cucumber—it tastes like washing!"

Our father was sitting under the window reading the evening paper. He put it down when we rushed into the room, and smiled at us with an expression which seemed to say:

"I know I'm not much, but sometimes, not very often, I admit, but sometimes I do bring it off. This is one of the sometimes."

"Hello," he greeted us, quietly.

"Hello, father," we answered.

Instantly our mother said:

"Now leave your father alone. He's had a busy day. He's tired. He doesn't want to be listening to your rubbish!"

"Nobody ever seems able to treat anybody else like a friendly human being in this house," said Anda.

"That'll be enough of that," said our mother in a voice of finality.

As always, she was seething. She was running in and out of the scullery with plates and pots and the kettle. She had an overall on over that puce dress of hers with the panels of glittering black beads. This was her best dress. Something of proud event had evidently taken place.

Our father was in his usual everyday navy-blue suit, and his shabby champagne-coloured boots with uppers of cream-coloured velour; he had bought them second-hand at a stall in the market. He was, as always, a remarkable sight to see. He was a man at whom people stared without end. They stared as though he were a unicorn, a phoenix—something stunningly heraldic.

Without doubt there was knock-down drama in his face. He had a brilliant magenta birthmark on his left cheek, the spread beginning right under his sparkling azure eye, and looping violently back like a stage curtain to the lobe of his ear. His hair, which was black, was cut in a fringe on his forehead. He was tall and excruciatingly thin. He seemed as though he had been boned. He seemed as though, when he stood up, he would break into halves at any second, so tottery he was, so uncertain-seeming, his tallness being too much for his thinness.

He was a silent, stoked-up man, with a character that people, and our mother in particular, declared was weak. This is easy to say, but who can know for sure. What could be said was that he was often afraid of life, often bewildered, and completely under the tyranny of our mother. Perhaps he had not a great deal of strength in hiding his weakness. Perhaps that's what *strength* really means—the capacity a person has for hiding his weaknesses.

Several combinations of implacable facts gave our father a conviction, often tearfully voiced, that life was too much for him. There was his private feeling about his personal appearance—the offensive remarks this often occasioned: there was his failure to hold down steady employment; there was the fact of his four children growing up without those things he would dearly have liked to provide for them; and, worst of all, there was his inability to cope with his volcanic, unloving wife. He knew his place: he was *le mari de madame*. She never let a day go by without reminding him of this. It all came out in the frequent rows, and when he was drunk.

He did not understand his children, either—or any

children—and he treated us with a pitiful kind of jocularity that set our nerves on edge. We felt only his brutal lack of taste, his unease before us, his curious, almost old-maid's amaze at the thought of consanguinity between himself and such ruthless, poised brats as we were. We were, of course, not reflecting enough in those days, to discover, understand, and sympathize with the sources of his nervousness and various disorders. Steve, with the utmost impartiality, once said of him:

"If we were all goods in a store, our father would be in the cheap remnants tray."

The elder two, who felt that this was apt, could not, however, allow their junior to carry off such an observation, and Robert asked the little boy just where he thought that he, Steve, would have a place in this store.

"I never thought about it," Steve replied. "But, no doubt, I'd be something rather special in the fine art and luxuries department—and just as useless as father in the cheap remnants!"

Our father had been out of regular work for years. He was not very strong, and if ever he did manage to get himself engaged for a job, he usually broke down after the first fortnight. He used to knock up a pound or so a week by working as a barman every night in a big public house. To augment this totally inadequate revenue he did his "studying"; and our mother dusted the pictures and bijouterie in an art dealer's shop from nine till noon from Monday to Friday. The art dealer was her brother Fred who had, according to our mother, turned out the most success in the world. Certainly she never forgot to hold him up to our father as an example of what mortal man can do if he "only uses his brains."

Now, too, Robert was helping a little with the house-keeping, having got his job in the office.

On this evening of our father's triumph, or rather, the triumph of the horse he had fancied, he felt giddy enough to want us to applaud and admire him, so swaggeringly, he said:

"And what have you little dossers been doing this afternoon while your daddy has been earning some money for you?"

But Anda could not allow him to have even this pitiful feeling of achievement. Throwing herself down on our broken sofa, she said:

"Your darling children have been airing their beautiful rags in the park, drinking treats of tuppenny lemonade, and wishing that their daddy would earn some money for them a little more frequently, Oh, haven't they just!"

He gave her an angry wounded look. He saw that he had said the wrong thing in an attempt to ingratiate himself with us, in an attempt to be thought a dependable man, an amusing sport. He knew that he had done wrong, but his look indicated that there was no need at all for Anda to have been so painfully direct. Our mother drove furiously into the scene, and said to Anda in her exceedingly acid way:

"Those that want the best had better be the best! You hold your tongue and get in the scullery with those filthy hands! Get them into water, quick; at the same time, pull up your drawers, they'll drop off you in a minute."

Having successfully brought Anda low, she turned on me. She had borne me a grudge all day from a little incident of the morning:

In our backyard some moss had begun to creep between the paving-flags. Thrilled, I had knelt down to look at it.

"What are you up to, Laura?" our mother called through

the scullery window, looking up from her explosive scrubbing brush.

"Oh," I said, "do let us ask the landlord to allow us to take up three or four of the flags so that I can make a little garden here! It would be a tremendous success!"

"Come in this minute and clean the stove!" she ordered. "There's no time in this house for rubbish like that!"

Remembering this with her dreadful concentration on everything that she imagined was an attempt to take some territory away from her, she now said:

"You're another who's got wants above your station. Get along to the cake-shop and buy six tuppenny custards."

She threw a shilling down on the table, and I ran out of the house. I always enjoyed going to make our rare purchases at the cake-shop. They specialized in custard tarts, and as you went up to the counter there was a crescent-shaped carpet that once had been smart but now all its carpet consistency had been squelched out of it by years of impatient feet, and what it seemed to represent as you stood upon it was a kind of metamorphosis, soft, marshy, and discoloured, of the creamy yellow custard in the tarts you were buying, a quite unimportant notion, but it added zest to the buying, for me.

When I returned we sat down at the table, and powerfully attacked this gala tea provided for us out of the blue by a nag who had run like the wind on a race-track in the distant country. In the steam from the brown teapot I saw those four long innocent legs pelting along to provide an extra-special tea for a hand-to-mouth family, the like of ourselves.

Steve had built up a little mountain of toasted cheese on his plate, and round this he was urging a ribbon of bacon with his fork. I could see the idea. The bacon was a coppery dragon swirling round the yellow cheese hill. At any moment, the dragon would make a sudden swoop and demolish the mountain, or perhaps it was the other way round, and the mountain would fall on the dragon. But our mother gave him a slap with her knuckly hand that knocked the fork to the floor. She was always cross to us.

"Don't mess about!" she bawled at him. "Get it down you! I don't buy good food for you to play with. Eat it."

He retrieved his fork, running his tongue down its tines in pursuit of lingering savoury morsels, and looking at her in a way that made me see clearly that children are not childish in their hearts.

Well, well, I thought, people ought to try and understand their own children, they ought to make things easier for them instead of adding to their muddles. Many children must be ruined for all time by their doting or demonic parents. Many children must hate their parents! Beatrice Cenci even boiled her papa in a cauldron. This, of course, is an old-time method of dealing with parents and rather one-sided at that! You cannot argue from a cauldron!

But it isn't everyone who has a mother like ours. She was a specialist whose specialities never touched the kind, the gentle, or the constructive. She was at her best when she was toppling the entire scene. All her dislike of us and the world in general was extended into whatever she was doing. Under her hands soap suds were angry, clothes sneered, steam menaced, crockery raved.

She was small and energetic. She did everything as though she were being scorched into the act. It was terrible if she did anything for you—buttoned your dress at the back where you could not reach, or if you were ill and she had to wash you or comb your hair. She came at you, and she did things to you, like an executioner, not like a mild good-natured mother such as, in the nature of things, children are led to expect. Not one of us had ever had a tender word from her. The older we grew the further we moved away from her and she was surprised and deeply indignant that her own ruttish world held no charms for her children.

On her best days she was waspish, on her worst she was murderous. It would be completely idle to say that her perpetual bad temper hid a heart of gold. She used all her energy in dusting her brother's pictures and keeping herself constantly in a rage. She had nothing at all left over for mere kindness.

She was managing and catastrophic and glum. As far as her treatment of my brother Steve went, there ought to have been some outside interference. His limbs were often impatterned with brilliant bruises from her physical cruelty. The other bruises done to his mind in her most ill-natured and rapacious hours were not seen until they had become the *actions* of his later life.

Our mother was sandy in colour, and by reason of dragging her thin frizzy hair up the sides of her head and harpooning it triumphantly in a sort of toadstool at the top of her cranium, she always seemed as though she had just been scalped.

Her face never lost that swept blotched look a person gets following a burst of tears; it was suffused and convulsive, and swollen about the eyes. Yet she never cried. She left that to others—she irresistibly made them.

Even when she was asleep she looked ready to erupt at any moment. She loved the sound of her own voice. She was always telling us how lucky we were that there were not twelve of us. She held a sort of threat over us that in case we did not behave ourselves, this dreadful twelve might yet materialize; she did this until it would have been absurd and impossible to carry out such a threat any longer.

Perhaps her worst day was washing day. Then she rushed round the kitchen like a yelping fox, though, of course, every day with her was what our father called "a hell and blazes day."

The mangle we had was, I am sure, notoriously responsible for her unusually evil temper on washing days. It was not a jolly small modern mangle with rubber rollers to ease labour. Just the contrary. It stood high and huge like a telescoped railway engine. It was a brooding, great article, sinister, even elemental. Like our mother, it positively yearned to do you an injury. The only difference was that our mother did do you the injury. The mangle couldn't if you were careful with it. And you certainly had to be careful. It wasn't at all interested in wringing clothes. It simply waited with joyful concentration ready to mangle your fingers, or fall on you, or lurch alarmingly, or drop some of its heavy parts on to your toes.

Our mother was fond of some things. She liked nougat, and she liked glasses of stout into which a red-hot poker had been plunged. But even so, she never ate the nougat or drank the stout as though enjoying these things. She gulped her pleasures down, then looked round in an offended way as though trying to hide the guilt she felt at having tried to enjoy herself.

No matter what she was doing she always wore long green glass ear-rings: these made a wild jigging accompaniment to her effervescing moods. She was stupefyingly ignorant and just as astoundingly sure of herself. Our next-door neighbour, an honest washerwoman, used to say:

"Your Ma's ignorance is only matched by her flaming arrogance!"

She was a terrifying yet a sad creature; how walled-in she was, how yearning more than anything for security in a world where the only thing that can be secured is insecurity. She had nothing, chiefly because she gave nothing. Her little world of hullaballoo had never been consonant with any real or mental vitality. She saw almost everything as unseemly, or nonsensical and ignominious. It seemed to her that all the world had just trodden in a mess. She found it shameful, askance, wanting.

It seemed that after our splendid tea, as the tailpiece of the treat, we were to go to the cinema, to be tenderly conducted there by our mother. Our father would not be going, as in his capacity as potman in the tavern, he went on duty at seven in the evening until closing-time.

We were all delighted at the prospect of going to the pictures. The right pictures were sops to our different dreams. For the modest sum of ninepence you bought admission into a place gloriously dark, with very bad statues of terrific heroes and the more virtuous of the Greek goddesses holding aloft frosted glass torches, which burned with a refined ecclesiastical kind of strawberry-coloured light between the films: you had a plush seat entirely to yourself, and before your pleased eyes the most terrific events jolted across the screen.

"Oh, shall we go to the Playhouse cinema?" Steve asked our mother with great anxiety. "They've got a glorious film there—'The House by the Fens'—with four murders and one suicide! Do let us go there!"

"You funny little carcase," our father laughed at him, "you don't want to go filling your head with stuff like that!"

But it turned out that Steve was not going with us, after all.

"It'll be too late for him to be up," said our mother. She looked at him spitefully. He was mopping up the grease on his plate with a crust. His fingers dug into the bread. He did not look up.

"Amn't I going then?" he asked softly, eyes on his plate.

"No, you're not," she replied, crushing and final. "You know your bedtime—eight o'clock sharp. We shan't get out of the pictures till past ten. Too late for the likes of you."

Our father picked up the plate of custards and thrust the tempting confectionery under Steve's nose.

"Here," he said, uncomfortably, "have a custard."

"Hoo, I don't want one," said Steve, brightly. "You must be making a mistake, father, offering the custards to me! For one thing, I'm not hungry now, and for another, if I took one it would upset our mother so much it would spoil the films for her. I should hate that! She works so hard, she is so kind and good to us, I am sure she deserves all the pleasure she can get!"

"Well, you little whelp!" began our mother at his poor little attempt at sarcasm. But he turned upon her and said:

"What's the matter? *Aren't* you kind and good to us? Have I exaggerated, perhaps?"

She, in a trapped kind of way, stared at him furiously, and before she could marshal her resources, our father turned his brilliantly-blighted face to her:

"Now, see what you've done!" he said. "It never was my intention to stop him from the treat. That's your idea. You're so damned anxious to keep him down that you overreach yourself, and he talks to you in as ugly a way as I ever heard from a child. That's no way to speak to your mother," he said to the little boy, "tell her you're sorry, then maybe you can go along with them."

"What's the use of apologizing," said Steve, "if you're not sorry? That's rot, isn't it? I'm not sorry for what I said. I'm treated unfairly, I turn nasty, and what are you surprised for? But I know what's the matter. I'm only eleven years old, that's what's the matter. Well, I won't always be eleven! Some day I shall be able to go to the cinema every night, and not with a crew like these!"

He included us all in a scornful sweep of his eyes.

"Even if I'd gone," he continued, slipping from his chair and going to the door that led to the lobby where the stairs were, "they wouldn't have let me enjoy it—well, Laura would have. But the others 'ud have made me sit in the seat with a tall man in front, or a woman with a big hat on, stopping me from seeing the screen. They'd have ignored me all the time, not letting me say anything about anything. No one'd have been jolly with me and asked me to join in things. So what am I missing? I'm better off alone, by myself."

He went out of the room and up the stairs with his sorrow that was proud.

"He's too impudent," said Anda, virtuously.

"You can shut up, too," said our father. It was one of his rare times of being thoroughly roused. He turned back to our mother:

"I don't often say much in this house. I know who's the boss here, same's the kids know. I'm only a kid, myself, come to that. Anyway, I'm treated like one, and I can feel like a kid, too. The one boast is that I've got the guts to find in the neglect of myself something challenging—and comic! But, like all other children, there's one thing I can't forgive, and that's a hard, cold heart! A person can get over being treated bad-temperedly because tempers pass and there's a bit of love at the end, a few sweet words to make it up again; it's only when you know *there'll never be any change* that you lose faith, hope, and bloody charity as well. This was meant to be a happy day—a rare event in *this* house—but you've been and toppled everything. It fairly wrings a person's heart, so it does!"

He had risen from the table and was looking for his scarf and cap to go to the pub. His hands were trembling. He looked as if he would be glad to go away and have a good cry somewhere.

He found his things and went to the door. From there he turned his sorrowful, quixotic face to us children, and he said:

"Well, I hope *you* have a good time, at any rate. That'll be something!" and he went.

I began to clear away the tea-things.

"Oh, leave them!" our mother shouted. "Let's get out of this house, for goodness sake! Go and put your coat on."

"Aren't you going to take him?" Robert asked, jerking his head ceilingward. His decent sense of life was always coming near to being overthrown in his own home.

"Oh, all right, all right, damn it," she shouted. "I can't say or do anything in this place without interference from somebody! That's good, that is, considering I'm the mainstay, as well. Go and tell the little imp, one of you—you go, Laura."

I went up to the little back bedroom that Steve shared with Robert. He was sitting near the window, looking wanton; a book was spread open on his knees.

"Just off?" he asked.

"She says you can come," I told him.

His face became pleated like some angry perplexed parrot of an old man.

"Isn't she kind!" he exclaimed; and then he demanded with a shocking, unchildlike anger:

"What does she take me for? First I can't go, then I can! You see the injustice of it, do you? I'm simply dragged about to please her moods, I'm made to feel a fool at every turn. I submit very industriously to all these insults, I can't help myself, but it won't be like this always! I dream of the by-and-by! And I'm not going with you! I've got a good book here, and, really, you know" (he brought this out with a spasm of vicious joy), "you are none of you so extra that I'd prefer your company to reading Oliver Goldsmith on 'A Party at Vauxhall.' Things aren't completely intolerable, you know!"

We had asked for all this.

"All right," said. I went downstairs.

"Oh, the little hyena!" our mother said of him, when she heard that Steve would not go with us. "What can a decent Christian woman do with an imp of Satan like him?"

"Treat him like another decent Christian, I should think," said Robert, who was so ill-pleased by the injustice done that in a minute he would say he wasn't going, either. I caught at anything to save a row, and I bustled us all out of the house before there was a further uproar.

When we were waiting in the queue outside the pink plaster cinema, some vendors came and set up a little trading colony in the gutter, offering apples, oranges, sliced cocoanut and bananas to seduce us. A handsome trade was soon in full swing, with great good humour on all sides, the queue in a happy maze anticipating good entertainment very shortly, and the vendors in their enthusiasm for their goods and pleasure in the appreciation of the crowd.

Then half a man propelling himself on a little wheeled

platform came up to share in the largesse. He was selling paper sacks of dun little seeds which, when dropped into a glass of water, would instantly bloom as though all the rainbow were caught in one little tumbler. I bought a packet as a present for Steve.

"What d'you want going wasting your money on that trash for?" said our mother to me. "And buying off that legless freak as well! You should turn your eyes away when a monstrosity like that goes by. God curse him—he got that way through sin of his own or his parents!"

Of course our mother had no more religion than sand in a sieve. This was not to say that she was not friendlily disposed towards God. She was one of those who saw God as the most benign old party in the world, sitting on a high stool in some celestial pledge-office, waiting to redeem to her the good time in life which she had put in pawn the day she married Mr. William Valley. So she thought.

Meantime, I stood chafing under her unkind words about the legless man, restless in a sudden sense of a non-loving, non-pitying world. What came to my rescue then was the vivid memory of the clotted clay on Steve's shoe that afternoon in the dell. I recalled the *something else* that it had conveyed to me. And in a sudden gush of happiness, I no longer felt invaded by our mother's brutality. I no longer felt belonging to her and all the cruel hugger-mugger she represented. I only had a tremendously firm and valid feeling of belonging to myself, of possessing my own unconquered soul in peace. Using the memory of the *look* of a lump of clotted clay with a bit of bright grass stuck in it, I catapulted myself away from existing misery on to a plane where misery was not.

And then I looked down and saw the gaudy packet in

my hand. I stared and I stared at it till I made it do the same for me. I made it speak of that *something else*.

As we moved into the cinema, I was thrilling with the thought that *anything at any time* could be made to do this for me—*if I wanted it to*. In all my life it need never be lost. I could use it, I could intensify it, and the more our mother did to me the stronger and the ampler would she make my escape!

The film pleased us all, except our mother who said, as we came out into the streets again, that it had been a waste of good money. But we had seen that marvellous man, Charlie Chaplin, in one of his early comedies, a comedy with unseen tears strewn through the excruciatingly funny sequences.

On the way home we stopped to buy a parcel of savoury fish and chips as a festive ending to this day of strange event.

I popped these into the stove on plates when we arrived home, and while our mother was brewing some cocoa, I stole upstairs to see my brother.

His little room was all a-wash with the rising moonlight. Slip-slop over the one broken chair lay his poor trousers, old ones of Robert cut down. Steve had never had a suit of clothes that had been bought and made exclusively for him alone.

But this judged and despised scrap of humanity was standing up on the bed, under the four-pane window, splendid in what nature had given him, not even his night-shirt on, preening and gesticulating, and using the moonlight as unction to restore the stupefying nonentity to which our mother had reduced him.

Regarding him, I was struck anew by the thought that though he had become a kind of changeling through the misfortune of constraint and ill-treatment, yet there remained with him a touching air of dignity and worth.

He had not heard me come in. He was talking aloud, exhorting heaven knows who or what, and pausing now and then as if to catch answers.

"Steve," I said, softly. "I've got something for you, dear!"

He looked over his shoulder to see who it was, face frowning with resentment.

"Can't I even talk to myself, now, without someone interrupting?" he demanded. "You needn't come bothering."

He turned from me and said in a quite different voice to someone or something invisible:

"It's only Laura!"

He brought his attention back to me, sighing.

In the moonlight his face was like a depigmented pansy, and his thick brushed yellow hair was turned to a shining slab of silver above his high blanched forehead. His eyes shone like crystal when he turned them up to the moon.

"Well, what do you want?" he asked. "Look here—she went out and never even left me a night-shirt! I suppose she hasn't ironed it, or washed it, even!"

I helped this untended little boy to find his clean shirt. Our mother had stuffed it away in the chest of drawers without telling him, leaving him to go to his naked bed. As he slipped it on, he said, conversationally:

"This is what I like, 'cos it's eerie! It makes a nice scene, doesn't it, the moonlight? It makes everything seem different. I was *thanking* it before you came in, for having gone to all that trouble to make things seem different— heaving itself up out of nowhere to arrive somewhere—and do something!"

A star now appeared at the pane, shining like the thumb-nail of a crystalline god of the night.

"There's one thing about stars," said Steve, noticing this

brilliant entry, "our mother can't interfere with *them*! That's something, don't you think?"

"She can't interfere with you, either," I said, "not the hidden, private, real you—unless you let her!"

"If I was clever, like you," he said, "she couldn't. But I'm not like you, so she does."

"I'm not clever," I said. "It's just because I'm *not* clever, because I let myself be like an old stupid bit of wood, or soap, or coal, that she can't make free in *my* secret places!"

That's what I call clever, at any rate," he retorted, thoughtfully.

"Well, what have you been up to while we've been out?" I asked, interestedly.

"I've been *away*," he said, dreamily, pleased.

"And what did you see while you were away?"

"Oh,—long grass. I saw the long grass streaming over—tombs. You can see the shape of the wind if you watch grass blowing. Beyond the tombs there was a heath, and on the heath three gallows—men hanging on 'em in the moonlight."

And here he recommended his nods and beckonings with his hand to Lord only knows what. I gave him a nudge to bring him from this sinister indulging of himself.

"Were these men dead?" I asked.

"I don't know," he replied. "But I could hear them talking. 'Fancy,' they were saying, 'Fancy! We'd never have come to this if we'd been kinder to our old friend, Steve Valley.'"

He looked at me with curious, cross-eyed malignity, withdrawn and unforgiving.

"Good heavens!" I exclaimed, upset.

"Oh, never mind," he put in, haughtily. "When they said that I felt sorry for them. I asked them should I bring them a drink. They said, By God they would enjoy that, but what was the use since I couldn't reach up high enough. So I left 'em, cursing!"

Thinking there was enough vim in his imagination for ten, I lit the candle. The little cool flame scurried about at the top of its long white waxen pillar, and tall shadows began to crane at us from the walls, ranging up and down very determinedly.

Colour flared in a corner where the little boy had tacked up pictures of foreign lands which he had cut out of free travel agency brochures. It was his regular practice to enter these handsome offices and snatch up a handful of the gay adjurations to holiday in Lucerne or the Dolomites.

Intimations of romance also came from a small up-ended soap-box in which stood a little library comprising "Treasure Island," "Moby Dick," two volumes of "Chatterbox Annual," "Hans Andersen's Fairy Tales," and "Gulliver's Travels"; there they stood in entire pride.

I tucked Steve up in bed, and I gave him the packet of water-flowers. He was so instantly affected by this little present, that he began to bustle about with the bedclothes, and would not look at me for pleasure.

"Oh," he said at last, in control of himself, "this is just what I like! Something wonderful that happens in a second from nowhere! Go and get a glass of water, Laura, and let us try them."

He was sitting up in his delight. But just then our mother called me with much asperity.

"In the morning," I said. "It'll be something to look forward to."

"Why, so it will," he said. "Oh! Oh! I don't often have anything to look forward to. You never get what you really want—only something like. You always get something with something missing. Perhaps it's better when you grow up!"

He leaned and doused the candle with a smack of his hand. Very quietly, the moonlight asserted itself in the little room. I began to go downstairs, but he called me back.

"You *tread* kind," he said, grudgingly.

I left him sitting undismayed, crafty-eyed, his hands gone to the support of his head, plotting with himself, hunched in the moonlight.

That was the early land.

Chapter II

"Thou art a Man: God is no more:
Thy own humanity learn to adore.
For that is My spirit of life
Awake, arise to spiritual strife."

WILLIAM BLAKE

FROM that summer's day in the park until Christmas an uneasy calm, stretched tight and thin, lay upon our house. Steve, who was usually the flaming faggot to fire the sluggish oil, seemed to have found in his new studies at the Grammar School a haven into which he could and did retire from the street, our mother, and all that was a torment to him. Since he had been at the Grammar School our parents had also been compelled to make efforts to clothe him like a Christian, and so, for the first time in his life, Steve had the comfort of decent pride in his appearance.

He had made several friends at the new school, not among his contemporaries whom he found exceeding dull, but among the senior boys of sixteen and seventeen, one of whom, before very long, succumbed to a classical and romantic failing inspired probably by Steve's good looks.

This experience, faithfully confided to me, made the little boy cringe with offence. All his buildings tumbled down, and great wheels turned and roared.

"Never mind," I said. · "If you do not want to be miserable, you'll forget it. It happens to everyone at some time in life. But you take the knock and carry on. That's what it comes to!"

"Carry on! It's easy for you to talk. It hasn't happened to you!"

But of course it had. Why not? One school is like the next for sentimental friendships. But I got over the way laying, and a curious, frightening exhibition of high-pitched emotion, by plunging with greater vigour into my mental vagabondage.

Steve, however, being too rational for any such method of escape, allowed his analytical, depressed, and sarcastic thoughts to run upon his experiences till he had savoured the full horror, and then it all quietly crystallized as yet another testimony to the worthlessness of all life and living creatures.

My brother was also being patronized by the Classics Master first because he had much more than the primitive intelligence of the average lad, showing real genius in his mastering of the Greek language, and second because the master's wife was an artist and used the little boy as a model.

Steve's enthusiasm for Greek was lovely to see. It was a joy to him to write down the beautiful characters of this language and to read aloud to me the simple sentences he was put on to construe in that first term; by this reading aloud he confessed he got a delicious, satisfying feeling of sharing the credit for the wise and noble words he was uttering.

This was, indeed, the beginning of a new time for Steve, a time during which he fortified himself behind a silence of diligence and delight—a withdrawal into realms of learning wherein no one could stone him. If his existence till then had been like a desolate nightmare by Bruegel, now Steve moved in any summer landscape of Claude Monet, all his faculties aglow. Like a gay little serpent, he slithered out from the dark ruin into the sunny ferns, naked and bold.

From the first, Robert took a profound and very wistful interest in Steve's learning of Greek. With admiration and wonder he would watch the little boy doing his homework, and when Steve had gone to bed, Robert would often lovingly and blankly turn the pages of the Greek text-books. Robert himself would have given anything to learn and, indeed, for a short time, Steve tried to impart to him the rudiments of the language as he made progress. But, somehow, they never hit it off; their sessions ended in studied insults from both sides. Steve was too lordly and impatient, Robert too critical and slow. Robert would ask a question, Steve would rattle off the answer. Uncomprehending, Robert would ask again, and Steve, remembering how until now he had been nobody, was not disposed to unbend towards his elder brother so strangely humble before alpha and omega.

Besides, Steve's interest tended towards the philosophical and scientific, whereas Robert cared for nothing but the historical. Steve's gods were going to be Plato and Aristotle, but Robert's were Herodotus and Demosthenes. So the lessons came to an end.

But on a December evening, two days before Christmas, Anda was to blow a hurricane right through our house and family. She had reached sixteen and had left school with the ending of the Christmas term.

At the art school she had been studying textile designing, with our parents' fond hope that she would be able to fill a post in one of the great cotton warehouses and use her knowledge in an interesting and remunerative fashion.

I don't know that Anda had done so well at this work. It is true she had decorated the whitewashed walls of our scullery with a recurring design of what she called abstract angels, that is to say, all that appeared was a heel and a wing; it looked jolly in glistening azure paint, but it meant nothing, certainly not any harm, and it was all we had ever seen of her artistic endeavours.

Now on this night, we were all sitting round the table eating our supper which, as Christmas was so near, consisted of some advance mince-pies besides bread and jam and cocoa.

Our father, drunk, had not been in long from his evening's work in the tavern; he had brought home an armful of holly to wind round the pictures and the gas bracket. This lay glistening and darting beauty at us from the top of the piano.

The general feeling was one of good event; our father, though drunk, was only mildly intoxicated, and had most of his faculties about him.

When he was badly drunk he was a terrifying sight to see. Then he had a strange doll-like personality, and this was the most terrifying thing about him—he had no sense! A grown person without any sense! He would carry his head on his shoulder. He twitched and twirled. His hand went to his bootlaces, then soared to his poll. He gave off loud shoots of laughter when there was no cause for amusement. His two eyes strained madly to get out of his head. The head tried to swoop off his shoulders. Everything he had wanted to escape from him. He used his limbs like a marionette, as though he expected them to drop off at any minute; and his locomotion was a series of hops and skips that could be entrancingly funny, unless you happened to get in his way when he would fall against you and knock you down. His voice became hoarse like a gnome's or a patriarch's. Sudden hawk-swoops of his head seemed to indicate that he was trying to get away from his own thoughts. Some fateful and ultimate purpose emanated from him. Fateful enough! You could almost see him trying to make up his mind to murder our mother.

But on this evening he had not reached that breath-taking stage. He had left the table and propped himself up against the mantelpiece, his untamed face shining with sweat. He was recounting a thing that had happened to him on his way home. It seemed he had stopped in a doorway and begun to roll himself a cigarette by the light of the street lamp.

"Aye, there I was, and a tall woman in a fur coat, with a face just like a ... a white fiddle, came up to see what I was at. Her hair was all tidy, and her hands polished: I'll bet she was as clean as that *all over*! Toffs, eh! Give themselves no peace. All that toilet and tittivating before they can begin the day. *Me*—I just get up! Well, she stood till I had to say something.

'Good evening,' I said. 'Lovely weather we've been having in spite of the rain! You think you know me or something?'—I said.

'Are you saved?' this woman asked me.

'Who? Me? I said, roaring with laughter.' That's the second time I've been asked that tonight! It must be the Christmas spirit getting out of hand! Well,' I said, 'go on—I'll buy it!'

'Are you saved?' she asked again.

'How should I know?' I said.

'By the peace of the heart,' she says, very lofty.

I blew a cloud of smoke at her, but she was past taking hints. She wouldn't go away—not she! So I said:

'Oh, I usually get this peace of the heart, as you call it, every time I eat a good meal, especially if it's soused pig's ear—soused pig's ear eats very sweet, ma'am; and every time I have a good smoke, a good drink, and a good something else! Seems to me,' I bawled, 'I'm saved on every count!'

'I didn't mean that,' she said, very chilly. 'I didn't mean beastly pleasure!'

'Hoo! I see,' I said. 'Fancy,' I said, 'and you *look* like a Christian, 'cept for that fur coat!'

'Have you found God?' she shouted.

'Well, I don't see what it's got to do with you, one way or the other, standing there wobbling about,' I said. 'Anyway, let's be hearing where you can find God, first. Where is God? Go on—tell us.'

'Oh,' she declared, very disdainful, 'God is on the mountain, on the snowy peaks, on the untrodden paths!'

'Snowy peaks my bloody eye!' I says. 'God's strewth! Some of you people don't half kid yourselves! God goes where it's trodden and well trodden. It's never 'Keep Off the Grass' with God, as it is with the likes of you. He's down here in the dust, in this doorway. Only a minute ago as I rolled my smoke, God leaned there against the wall, and He says to me very jovial, He says:

'That's right, William Valley, that's the ticket! Smoke your smoke! You're meant to enjoy yourself, you know. It's very important that you should, you know. Hardly anyone realizes how important this is. Well, *I'll* tell you—it's a sin if you *don't* enjoy yourself.' That's what He told me,' I said to this woman.

'It's positively indecent to talk like that,' she lets on, shocked and severe.

'Just so,' I says peacefully. 'There's a lot that's illegal about me, I daresay, but I'm nobody's fool. Still, it's a shame, and it doesn't become a comical old bastard like me to go putting the ki-bosh on your Lady Bountiful. What a world, eh, where the poor are judged harshly, and the bloody rich judged rashly! I don't know! 'Course the rich have a very queer habit of calling it their soul when they mean something else, arid the poor aren't supposed to have a soul at all! Have you got anything else on your mind, ma'am?' I says.

She turned away then, she saw I was a hopeless case. But I poked my head out of the doorway and I shouted after her:

'Here! A minute!'

She came back.

'What is it?' she asked, very cold.

'Are *you* saved?' I says, simple; but, without answering me, she turned away quick and never came back."

That's a nice tale to tell your children!" sniffed our mother.

"It's a nice tale to tell anyone," he retorted with humorous gusto, smoking and grinning in happy wantonness, the brilliant maltreatment of his face having a look of being varnished over through the heat.

Before our mother could protest further, Steve, making sweet eyes at me over the rim of his cocoa-cup, said:

"Laura, I say! Are you saved?"

"I don't know," I replied, "I never thought about it; in any case, it isn't the sort of thing you could have certainties about."

"Well, then, tell me something else. Tell me this, could you be a martyr for Our Lord? If a persecution came, should you betray Him? If they were to torture you, should you break down, do you think?"

"Oh, I should," I replied fervently. "I should break down and betray. At the very first turn of the screw or taste of the flail, I should tell all."

"I'll bet Robbie would bear it!" declared Steve. "It would be beneath his dignity to howl. Wouldn't it, Robbie?"

He had to ask Robert twice. Robert brought his nose out of his book.

"I'm not reading with all my nerves," he said, "I heard you the first time. What a silly question to ask; a person can't truly say how they would act in advance since we can only draw on experiences we have *known*!"

"I daresay I ought to be bowled over by that," said Steve. "It was most impressively said. But do tell how you imagine you would behave."

"I imagine," said Robert, filling his mouth with bread and jam, "that I'd do exactly the same as Laura—betray the lot, though, of course, I'd like to think I'd make an heroic stand and go down to history as a beautiful example!"

"So would we all," said Steve, and was about to call forth Anda's views on the powers of her endurance, when our father, who had something more imperative to ask her, went before him.

"Now," he said, "those questions of yours are pretty daft! Don't keep on asking 'em, my boy."

"But I want to," replied Steve.

"Yes, but you don't want to keep on wanting; you just be God's good boy, eh, and hold quiet while I ask Anda something. Look, Anda, tell us what you are going to do now that you have left school for good."

She was absolutely ready for him. Impudent, credulous,

and chaste as she was then, she had her life planned before her. She leaned back in her chair and, turning her fine eyes upon him, she said:

"Well, I hadn't anticipated this heart-to-heart talk till after Christmas, but we might as well get it over with now."

"Sounds quite threatening," smiled our father.

"Oh," declared Anda, "it needn't cause a sensation. What I'm going to say is nothing but common sense. If I go into a textile firm, the chances are I shall be running round buying buns and making tea for the others for the first year at ten shillings a week. You can't see them employing me as a full-blown designer the first morning I walk in, can you? Besides, you know, I haven't got a scrap of originality. I shall never set the textile industry alight. My being trained as a textile-designer has taught me one thing only—I shall never be a textile designer!"

"Well," said our mother, fiercely, "that's a nice way to talk, miss! That's a fine way of repaying your father and me for ..."

"All that you have done for me!" finished Anda for her. "Oh, don't let us have all that! I'm trying to talk sense! Now, what I can do, and what will bring you a quick return for all that you have done for me, is to turn to account what I have got, instead of drudging for what I shall never have. I've got a nice face that they say God gave me (but I don't believe in God), and so, I'm going to use my own sweet mug! I'm going to sit for an artist. One has already offered me employment; he is connected with the art school and his name is Claude Maccabeus—the famous painter, so I won't be going to any Tom, Dick, or Harry. And he'll pay me five shillings an hour! Four hours a day only will equal one pound a day, or five or six pounds a week. D'you see? Riches!"

"Well, God Almighty!" said our father, heavily. He sat him down in a chair; perhaps he felt he could no longer stand up after news like this. "He wouldn't want you to sit ... to sit, well, dammit, without your clothes on, would he?" He stared at Anda with all his might.

"Certainly he would," replied Anda. "What do you suppose? The world's best art has no clothes on—ask our mother. She spends all her time dusting it down in uncle's shop! Of course, I shouldn't be without my clothes all the time. That would be too dull! He'll paint me in all sorts of costumes. He says I was just made for his pictures. He says he has been looking for a model like me all his life!"

"I daresay he has," said our father, seeming to lose all interest in the proposition. But suddenly he leaned forward and down on the table he smashed his hand that he had made into a fist. Some spoons gave off an agitated trill.

"You're not going to do it," he roared at Anda. "Do you hear me?"

"It would be difficult not to hear," she retorted, calmly. "Whatever are you bawling at? There's no need to wreck the home! What's the matter? What have I said wrong?"

"If you think," replied our father, "that I'm going to allow any child of mine to disgrace herself by sitting stark naked while some man, a stranger to her, throws the whole shameful scene on to a canvas, you've got another, guess coming, my girl!"

Anda went off into a shout of laughter.

"Oh, father," she said, "you make it sound as though I were going on the streets!"

"It's no better than that," he cried.

And here, our mother, feeling that a lot of unpleasantness was going on in which she had no part, determined to have her show, too, and made a start by ordering Steve to leave the table at once and go to bed, the talk not being exactly suitable for his hearing.

"Oh, I'm just going," he drawled. "There's nothing here to hold a fellow."

He did not even look up, but continued to turn the leaves of the Christmas number of a literary journal he had persuaded me to buy for him.

"Well, then, get off to bed at once," said our mother. "This is no place for you!"

"I myself always said that," exclaimed Steve, getting ready for the stairs. "Anyway, what a fuss about nothing! It won't be any come-down for Anda to show her pelt to a painter! She's the sort that goes dressed in order to be undressed, and most times this is done to her just in a look! It's amusing anyone worrying about a little matter of sitting for a painter! If that's the worst she ever does, how lucky you will be, father!"

The concentrated impudence of this statement set both our parents effervescing.

"Well, for evermore!" exclaimed our mother.

"My beautiful and respectful children!" said our father.

It suddenly came to him that the one who had uttered this last cynicism was Steve, his youngest.

"Go to God!" our father shrieked, his eyes bulging. "I don't have to take that from you," he said. '

He got up to go and hit the little boy, colliding with our mother who was half-way on the same errand, while Steve, snatching up two or three mince-pies, made a thunderous exit. We could hear the protesting hup-ha hup-ha of the stairs as his feet pounded upwards.

Our parents returned to the table with as much dignity

as they could muster. Our father, running his hand through his hair, kept saying:

"The young devil, the young devil!"

All at once he turned on Anda:

"This is all your doing," he shouted. "You're a bad lot, you are!"

And Anda, who felt that a very sensible proposition had been received not only with the direst ingratitude, but insult as well, stood up in a rage:

"It's a nice thing," said Anda, "to be told I'm a bad lot—whatever nastiness you mean by that—when all that I've suggested is a way to bring some money into this hovel, and, oddly enough, more money than either of you who condemn me, have ever earned. You," she said to our parents, "have plenty of room to criticize anybody! One could understand your nice feelings if you were keeping us in style, or even keeping us decently. There's always been enough money for booze and betting, but never enough to take us out of this street. We've never had anything nice or exciting to own, or live with, or look forward to. We have been cut off from pleasant friendships because we never could invite people to this awful house; we've never had colour or ease or beauty. And yet, and yet," she cried, passionately, "this awful home, this dreadful street could have been endured, if we had been loved, and made to feel—if only *sometimes*—that we mattered, that we were just a little important, just a little necessary. Instead, we've never heard anything but what a nuisance we are, how detestable we are, and what wonderful persons you are to put up with us. But *why* are you wonderful? What have you ever done for us? Our education was provided for ourselves with such brain as we could salvage from the petrifying atmosphere of our home! All you've had to do has been to provide us with food and clothes, and we've never had enough of either. You had us children not as children to love and pet and make happy, but simply as an insurance policy for your old age! And now, when I can earn some money that would enable us to move from these beastly surroundings, just because the way of getting it does not meet with your bad-minded ideas of what is proper, you object and begin to call me names. Morality is only *appearances* with you! In actual fact, you're two of the most immoral people in all England: it's immoral to neglect and scold and drive children the way you have neglected and driven us. I don't suppose it occurs to either of you that it's *your fault* I'm placed in the position of being offered the very job you're so offended about. It's your fault that I have to work at all before I'm really equipped to take my place as a useful citizen. At sixteen you're still only a child, or you ought to be, not a knowing old woman before your time, like I am. At sixteen you haven't made up your mind, you ought to be given chances of further education—chances of the university if you wanted to go there. It so happens that I don't. It so happens that I shall be very pleased to accept the job that's been offered me. But what about the others when they come to school-leaving age? They'll be just like poor Robert—shoved into some hole-in-a-corner job to eat out their hearts, watch their talents die, miss opportunities—all, all because our dear parents have never worried about providing even a little for their precious children. Of course we, the children, aren't, I know, supposed to have any preferences or feelings at all. We were brought into the world to suit you, not ourselves, to run at your orders, subject to your stupid, pig-headed tyranny, to your whims, to your ignorance. If I have to take a job, if I have to help to provide for the family which you have failed to do, then, at least, I may choose the job I must take.

"Yes, you can blame economics, as you call it, blame the government, blame the country, but there are things that are more important than economics and governments; all that matters to children is *love*, and we've never had it, never. And that's your fault. Everything is your fault, and to cover up your faults you've the gall to name me a street-girl when I offer to take from you the responsibility which neither of you ever accepted."

I had listened intently to every passionate word uttered by my sister.

Well, I thought, what she says may be the sacred truth for us children, but nothing can mend it now—certainly not words. And, in any case, we must not let such a set of circumstances be too important to us; they must be taken as little ugly events on a journey, and not affecting the journey's end. We shall have to take the staggering handicaps of our life as something which we, for a reason, were *specially chosen* to bear. Many other children would not be able to endure it; so they were given happy, unaffrighted homes. Their eyes are glimmering, but ours are staring wide open.

As well as trying to mend our lot, we must keep our distance from self-pity—and we are *not to be pitied*, either! Just the opposite. We are to be envied! Something has happened to us that happens only to the favoured. Just as in those battles in history books, the bravest men are chosen for the worst job, so we children have been selected for parents like these. It's a role requiring spirit, and it's a role that will bring us adventures of so rare an order that most people would never dream they were adventures at all.

So, having seen plainly that Anda's words and the truth

of them must not be allowed to submerge too much of my being, and her words having had their proper share of consideration, I dismissed them, and fell to thinking about the wind that was getting up outside in the dark street. The wind was not just a casual noise to be swallowed up and forgotten with the other noises of the street. It had risen in the thin blown-glass of waves meeting a far-off shore; it had travelled from beaches where the sea slid forward and fled back again, grinding the shells to sand; this wind had boomed in slippery caves with hanging seaweeds for aeolian harps; it had blown across wild heaths setting tattered winter weeds jigging, careered through copses and wild wood and quiet country cemeteries where tombstones listened to it impassively in the moonlight; it reached the towns, roaring round theatres and churches, past shut shops where quails and shrimps and sheep's brains and forced strawberries were all quietly waiting to be bought and devoured and so become the blood and thoughts of men and women. And it came at last to shabby streets like our own, shrieking aghast through leagues of brick and hovels, whipping the waters of lonely, warehouseenclosed canals into long stiff ridges of black cream, and finally going off blustering and spent to the hills beyond the town.

And this little gaslit room of ours, this ugly domestic interior, fraught with rags and pain, the chairs, the carpet, the shush-shushing fire, the ceiling—all listening to the truculence and idiocy of the mortal event going on—all these projected against the immensity of the wind and the night and the starry heavens, were reduced to what they really were—a few unkind hours that would pass, and could not affect or change the immutability of those eternal essences pressing round us on all sides, asking only to be recognized and promising happiness beyond all understanding in return.

These were not the thoughts of a child who had known every security; they were the inarticulate thoughts of a child who had never known a minute of security, and they would have never come at all without that insecurity.

I felt glad and comforted. I went and took Anda by the arm, and helpless with anger as she was, she allowed me to lead her upstairs to the exceeding small bedroom that we shared, leaving our parents below, our mother muttering over and over, as a straw to clutch at:

"She said she didn't believe in God, she said she didn't believe in God—and *that's why*!"

Without any words, Anda and I undressed and got into bed. Now that the wind had dropped everything was very silent, but presently a new sound stole upstairs to us, who ought to have cringed at it, and rushed with love to comfort it; but this sound came to us boringly. We had heard it so many many times; its pathos and weak cause meant nothing to us. It was the sound of our father—crying.

A short time afterwards I fell asleep, and it seemed but a minute later that I was wakened to find Anda bending over me tearfully, the candle lit, and herself fully dressed, even to her old plaid coat, and she had a bundle under her arm.

"I thought you'd never waken," she said. "Look, I'm going. I want to say good-bye to you, Laura, and tell you about meeting later on."

I nodded stupidly. It all seemed like a sight in a peep-show. The little window had squared off a section of the brilliant ultramarine night including a faint powdering of stars, and in the rich candlelight this beautiful face of my sister was bending over me, dewy-eyed and tense for departure.·

"I'm *running away*," she said, and waited for the drama of the thing to sink into me. I nodded.

"I'm running away," she reiterated, "and there you sit like an owl! It's very important!" she said. "Do try to listen. I'm going to live with Claude Maccabeus. He said I could if I found it too difficult at home. He knows what it's like here, for I told him. Oh, Laura, I have been so unhappy. Going away from this home will be like going to heaven. I'm sorry to leave you and Robert, but after Christmas when I've settled down, I'll write to you and you shall come and visit me. There'll be no fear of their seeing my letter for you always get up first in the morning, and I'll post it for earliest delivery. And look, this note is for them. It tells them I shall never come back again, and it's useless of them to make me. I've said if they try to make me return by force, through the police, you know, as I'm under age, I shall tell about our mother beating Steve, and Oh, I shall tell about everything. I'd rather go into a Home than return here. But, you'll see—they'll leave me alone. I must be off now. It's nearly half-past four. The workmen's trains will be starting soon, and that's how I'll get to Claude's. You'll come and see me after I write?"

"Yes, yes," I said. "Good luck!"

She tiptoed out of the room and went downstairs. I heard the street door close quietly after her, and her quick light footsteps dying away down the frosty street.·

I hoped that Mr. Maccabeus would be kind to her. He was very famous. Three of his paintings were hanging in the big art gallery in the town. Some were also in the Tate Gallery in London, some in the Louvre, and some in New

York. I couldn't help thinking: fancy anyone as important as all that taking up with one of the Valley children.

I gave the note to our parents next morning, but they made no comment to us on our sister's flight. They did not notify the police, either.

Through Christmas Eve and Christmas Day our mother was better to us than we had ever known her in all our lives. She was gracious, or did her best to be, even to Steve, as though trying to demonstrate to us what an excellent person she really was—only requiring a little understanding from her inhuman children.

But all the graciousness and attempts at humanity flew away in the evening of Boxing Day. Steve, who had been out for a solitary walk in the cold, foggy streets, returned with a pitiful little waif of a pup he had found wandering forlorn, homeless and starving. It stood on our hearthrug, a shaking little bag of bones, with a short stiff tail and tearful eyes that stared violently at everything—the fire spitting, a finger held out to it, and, best of all, a good saucer of food hurriedly prepared by Steve and me in the scullery.

Only Robert and I were in when Steve returned with his waif, our parents being gone to visit the rich uncle.

"Oh," said Steve, looking with rare love at the scared, gulping animal, "do you think she will allow me to keep him?"

Robert and I did not dare to say. But she, coming in shortly after tea, settled the matter once and for all. In next to no time she had the pitiful little dog out in the dark dreary streets where we could hear him barking as though his throat were full of grace-notes.

Our mother came back, scolding and harassing Steve, telling him how she had to work to get enough for him to eat without taking on any flea-ridden whelps of the streets as well.

"And who did you think was going to pay the seven-andsix for his licence?" she shouted. "Do you think we are made of money? Do you think your father and I grow seven-and-sixes on trees?"

And so on, beginning every fresh sentence with the maddening "Do you think?"

At last she went and sat in her elbow-chair by the fire. Our father had gone on to his work in the tavern, and presently she would be going there for a holiday treat of bottled stout.

She had brought some presents for us from our uncle, but none of us could bear to look at them, thinking of that little dog wandering in the wastes of the big town.

Steve, who had been hovering helplessly in corner after corner ever since, in her friendless way, she had ushered the dog into the street, suddenly gathered himself together, and came on tiptoe over to her, his fine narrow head with its shining gold hair leaning down to her like an angel's. Startled, she drew away from him, and well she might; for, with stunning, youthless control he said to her very civilly:

"You can't think what *fiery*, what pit-of-the-stomach *loathing* I feel for you."

Such words make a racy conversational effect at any time, and it was no little thing for a mother to be told this, to see such a look in the face of her child, especially this face that had looked everything in its time—everything—except a little holiday face.

At this authoritative and mercurial statement, our mother had looked towards Robert as though drawing strength from his aloof and compact personality. Above her parted mouth her big nose looked bleak and angry—it all seemed to be too much for the nose in particular. She had nothing at all with which to meet this situation. She could only make use of her old resort when Steve became too much for her:

"Oh—you nasty little tiger!" she cried. "Go to bed directly!"

He went, and after he had gone, she said to Robert and me: "To think of him saying that to me!"

Whereupon Robert replied with unusual bitterness:

"Oh, well, in this house, it's just as Anda said it was—it's beastly!"

His eye that was set in the fixed stare looked towards her with an intense sadness; he twisted his hands, and continued:

"What is so awful is *not* what Steve said to you, but that *you* turned that pup out into the streets. I'd have paid his licence, and he wouldn't have eaten as much as would have mattered! Oh, if only you knew, if you only knew how sad you make us!"

"Sad? You!" she exclaimed, jumping to her feet.

"What have you to be sad about? I'm the one to be sad at having brought such an ungrateful pack of brats into the world! You've got no worries, have you, like your poor father and mother? You little devils have the life of kings—all of you! And what thanks do I get? None, none at all. Oh, I'm going out," she declared, screaming and muddled. (She was going out, anyway, but she made it appear as if we were driving her out.) "That's what it comes to—you cause your own mother to walk the streets, instead of being able to sit quietly at home with good decent children!"

Challengingly, her red face turned to left and to right, then she banged out of the house, and we heard the high heels of her white French velour boots knocking furiously down the pavement.

When you had known our mother any length of time, you discovered a thing about her that stole upon you quietly, so quietly that it seemed not out of place until, with a loud noise in your brains, you saw what an awful thing you had realized. It was that our mother could not possibly have been a little child—ever. It seemed a sure thing that she had always been a red-haired, iconoclastic, insensitive, ferocious little woman.

What she thought about as she tore through life only God and herself knew. God does not tell and our mother was inarticulate, but it's a safe bet that she never thought of rooms everywhere, people alive in them, people and their affairs aslant between the earth and the sky. She had *wonder* about nothing—not even about herself as *herself*. She knew, of course, that she was remarkable, even splendid, but this she took for granted. Never, never had she allowed the birds of fancy to nest in her hair, nor did she look for meanings in things. The ancient consideration of Yea and Nay did not trouble her. Yet she longed, you could sense it, for a vague something to fill and complete her life, but what this was she did not know. She threw off the impression that something was pent up within her, but it was not deep or important. She used to say:

"I love music and I never hear it!" This was because she would not allow that to hear you must listen. Her indwelling foe was herself.

After she had gone out I made some tea and took a cup to my brother Steve. He had lit the candle and was sitting before it with his hands clasped, thinking.

"Oh," he turned to me, "think of that little dog roaming the streets, having nowhere, no one!"

"Well," I coaxed, "if nobody seems to care God is looking after it, as He must seeing that He made it."

"I don't doubt," he said, "that we feel for it so much because we are all in the same boat, having nowhere, having no one."

"We've got one another," I said.

"Yes, but that doesn't make us feel *safe*, does it? It's important to feel safe! And don't talk about God caring. If He cared for us the least bit He would never have allowed us to be born to such terrible people! Oh and when I think of that little homeless thing—I'm strangling to think about it—how can I believe in God or anything? One day, you'll see, I shall not hinder myself from taking revenge upon everything and everybody!"

"But even ... even, Steve," I said, warily, "even if something that seems to be harm should come to the little dog, that was the best thing that could have happened to it. If, for instance, it is dead now, that is better than wandering starving and homeless."

"Who the devil said so? That's no consolation to the pup, as it does die!"

"Anything seems better than what is happening to us," I said in despair. "And it's very hard to recognize consolations. Listen: don't you remember what your friend said—Joy Considine—she said that death isn't death unless you want it to be—it's going home for those who have no home. Well, think of it like that for the pup."

His face took on a serious, tender look. He said nothing.

"Oh, why should we have to talk like this, so desperate and grave," I cried, "and have to think things out for ourselves so frenziedly with no guidance at all. Everything ought to be merry and uncomplicated. Try to help me, dear Steve.

Don't be stony! Oh, dear! When I tell myself things I can make myself understand so very well, but you are another matter. I can't explain why God allows this and God allows that. How can these things be *His* fault when He gave the people the free will to treat a dog well or badly. It's our mother's fault and the fault of the people who turned it out in the first place. Anyway, God knows and understands everything, but we only see the bit that happens to us. So don't let's start blaming Him or saying we don't believe in Him, as often it's all you've got left—the belief that there is Someone Else. I don't know how any of us could ever have got by, Steve, unless ... unless we'd had someone or something to believe in."

He began to cry.

"It's only sometimes I don't believe," he sobbed. "I'm not trying to run the Blessed Trinity out of business, but such things happen you can't help asking where does all *that* get you."

"Never mind, never mind," I said, going to him, and comforting him. "Religion, anyway, isn't gabbling from the Bible or a permanent seat in a pew—it's simply how a person behaves. But don't let's talk about all this any more. Let's just be glad we're together. For even if you feel that God doesn't love you—feel that I love you, for I do. And, Steve, couldn't you be glad just because you are—*you*! Never mind about things not being fair. They never are for anyone, I'm sure. But, in spite of all, aren't you pleased that you are you, such a good runner, such a one for holding your own, and so good at Greek? They've never had a boy in that school as good at Greek as you. Isn't that something?"

"Yes, it is," he admitted slowly, staring at me with his crying eyes. "Yes, it is something. I never thought about it before, that way. It's jolly ... jolly suitable of you to talk like this! You are ... awfully decent, Laura. It is something to be yourself, it's a lot, the way you put it. Even so ... it's not enough—not for me!"

"Well, drink your tea, and if you like, Robert and I will bring our cups here to your room, and then, if you feel like giving us a very special treat, you could read to us from your Greek book—you know, the one that gives those little extracts from Homer and Plato. Of course, we shall not be able to understand what you are saying, but the sound of the Greek is so lovely."

His face had begun to flame with joy. He hurriedly drank his tea, and I went down for Robert. We sat with him for an hour, listening while he read the glittering words of Plato, rocking himself with delight.

All this time I was anxiously waiting to hear from Anda, getting up extra early every morning as though that must infallibly charm the postman to call. When it was January-end and still no letter had arrived, I began to scan the newspapers thinking she had come to a poor end. I expected, perhaps, to read an account of the "body of a beautiful young girl" having been taken from the sulky keeping of some dun pond. Then, happily, I remembered how well she could swim, so I turned to reports of gas-oven cases.

Just when I was on the point of going to the art school to obtain the address of Mr. Maccabeus, a letter in Anda's unmistakable scrawl shot under the door one morning. She invited me to tea at Claude's home in Cheshire on the coming Saturday. She did not say how she did, or if Claude was using her kindly. She simply asked me to go, alone, adding: "You had better come, too, if you know what is good for you!"

Therefore, borrowing my bus fare from my obliging brother Robert, and giving out to everyone that I was going to spend my Saturday afternoon with a school-friend, I boarded the bus for the Cheshire village where the artist lived, sitting in the cold tawny sunlight of the winter's afternoon, watching the road rise through the suburbs into the smoking sun on the western horizon. I sat sending out glances across the frozen fields, retorted to by perishing little birds, gaunt trees on the fringe of leaden ponds, the greasy white ice in the ruts, and a little cloud like a scroll upon the reddening sky.

I kept an open mind as to what I should find at my destination. I went up the country lane to the house, stopping to thrill before a still, laden holly tree, its berries shining among the dark, solemn leaves, and sniff the aromatic smell from evergreen growth above a sluggish ditch.

Good it was for the young town girl to stand in that moist lane when the winter's day was drawing to its close, to smell keen country smells and some damp whiff from a distant marsh, to see the trees waiting proud and hushed for the long lonely night, to hear cattle snuffling, see frost binding the grass, and a sticky, dewy swan sailing away on running water under the trees: knowing that in a few minutes there would be a place in front of a roaring fire, with tea, and words of welcome.

All my nature went out to the quiet, intense livingness round me, fusing, losing the unreality of the daily round in the sturdy reality of sheep and trees and frost and a new moon coming out with charming archness above a distant coppice.

I stood, gathered into the everlasting spirit of these good things, and I felt such security, such a tide of rapture rising in me, that if all dear to me were then swept from me, the handful of rooms I called home, my school, my books, the whole romance of learning, my little brother Steve whom I loved most of all, if I found my sister no longer as my sister but as a strange wicked young woman, still from me could never be taken these magical personal sensations setting at naught the world and every disaster.

Was this a useless dallying? But it gave me such strength, such zest to go on. Does it matter from where this radiant tide comes so long as it comes at all? It was like where Thomas Traherne said in my anthology: "I within did flow with Seas of Life like Wine." Oh, how did I so enjoy being *me* among my own bones, and the me that *was* the sugary frost upon the grass, the me that *was* the woodiness of the coppice, the me that *was* the astringent lemon-coloured moon.

And then there was the house, waiting to see how it would be received at the end of the lane.

I had got the odd notion that if my sister were living "in sin" with Mr. Maccabeus, this circumstance would be signalled by something violent and heraldic, imbuing even the outside walls of the house, and peculiar to the very chimney-smoke.

But, by then, I had come to a state of mind when if they were going to give me a meringue for my tea, I should not mind what I found, for in those days I had a great fondness for sinking my tongue into the crisp, creamy mashed lusciousness of a meringue and, of course, I almost never had one.

Claude's was the only house in sight, which gave it a special distinction in my eyes so used to regimented rows of bandboxes under the denomination of houses. I knew from pictures in Robert's history books that it was a Regency house, and the old mellow bricks told me so, as well. There it stood, glimmering among the fields in the dusk, beautiful, wistful, with sallies of trees, on its sloping lawn, and a wych-elm in full grace and mystery beside the front door.

Lingeringly, I went up the path. It was my sister who answered my ring—Anda, and yet not Anda. Whatever I had expected, I had not anticipated this radiance, this blossoming, not of being sophisticated or grown up, but of having found herself, found her childhood. There she stood on the door-step in coloured, audacious clothes, larky and released.

As the daughter of poor people, she had never had time to be a child. From the beginning, Anda had been old and petulant and disillusioned. Of course, in a street like ours where circumstance was so ugly, exacting, and joyless, to act as a child would be tantamount to behaving like a lunatic. For my part, I had had my childhood to myself, without word or gesture, locked up as a treasure in my own heart and mind. But, for the majority, the children of the poor have no childhood unless, *after* they have grown up, enough skill or drama comes to them to enable them *then* to find their childhood.

Anda now had had the great good luck to become a child. That was the immediate thing to be noticed about her. She greeted me with a joyfulness and, above all, with a tenderness I had never known in her.

"Come along," she said, leading me into a spacious sittingroom where a great fire was leaping on the bricks of the open heart—a fighting confusion of flamelets like many golden lions. "We're having a party as soon as the children arrive."

"The children?"

"Oh, yes. Claude would never dream of having a party

76

without children. Whenever he's having one, the children of the neighbouring houses are always invited. He says a party is no party at all without children."

"Why didn't you let me bring Steve, then?"

"Oh," she said, wrinkling her nose, "another time, but not for the first time. Not yet. He'd go and forget himself, wipe his nose on his sleeve or say something with unforgivable candour. And he tells lies as he breathes! Besides, Steve isn't a child. He never was. You know that."

"Well, you weren't one, either, till you came here."

"It's cute of you to see that change in me, and to understand. Well, you always knew more than any of us! We've all of us, in one way or another, pinned our faith to you. Steve can come another time, I promise you. Claude is out, just rushed away to the village for cigarettes or something; he'll be in directly."

"I don't need to ask if you are happy here!"

"Oh, you don't, you don't, Laura dear," she answered. "You know," she went on, her face turning sad, "you and I and the boys have never known what it is to be alive!"

I didn't say anything. I thought: It would be completely wrong to believe that to *live* means to own a lovely home like this. Perhaps the right way *to live* is to demonstrate to yourself that you can manage without such ease and beauty. Time was when, like Anda, I too, would have thought this way of living a magnificent way, indeed. But in the last year or two, I seemed to have gone on to other roads from where I was beginning to see how beautiful it was to own nothing. Existing. conceptions of what constitutes bliss in comparison with our hand-to-mouth methods, were tending to become wiped out, and I was beginning to be so acutely aware of my immense advantages in possessing only myself, that the comforts and amenities of upper middle-class men like Mr Maccabeus, the result of money, art, and fame, seemed excellent in their way, but not for me. Those who have nothing but life understand best how to live.

Of course, I saw how different everything was for Anda and Steve, how the world of Mr Maccabeus was their own true world, and I should not have dreamt of persuading them otherwise.

"But, listen," Anda was saying, "we're not going to talk about our people. I've left them and what they represent. I shall never go back again. I love Claude, he's been wonderful, wonderful!" Her face took on a specially happy look. "You don't know the half of it! I don't love him like you say you're *in love* with a person, but I *love* him, simply that. I would gladly lay down my life to bring him even a minute's happiness—if such a thing were required of me. You'll see why I say this when you've known him half an hour. Now come, and I'll show you the house."

How well she talked about all the house's treasures—pictures, carpets, books, furniture, views from windows. Transformation into this lovely, leisurely new world had given Anda delight at every level of her apprehension.

From her bedroom at the top of the house to the basement kitchen where the housekeeper was creaming jellies and putting sweets and almonds on top of a gigantic trifle, the whole place held charm and happiness. I kept marvelling at the amount of space everywhere. "Why, do you know," I said to her, "if everyone had as much space as this in their home, there'd hardly ever be bad tempers and high words!"

Five or six children hurried in just then, ages ranging from seven to fourteen, good-looking, well-spoken children, interesting and imperious, the kind who looked down on

Steve and me at school. But they swarmed round Anda with enthusiasm, met me politely, forgot me instantly, and began to career about the house, absolutely at home.

But if the children had been noisy, Mr. Maccabeus came in like a hurricane. He was like a whole hill of a man, gigantically fat, and hung with parcels. He had a huge pale face, solemn and intent, but he was nearly always smiling. He had large, green eyes, a forehead like a church-steeple, and a mass of ash-coloured hair as light as goose-down. There was a little fleet of warts by his nose, but these were not grotesque, they seemed to be extensions of his jollity.

He swung off his hat and coat, threw the parcels in all directions, and immediately began playing with the children, including me, without waiting to hear who I was or whence I came.

After a spell of boisterous fun, from the hearthrug where he was sprawling with his red tie like a piece of string hanging down his back, his shirt sleeves up to the elbow showing fair hair streaming off his arms, he thrust children from him on all sides and, drawing Anda to him, he peered into her face with great sorrow, and said:

"Anda, wasn't a sister of yours coming to visit us today?"

"Yes, well; she's here. You were tweaking her hair just now, I saw you!"

"Was I really? Now let me see—but, look here, Mrs. Anda, I have tweaked every girl's hair in this room in the last two minutes. Show me your sister."

Sweeping off another avalanche of children, he puffed his way to his feet and, catching me by the hand, he brought me to him pretty smartly.

"Lor!" he exclaimed, "this is no way to treat a guest! An honoured guest, moreover. How d'ee do, my dear. The rest

79

of you do what you like till it's tea: Anda's sister and I are going off by ourselves to get acquainted."

He took me by the hand and we went out of the room. We came to a locked door on the first floor and, drawing a key from his pocket, the artist said:

"Now you go in there and amuse yourself for a minute while I tidy myself."

"I was wondering where your studio was," I admitted. "Like a stable without a horse—an artist's house without a studio. My! Have you painted *all* those pictures?"

"Me—and the Holy Ghost," he said, biting his wrist and making a finger-ring he was wearing flash and flash with that melancholy fire hidden away in blue gems." I have to keep this door locked, don't you see, else the children would wreck everything. They wouldn't mean to, of course, the thing would just happen. Then they'd be so upset. Children aren't unkind, never imagine it, they just don't think. And why should they think? Childhood isn't for thinking in— it's for living in—the thinking comes on after when there seems nothing else to do. In you go!"

He left me in the large studio. With his departure I was taking his soundings. I had a mental awareness that he was honest, rather anti-social in some of his ideas, affectionate, sensitive, astute, and spry. He was not afraid to walk the whole world with himself, was devoid of all flunkeyisms, was a rip, a mystery.

His pictures stood everywhere—pictures of children and young girls—children skipping, flying over fences, gravely fishing, children going to bed, stooping, arguing, being read to—a methodical radiant crowding of children. And there were girls and young women with poetical hips and flanks—lovely and fiery and strange. But it was what he put into the faces that counted so much: they were all radiantly alive.

My sister Anda was on the latest easel, right in the middle of an almost finished picture. He had painted her as a splendid kind of angel person, and on either side of her was a declension of dogs–all kinds of dogs, from mastiffs to meek dachshunds with brief, elaborate legs. It was a strange, curly composition, hit off in thick lines and slabs of paint—browns and gamboges, with Anda in the centre in smooth airy gold.

"Ah!" exclaimed Mr. Maccabeus, coming in, "do you like it? We're going to call it 'The Angel Who Guards Dogs.' "

I told him I liked it very well, I liked everything that I saw. This artist was a genius whose medium was the monochrome, and for this reason I saw how the colouring of my sister suited him uncommonly well, being a whole code for him, as it were, on the shades of gold and brown.

Another speciality of his was his wonderful flowing line—just like Daumier. I was scheming how to say all this to him; finally I got it out, standing before him where he was sitting on a high stool. He listened to the halting end.

"Well," he said, "that's wonderful! You have a sense for these things. Do you paint? Do you think of being an artist?"

"No," I said, smiling, "I only think of being alive."

He suddenly took my face between his big, beautiful hands, and looked at me very earnestly for a long time.

"To think of being alive, and to be alive, is to be the best artist of all," he said at last. "It's glorious of you to say what you did, especially with your background. Anda has told me all about you—Laura, Laura dear. She said, with uncommon wisdom for our thistledown Anda, she said that you were the only one of your family who had managed to escape that appalling street without ever leaving it. This puzzled me at the time, but in those few words of yours I see, I understand. Aren't you nice!"

"Aren't *you!*" I said. "I'm so glad that Anda has come here!"

"I should like you to be with us, too, and your brothers, all of you. Laura, tell me, don't you ever get lonely for people, for nice people? Eh, Laura?"

"Oh, I don't think so," I said, laughing at his serious face. "When all the people have gone, you've always got yourself to go back to!"

"And is that how you like it?"

"Yes, I do. Being alone is being lucky and strong!"

"If you know *how* to be alone!"

"Yes, if you know how! To be sweet on yourself, I don't mean selfish, is … why … Mr Maccabeus, it's *distinguished!*"

"Oh, my God, Laura, where did you learn all this? Bring me the one who taught you! But there, that isn't the kind of thing that's taught! It has to be revealed! You must have gone down to hell in your short life, child, to come to such terms with life already. What a woman you'll be, what an adorable, wise little creature. I hope I may not know you then: you'd give a man no peace—a man like me. You'd destroy me, so you would!"

His face had broken into such tender smiling, it was too much for me.

"I don't see what on earth you have to praise me for," I cried. "You ought to meet my brother Robert who is wonderful at History, and my brother Steve who is so brilliant at Greek. As for me, I shall not grow to be a Helen of Troy to harrow up the hearts of men. I shall just be—me, just Laura, as pig-guzzling and petty as anyone else! But let's leave me alone, you make me feel so shy! I should like Steve, above all, to be here with you. For Steve and Anda need something different from Robert and me. We don't want anything, but to be nested down somewhere out of the cold—and have a book. They need something else ... love, I suppose. They need tender people."

He drew me to him.

"Everyone needs love, child. Circumstances can make you imagine life without it, but the plain fact is, we are all loved. For if those you see don't love you, there are those you *can't* see who *do*, and it's their love that gives you your splendid insight and independence. No one is alone, no one is unimportant. Oh, I am so glad to have you in my house. You must come again – often. We shall not talk seriously any more today. But what we have said has been fine—fine for me! You're a dear girl. And now, let us go and have tea. There's trifle, I know, and heaven knows what beside!"

"Is there ... is there ... meringue?" I asked timidly. He looked at me very happily when I said that. "Oh, do you like meringues, too! I adore them! They're my favourites! There's a whole mountain of meringues, and you shall eat as many as you can hold. Come along, darling girl!"

We went downstairs hand in hand. Before we went in to the others, he said:

"Come here often—often! For you and I—Oh, we shall always get along *magnificently*!"

Then he burst open the door and rushed in like a madman.

"It's teatime," he bellowed, and we all pounced into a breakfast-room that had become a tea-time room, and we devoured a rich and enormous tea.

After that, languid and sober, we sat round the fire in the

big room, and Mr. Maccabeus told ghost stories and fairy tales, and drew every child something personal on large pieces of brown paper, with brilliant chalks. In less than no time everyone had a drawing, done like lightning. Mine was the head of his Siamese cat who had azure jewelled eyes and was called Peregrine.

When I was jogging home in the bus, a lady climbed in with a hideous little girl who had huge, swollen, radish-red cheeks, bolting eyes, and long hair in two pigtails. But the kindness with which her mother used her could not have been greater if the little girl had rivalled Helen for looks. I thought:

Good for that mother, and good for the little girl, for she will need a lot of love to make up for that face.

And I saw, with sharp regret, how it would be better to be desperately ugly and have a loving mother, than to be as beautiful as angels as were my sister and Steve whose mother cared for them not a jot. The wheels of the bus roared approval.

Well, I thought, it's been a pretty outing! But the best of all had been when I stood by myself in the lane, and the best of it was now, seeing the frosty fields shaggy in the dim moonlight, seeing lamps winding on distant roads, and the high stars above all.

Milestones squatted like hens in the ditch. The ditch gave way to suburban gardens and these to the lights of the town.

Alighting at the terminus, I struck off into the dark streets for home, dodging traffic wheels, flying dark doorways, listening to tango music from a caretaker's rooms above a warehouse, stopping under the blue official lamp shining wanly and correctly on its bracket outside a police station to read a printed exhortation to deliver up—supposing you were sheltering him—Mr. Eugene Luritas, wanted for murder; hearing the stamp of my feet on the paving-flags of shabby, lonely by-ways, noticing the pool of aquarium light at the foot of every street lamp, reflections like great water-lilies waiting to swim away into the river of dark flowing along the gutter. And once again, I got the thrill of the country lane—that thrill in being *me*, in being a girl alive, walking in the night, able to see and read and understand hieroglyphics which resolved themselves into a description of a man— wanted for murder.

I got such a feeling of immensity I felt carried away.

"I'm me," I said to myself. "I'm Laura. When I get home father will be drunk, since it's Saturday night, and he may have done for our mother at last! Or he'll have burnt the house down! It won't matter much—whatever I find. I'm not afraid. Anything can happen. He can murder me if he wants—and he might! I'm fourteen which is no age at all in a clever world. Children make fun of me and grown people don't like me as a rule. I don't mind this. I only mind that dead or alive that *me* inside me, which they say is the soul, finds it good, *good* to be here, there, or anywhere, so long as it is somewhere at all!"

Chapter III

"What other fire could be a better image of the fire which is there, than the fire which is here? Or what other earth than this, of the earth which is there?"

PLOTINUS

I WAS sixteen, nearly seventeen. I had left school nine months and had a job—doling out books to the public in a library—lowly and romantic service.

Our mother said it was stupid work, but she needed my wages, so she did not harass me too much.

But most people thought me stupid and inert, if not a downright idiot. The girls in the street looked down on me because I was not courting. In the back streets of any large town courtship and marriage come on early; in a life ravishingly dull, the prospect of marriage lifts the thoughts of the young above their poverty and insignificance. Most girls in our street had a large family by the time they were twenty-five; at that age they looked forty, and at forty their lives were finished.

Did I seem stuck up in this matter of young men? I wasn't. But I had never met anyone I wanted, and my mind was on other matters. I wanted to be *wholly* myself. I wished to live by my own volition, and not in what might degenerate into whining expectations and exactions of someone else.

As for the girls and young men among whom I worked in the library, they came of families far more prosperous than mine. They worked, indeed, simply for pocket money; they wore smart clothes, they were busy with all sorts of social occasions—parties, theatres, rowing on the lake, dinners—and considered me a bookish and aloof kind of barbarian because I had none of those things that went to make up the happiness of the average human being.

But I was brazen in my poverty, for poverty is not a shame. One's fortune is to be judged by one's imagination.

Yet I could have redeemed myself in their eyes if only I had had ambition, if I had been competitive in any way; and, once again, I was found wanting.

"Life must be terrible for you!" my detractors would sniff from time to time. I said nothing. Coming from a home that was one round of blazing rows, I was shy of arguments outside it.

But I could not see that my life was terrible: I thought theirs was. They had no time to live! All the day and half the night taken up with things that were especially unloved by me! What was their life? Where did it take them? They were cooped—clamped to prevailing fashions, to social customs, to the itch to Reform, to herd-instincts and the niceties of class-distinction, to the paraded false front.

I went lucky and free. I explored my own thoughts and impressions to the limit. I never looked, but I always found!

All this was only my view, but even the poor scarecrow in the field may have his own crooked opinion about the stars that crack out above him and the disorder of daisies at his heels.

Of course, like many persons who are nearly seventeen, I used to ask myself:

"Where are you going, what are you doing?" And, for the life of me, I could not answer. I had no answer when I asked myself what was the use of such a life as mine in which I had only gone on consciously intensifying my childhood's rapture in the little anythings of daily life, the bright, tremendous little nothings or—what the world calls nothing; a life in which, with lasting wonderment and curiosity and greed, I made detailed observations not only of the beautiful omens of each passing day, but of every manifestation of life—nothing ever made into a habit, nothing ever taken for granted—trying to find affinities and harmonies with the inanimate as well as the quick, with the absurd as well as the exquisite; busy collecting far-off, precious memories of birds and winding roads, of old white gates of drives thrown back against the bushes in the rain, of the porticoes of old theatres, of crow-ruined trees on windy knolls, of the contained secret look of very old houses, of endless perspectives of lamps on roads.

Why was it that I put up such a cry after these evocations? Why hover over past experiences till they ran with the fires of significance? And deck present experiences with this creative faculty of joy. How could this pride and delight in life s mystery and sweetness and humour make me a good and useful citizen? It was not as though I were a poet to give them back to the world; no one would be better in their life-tenancy because of what I had found in mine. Who cared whether I saw paradise before I had died to inherit it, in an old mossy wall, a broken flight of marble steps, in the poor hungry soil of town gardens, in the right good look of certain anonymous hands stretched across the library counter for their tickets, in grass and bricks, and a starry sky over the town? Where was the virtue of such artless, undirected happiness, such awareness of life and earth such life and earth ecstasies!

I had no one to ask. But I felt I was right in my realization of the value and infinite possibilities of my continued childhood's activity. So, while other earnest young people were sitting for examinations or making such social contacts as would be useful to them later on, or courting cosily in front of the parlour fire, I myself knew of nothing more important than this directing of my life steadily towards those forms flashing ecstasy like lighthouse beams in the dark; I knew of nothing more important than to go on and keep on till the anguished insistence of one's own personal fate was hushed in something mightier, till any misfortune, any disease, or *any* death should find me unconquerable. The great thing was to make one's self so plastic that no person alive could harm one.

To make of myself, to bring myself to the *whole conclusion of myself*—this was my idea of my *duty* and success in life.

Our father, spying me enjoying the *private character* of a piece of coal or the salt glittering on the table under the gaslight, or enthralled by other homely wonders, used to say:

"Our Laura is always thinking! She thinks so hard you can almost *hear* her, but she thinks too much for a little one. Yet perhaps she is going to die young and is getting it all in!"

To this, even our mother had no answer, and having in her make-up certain talents, such as dexterity in intrigue, a sparkling spite, and an endless capacity for meaningless small talk which would have placed her in the front ranks of high-society women—she now brought a high-society woman's management to our father's comment: she ignored it.

One of my colleagues in the library often lent me her bicycle on Sundays, and I rode out in my blue cap, my shabby knee-length cinnamon coat and square-toed shoes. At such times, going about the country, I yielded to the battery of magic everywhere.

I would look with radiant affection and an abiding sense of adventure beyond telling, at the perfect fittingness of a ground fern lying coiled on the short turf like a lizard, a fire that tramps had built, the chestnut woods slapped into leaf by the late April wind, the benign ectoplasmic face in a cloud, a little stream getting ready to jump its first weir, a heaving pine clinging for the dear life to a hillside, its roots all exposed in their poverty and danger. My legs dug down into the soil, my blood streamed into the earth, my hands tingled in the wind, my arms were boughs, my legs the scraggy digging roots. "We are Us, that tree and me, we are fighting, we are one!"

Best of all was the wind that released a wine-dark torrent of memories, memories not only my own, but also those of my ancestors, of other peoples' ancestors, till I seemed to be invaded by memories of the English scene from the dawn of time, subtle and intoxicating.

I would return home when the night was down, lonely and forgotten, staring with unholy joy at the new moon setting early like a red finger-nail on the misty sky.

These were times when there came to me a hush of rapture so compelling as to be akin to pain. These were times to dream without end, when any sudden sniff of rain-soaked acres, any solitary poppy that had seeded itself on the shore of a wayside ditch, any sulphur butterfly would touch me to the soul. And these were times to tap the giant deposits of the consciousness of people who had lived centuries before me, lingering yet in places where they had been happy, where they had suffered fear, where they had lived and loved and died.

Why, I thought, too many people think that gems are all in Bond Street; they seem to ignore that gems are in the enamelled spots on fishes, in the eyes of birds, in the blackberry shining in the September hedge.

My occupations did not go unnoticed by my exceedingly curious brother, Steve.

"Oh, Laura," he would cry impatiently, "why do you spend hours and hours staring at a fallen leaf? What a fool you are! Do you expect it to turn into gold?"

But it did turn into gold or—something better than gold.

When I look at the fallen leaf it looks back at me, and though it is a small thing, it is a symbol of the whole wide universe, speaking to me of that hidden harmony binding all. The fallen leaf is a world in itself, a miracle of growing, unfolding, and dying to requicken the cycle, to begin again. Deathless it is, and beautiful; its poetic significance moves me in a look from mortal life into life everlasting. The creator of it created me—there are no barricades between my consciousness and its sentient life. Its nerves and my muscles are needled together; we, in our separate forms are totally related to One creative Idea which, however badly men have used it or twisted it, remains triumphant, positive good through time and beyond time.

It heightens existence for me, it makes me feel ampler, that fallen leaf. I am caught in no limiting boundaries of the sorrows and reasonings of my own mind. And I become conscious of One, *the* One who says:

"I am the understanding of them that understand, the splendour of the splendid."

To my brother, of course, I said no word of this, but to my gods I prayed that never would future possible wealth, or love, or art make it possible for me to forget how, in their own right, blades of grass and drops of rain had given me glimpses into the very heart and truth of life itself. The keenest loss would be to dismiss life, to find life wanting.

It was about this time I came across a man who, in a book, emphasized that nothing was more important than my method of searching for the innermost reality by way of the outward appearance of things. Through him I saw that the use of my gleanings, of my lucky choice of the role of a life-lover, of my cumulated stores of rapture, was to develop in me once and for all reserves of amiability and endurance—an endurance that one day I was to use to the utmost of its strength.

I found this book in the library; it was written by the Irish dramatist and poet—Bernard McCann. I found him dealing exhaustively with that happiness I had found in the world behind the world. Bernard McCann did not give me my magic, but he confirmed that I was right in collecting so reverently the riches of the little humble happenings of ordinary life. He confirmed that these things proved their worth if only in the intensity they awakened in the spirit of those who contemplated them.

He showed me that the only way to live was by this trick of making limitless horizons from sticks and stones, of seeking that loneliness in which, through silence, sunny incorporeal images made their beautiful journeyings.

It was the one trick whereby magic memories of the past cancel out the pain of the present and apprehensions of the future.

Through him I saw that it was vain to take and expect from the world—the art was to make the sanctuary in one's own corner of it, and intensify one's sense of endless livingness.

From the time of reading Bernard McCann, he became the giant who dominated the dream. His words made incandescent my happy loneliness. He opened up for me immense, byzantine vistas of the "Apple Tree, the Singing, and the Gold." I felt that he must have stood very near to that absolute of wisdom, serenity, and beauty that everyone looks for and seldom finds. At any rate, he made the world anew for me, and my own private landscape grew infinite, ever changing, ever more racy and wonderful.

I saw how right I had been to live two lives, one for the world, the other for the earth. And so I was refreshed and charmed to continue against all that was disquieting—and there was much—learning more and more how to barricade myself behind the airy walls of my own imaginings. I became expert at escaping from life into life. From there I could strike balances. This was necessary in living with a woman· like our mother whose need for daily commotion caused even hard facts to surpass themselves.

It is true she sometimes came very near to making a serious inroad, but she had no power against what already was my final conclusion: There is no one with me but myself! All the same, I accept. This will do for me.

This coercion of day-dreams, while making me what our mother called "a blithering idiot," did give me something that was nearly clairvoyant when it came to dealing with the false claims of the world.

Still, it took a lot of practice always to find the hidden harmony and relativity of things. Besides the horrors other people bring there are one's own private horrors to quell. The naked cruelties of wild nature could topple me; the inhumanity of humanity could douse light and hope for me.

Certain people and rooms gave off something that filled me with apprehension.

To my perception, the bedroom of the wife of our rich uncle—with its white lace bedcover, raspberry coloured furniture, and glittering glass, like the paper cover illustrations on libidinous French novels—was crammed with the oddest intentions. There was something in her room to untie chastity; the atmosphere was so loose and unlawful it seemed to dwarf your worst imagined possibilities of evil, so that nothing seemed wrong. I found there a curious lurking of revelations, of exciting parcels being undone with acute anticipation; first the glossy outer covering taken off, then the delicate white tissue paper removed, and at last the prize is revealed. Squawks of delight are given off and the cherished object curled in the arms.

This notion was presently given life-size proportions when, one afternoon, returning early from his picture-gallery through illness, our rich uncle came to this same bedroom and stood by while the glossy outer covering was taken off the delicate white underskirt removed, and the body of his wife received with squawks of delight by one of his friends. Our rich uncle burst into tears on the spot, but later he divorced her.

Telling of the scene that had brought about a court case, in the presence of Robert and myself, we being considered old enough to hear of such human infirmities, our mother was astounded when, at the end of her story I said, more to myself than to the company:

"Yes, I knew all the time!"

"You knew!" bawled our mother. "What do you mean? Were you acting as a go-between for the wretches? You'd better mind what you are saying, else you'll find yourself dragged into the witness-box, a nice thing, too!"

"I meant," I said, "I guessed!"

"And I'm not surprised," said our father, unconsciously coming to my rescue. "You had only to take one look at her to see what she was. He must have been hard up to go marrying that trash!"

"Now that's enough from you, William Valley," our mother put in. "Your family never had anything to boast about—in fact, it's the worst family I ever knew: no end to its shortcomings. It was a one-child family, as well—it was *you!*" And then followed the inevitable wrangle.

It was a strange world, indeed. Filled with merry, wonderful, and unaccountable things, such as I receiving some of my best and most beautiful thoughts in the privy, and laughing when I should have been crying if someone came and told me at their mother had been caught in a windmill. Life was life!

But now a long-extended conspiracy that had been working for the collapse of my brother Steve came to its shattering and inevitable climax.

He was fourteen. The high spots in his education were that he flourished at elocution, could paint with crude power and no taste, could write a bold essay splitting all infinitives without conscience and introducing descriptions of those areas of the anatomy that nice boys are not told they own let alone be encouraged to digress upon, and finally he was the most brilliant Greek scholar who had ever graced the Grammar School rolls. His Classics master and the headmaster predicted a wonderful career for him at the university. He himself had grown somewhat less cynical in his outlook.

Of his Greek he once said to me:

"When I say Greek, I say it in a soft voice, and caressingly, as if I told the best of all things to the best of all people. No one is in the room with me, except those I cannot see!"

Every week I saved something microscopic towards the time when he should be eighteen and ready for the university; what I had put together by then might help him, together with such scholarships as he would be certain to gain. I was not able to save much; most of my salary went to help the housekeeping. Nowadays our father was not very well: he was not always able to go to his work in the tavern. He had grown very lean and silent, and once it had seemed impossible that he could ever grow thinner.

It was the beginning of September, and I had just lit the gas on a warm mellow evening. Robert was sitting at the table affectionately working out some dates in history, and Steve was reading "Gulliver's Travels," the grown-up unexpurgated edition.

Our mother had the hearth to herself—this was usually the case. The children did not gather round her, they kept their distance: it was no family fireside.

Robert left off studying and began to read "The Importance of Being Earnest," enjoying it aloud, with numerous quotations.

"For heaven's sake, leave off," protested Steve at last. "Anyone would think that Wilde was the only man of letters with any wit, to hear you carrying on!"

"Mention a better!" said the seventeen-year-old Robert darkly.

"There's the man I'm reading now, for a start," retorted

Steve, "Jonathan Swift, and there are his friends Congreve and Addison! And what about Charles Lamb, and de Quincey? You ought to read them—Oh you really ought to read de Quincey; he is really sinister, he is fine! Begin with 'Murder Considered as One of the Fine Arts.' It's there where he says, for instance: 'It is absolutely barbarous to murder a sick person, who is usually quite unable to bear it!'"

Robert and I laughed loudly. Robert said:

"That school of yours is certainly bringing you on!"

"Oh, the place is all right," Steve said lightly, scared to say too much of what was so dear.

"I suppose you'll be in the Fifth when you return after these holidays?" said Robert.

But our mother, seething over her sewing, said to Robert in her hot rude way, not even troubling to address Steve:

"There's no need for him to begin bothering himself where he'll be next term, because he isn't going back to school—a good job, too, if that's the sort of stuff they're teaching him. I heard what he was saying about murder— the unnatural little devil! The sooner he gets out to work, the same as you had to when you were fourteen, the better! That'll knock the nonsense out of him!"

Silence. Terrible, packed silence, edging out from the fireside to every corner of the room. In this heightened moment we all seemed to shrink. I began to feel mown down with fear. A church spire suddenly mewed eight, and even that accustomed sound seemed wild and outrageous.

What unthinkable words were these? She had at last dropped the bombshell she had been preparing so lovingly for her little boy. But why, why? There was no need for him to leave school. We were better off now than ever before with both Robert and me contributing to the upkeep of the house. There were no fees to pay for Steve, and he always had managed to buy his text-books for a few shillings at second-hand shops. The truth was, she had no other intention but to outrage his heart, to give full vent to her peculiar dislike of him. He had got too far away from her, was too independent of her at the school. The thought of losing this highly satisfactory channel for the display of her own powers and whims was not to be thought of!

Undivided and grasping, she could not bear it when any territory was taken away from her, when anyone swung in a wind not of her blowing. She'd have liked all the world to lie wrapped in her apron whence, grudgingly, she'd have allowed a river or two to trickle away on its own course, a little man or two to leak out and live his own life. She'd have preferred to do away with any idea of her womanliness, for she saw herself as some super being of neuter gender, a power rather than a person. She would have liked to make men from clay and plot their lives to the end. But people demanded the right to be themselves: that was the scald! Most of the time she went about the world publicly asserting that fate had treated her mean!

Steve got up and came round to where she was sitting in her elbow chair. Although his eyes were entranced with apprehension, he said to her in a courteous way, with sincere concern to understand:

"I don't follow your meaning! Why must I leave school?"

Instantly her eyes caught fire and ran red with rage. She really could not bear to be questioned:

"There's no problem to be worked out—it's all quite clear—you're going to leave school. It's all been arranged with the headmaster. I wrote three weeks ago and this morning I had the letter saying they were going to release you. I don't know what you've been telling them at that school of yours, for he said he had always thought you were going on to the university. You! He came out with a lot of nonsense about it being a shame if you did not go on with your studies. It'll be a shame if you do go on with 'em! It'll be the ruin of you! He must think we're millionaires!"

She stopped to breathe, then went on with her ghastly extravagance:

"How much longer have your father and I to go on slaving for you? All your lazy life? You and the university! Anyway, I've put a stop to that! You're not going back to school. It's time you began to earn something. You're getting beyond yourself, you're too high and mighty since you got a bit of Greek into you. And where does it get you? Nowhere, except to make you look down on your elders and betters. You and your schoolmasters! You are a sucker-up, my lad! I've got your number all right, mister clever! I'm going to stop your little gallop if it's the last thing I ever do. Why should you have all that schooling? You don't deserve it! Robert never had it, and he deserves it more than you. Go on, get away from me! Don't stand there—staring. What's done is done, and you can't alter it. Get off, get away!"

This unpleasant woman was beginning to lose her head a little under his grave scrutiny. He had listened most attentively to the unexpected ferocity of his fate. Unless you knew him well, you could never have told that he was really listening to his doom. There was a look of mild surprise on his face. You would never have suspected, without knowing him, that something had come to him so sorrowful arid paralysing that he was experiencing what, for want of a better name, is often called a broken heart.

But I knew. I knew by the hands he was keeping out

of sight, how they'd be clenched, knew by the way he kept tipping up and forward on his toes, and by his bright, concentrated stare. I knew, too, his terror and anxiety now that she had taken away his only escape—the school. It was touching beyond tears.

Robert and I both began to expostulate with her at once, pointing out that it was not necessary for him to give up school. We offered to give our pocket-money to the house on top of the bulk of our salaries that we already contributed—anything to help, to keep Steve at school. Then Robert made the fatal mistake of emphasizing to her what a brilliant scholar Steve was, and how, if he went on to the university when he was eighteen, the world could not fail to hear of him.

"He's leaving school," she shouted at us, not less hideously than before. "He's *left!* You've all gone mad with this higher education. He's left, he's left, he's left!"

It was unarguably settled. After his first quiet enquiry, Steve had said nothing. He still remained by our mother's chair in a kind of shocked confusion, a spare little boy, quietly distrait.

"Oh, blast it!" she turned on him in a flurry of vindictiveness. "Don't stand there, looking as though you've been mashed! Else I shall really give you something to look sorry for!"

She was afraid now; she was afraid of what she had done to him, and, truly, she had cause to fear.

Under her last outburst, he backed away from her. He returned to the table and stood looking agitatedly down on his book. His hand went out to it, then fell to his side. Suddenly he came on furiously to cry and stumbled to the door.

Sombrely she watched the cringing little boy find his way out of the room. Nobody said anything. We could hear Steve travelling about upstairs.

"Now what's he doing?" our mother demanded of us.

"Better go up and see," said Robert, coldly.

"That'll do," she said.

In a few minutes Steve came downstairs, wearing his halfbelted overcoat and his cap with the broken peak. He was making for the street door.

"Where d'you think you're going this time of night?" our mother asked him.

He did not reply; he went out of the house, thinking to himself.

"The hateful little wretch! He won't answer when he is spoken to!" said our mother. The minutes ticked loudly by. She became restless.

"Do you think he'd go and do anything … silly, Laura?" she asked presently, not looking at me.

"I think it is extremely likely," I said.

"What? Chuck himself into the canal?"

"No, he's a good swimmer," Robert came in with calm malice. "He's more likely to throw himself under the wheels of a train! You've just about smashed that kid. If you do that to a person—at any age—they're apt to show frenzy and lose their reason!"

"Go to God!" she exclaimed, jumping up. "You two would drive anyone dotty! Talking like that! You must be mad!"

"Perhaps we are," said Robert, "all of us!"

Our mother went and put on her outdoor things; she declared she was going to meet our father as it was too miserable at home.

Robert and I were left alone.

"Do you think ..." I began, but he said, quickly:

"No, no, Laura! Don't think it! He wouldn't do anything. But I couldn't resist being cruel to her. Oh, she deserved it, she did, indeed! But Steve's too young for ... that!"

"He was never young," I said, "never, never. He was never too young to think of anything. He'd go and commit suicide as easily as any grown person. Oh, Robert, I must go out and try to find him!"

"No need," said Robert, "here he is!"

It was half an hour or so since he had gone out. Now that he had returned, we could see at once that he was quite different from the boy who had left the house. Not that there was any dramatic change, no distortion of limb or features; but now he had the utterly contained bearing of a person who has *finally* reorganized himself, and he gave off the terribly disturbing impression of no longer being a boy, but an incredibly beautiful little grown man, who had very cynically worked out all the answers, found everything wanting, false, and loathsome.

"Hello," said Robert to him, not oblivious of this new blow, but acting as if resolved not to notice how wrong things had gone. "Laura's just going to brew some tea. Will you have some?"

"Certainly," replied Steve, "when I come down."

He smiled at us coldly. He had had time to come to himself. He went upstairs. In a few minutes he began to climb heavily down again. He came in submerged under a mountain of books and, staggering over to the fire, he pitched the lot among the blazing coals.

But it was too much to see books, any books, being burnt.

"Ah, don't do that!" I exclaimed hurrying to the fire to retrieve what I could. Steve barred the way.

"I'll thank you, Laura," he said, pleasantly, dangerously, "to leave those books alone. They are my books, I can do as I please with what's mine. Don't upset yourself, either, I do this with no biting regret!"

"But it's such wanton destruction, it's ..."

"Mind your own business," said Steve; he began to laugh. "Wanton destruction! Wanton destruction—Oh! damn' funny!"

When he saw that nothing could be saved of that pile, Steve went upstairs for the next batch. I could not bear to see any more. I went into the scullery and began to make the tea. Four times I heard him come down with material for the holocaust—the one gesture he was deeming worthy of the magnificence of his despair.

As the last of those once-treasured volumes were burning, I went in with the tea. He was prodding the burning pages with the poker, smiling faintly, but, judging by the expression in his eyes; his heart must have been lead. He turned to us:

"Well! I have finished with all that! From now on, I've done with books! With good books! I've left one school for ever, but I shall start in another. I've saved one text-book for my studies there, I've saved 'Gulliver's Travels.' I shall be like its author—I shall love hating everybody! There is sense and clarity in that!"

He had gone to the table and was drinking his tea. Over the rim of the cup his eyes looked at us treacherously.

"Well," said Robert, "no one can doubt that you have just had a facer! And no one would deny you've some cause to agonize about it! But don't take it the hard way. Hating everyone won't make you feel better—you'll only feel worse, you'll go down!"

"Ah!" said Steve, softly, "now it is time for us to try and remember what our pastor told us about staying up! Staying up in the light! But, Oh, how I like that last phrase of yours, 'You'll go down!' Oh, how attractive it is to me and all that it implies. *Going down* is just what I'm getting at, and it's unusually astute of you to fear it. You aren't nearly so thick-headed as I have always thought you were!"

"You're a fool if you play into her hands," said Robert. "That's just what you are doing. She wants to make you what you intend to make yourself. She wants nothing so much as to loaf, as it were, in your mind, fouling all the landscape, and here you are—giving her permanent admission. Don't you be having any! Don't talk about thick-headedness, my boy, you're much more stupid than I am if you give up now and give in!"

"No doubt you mean well," said Steve, kindly, "but you are doing no more than spitting against the wind!"

"Mean well? Oh, what a fool you are. You're the one member of the family she really has captured. Anda ran away, I have my own defences, and so has Laura. Laura has learnt how to *dissolve*. What has been hardened can be broken. Don't get hard, Steve. If we all dwelt on what goes on in this house, we'd all go dotty and bitter—just like you!"

"I'm not going to say that she destroyed me," replied Steve. "We can all be safely trusted to do that for ourselves: her deadliness is that she has taken away from me the hope that tomorrow would be different. Yes, I used to hold a long-continued, nourishing hope that tomorrow would be different, but now I see that it will be as it's always been!"

"Oh, for God's sake!" exclaimed Robert. "It's up to *you*,

not her, to make tomorrow different—or not. Can't you see? Look here, you know more about Greek than the fellow who taught you. Go and work like she said, go into some miserable little job, but if your dreams are strong enough you'll ride over everything on them and come into your own at last." He became fervent upon his subject. "You've burnt all your books, you ass, but I'll replace the Greek ones, so that you can go on by yourself. It'll be a retreat, it'll be fine to remember that you're a fluent Greek scholar when people try to make free with you and bring you low. You've been marching behind that banner ever since you went to the Grammar School, escaping from her into your learning; I know, I've seen, I've understood, and good luck to you. All you've got to do is to continue the same way. Everyone's got something to put up with, worse than you, perhaps, but a person has to ... to meet things!"

Steve, who had listened to all this in respectful silence, said, thoughtfully:

"That is very beautiful! It may be the sacred truth for you: it means sweet damn' all to me! By the way, where *do* you get hold of such clap-trap? At any rate, it's a pity to waste it on me, for l haven't the faintest use for what you have just said, or, for that matter, for *anything* anyone may say! What took place this evening was an affair of the most insistent order and leaves a carbon copy on the mind!"

"There you go again!" cried Robert.

"There I go again," replied his brother, peaceably. "You see, I can't rise. I'm not one of God's collaborators like you! I can't reach those heroic heights on to which you have been shoved by your personal ill luck! It must be wonderful to be you! What a destiny! But I, who am by no means a descendant of Sir Galahad, I don't understand adversity, I don't like it, my badly-balanced mind can't make the best of it, and it's too much trouble to keep on trying. Life is too complex and dangerous to *make the best of it*. Yes, I know what you're going to say—that I'm too small for my part. Well, I am. Like everyone else, I was born with a positive bad streak, but I have been *made* worse. When I went out just now everything seemed frightful. I thought I should run away—but—where was I to go? There was nowhere. It came to me how strange life is, how distasteful, how evil. Something I had cherished had gone beyond any retrieving, and there is no compensation. At the same time I saw what I could do. Since life is so mangy and cruel and bad, I shall shape my way of living to life. If life is bad, I shall be worse! Where I can't put it into practice through lack of opportunity or fatigue, I shall retain it in my imagination. Oh, Oh, I didn't read Homer for nothing! Everything that *is* was in the imagination first! Old naturalists tell, and I believe it's in Herodotus, too, Robbie, that the humming bird and the lapwing enter without fear into the wide-open mouth of the crocodile and they are not crushed by the monster because they are there to pick its teeth! That shall be for me, too. The monster, Evil, will let me into its maw and will not harm me, because I shall have come to pick its teeth! That's the sort of an aspiration to cherish!"

"You're laying it on pretty thick, aren't you?" fumed Robert.

"And you're taking on as though I minded what has happened when, all the time, I don't care. You're making an over-solemn occasion of this! I don't care about anything any more. I simply don't care! All the action assembles at that point. If you can get that fixed into your head we shall

106

get along very prosperously. Laura, is there any more tea? And I'm hungry! Make me some toast, eh?"

I thought, well, thank God, he's not too dehumanized to want something to eat!

At about half-past ten our parents came in. I had made some supper for them. Our mother entered the room and her eyes flew before her, like agents sent on ahead by her anxiety to find out how the land lay. You could see the eyes returning, subsiding, when they saw that Steve had come home. Those eyes saw a boy quietly reading "Gulliver's Travels," not lying at the bottom of a pond or mangled on the railway. It seemed to them that a boy reading "Gulliver" was better than a boy dead, but they were eyes that had never known the value of anything.

Our mother's relief was wordless but loud. Both our parents had had a little too much to drink. Our father smiled at us in his vague lost way. Immediately he began to eat his supper.

Our mother joined him. Munching, she presently said to Steve, bringing it out as brightly as she could:

"Your father and I have been thinking ..."

She paused. Steve looked at her with polite interest.

"We have been thinking," she resumed, "that since you have left school you won't be needing all those books that make such a nasty clutter in your bedroom. So—we might as well sell them. No use to you now."

"I didn't catch all of that," Steve said, and with ceremonious insolence he leant his ear to listen. She delivered it again.

"What a pity," said Steve, "that you didn't mention it before you went out—not that it would have made any difference. But, you see, when you told me how beautifully you had arranged things I decided to play my part, too, and I've burnt them."

He looked at her with a sort of suppressed convulsive glee. "You've burnt them?" she echoed, looking about foolishly. "You mean—*burnt* them?"

"Yes," he said, "simply that!"

"And who gave you permission to burn them?" she asked.

"I gave it to myself," he replied. "My days of *asking* for permission are over."

"Well, you impudent, destructive little hound!" she exclaimed. "What d'you mean by going and burning all those books that your father and I slaved to buy for you?"

"Excuse me," he said, "you seem to overlook that all of those books were bought for me with Robert's and Laura's pocket-money, money that they earned, having nothing to do with your 'slaving.' But now they are burnt—nothing will ever bring them back again!"

Our father looked at the bleak loaded face of his youngest son, and what he saw there made him cry with violence when our mother made to rage at the boy anew:

"That's enough, that's enough! Be done with it! You've said enough and done enough for all time, judging by what I can make of it!"

"That's a nice thing to say after I've done all the dirty work for you," she said, indignantly.

"The dirty work!" he repeated, dreamily. "The dirty work! Aye, you've always done that, I think!"

"You wanted him to leave school as much as I did," she retorted, maliciously.

"Nay," he said, lifting his face with its strange, imperishable disfigurement, "let's have no lies. It was all your idea and I told you I should have nothing to do with it. If I was half a man I should have had something to do with it—I should have stopped it! But you always were the boss here, and I reckon it takes more than I've got to break the habit of a lifetime. What's happened is between the boy and you. Leave *me* right out of it." He turned to me. "Laura, my dear, have you got a bit more ham? There's one thing, if you've got no comfort anywhere, there's always a bit in a mouthful of food!"

I gave him another helping. Steve, catching his harassed eyes, said:

"Dear father, it is kind of you to state your mind so freely, but, hereafter, you will have no cause to reproach yourself on my account; you will have no cause to be proud, either!"

Our father sighed and looked at him with trepidation and pity, almost as though he understood, as though he saw how out of all those anonymous hours of rage and dislike and galling disappointments there had arisen between Steve and his mother a skulking entity, out for no good, an entity that tacked itself on to Steve's life like some brilliant, evil fungus, he being the younger, the less-armoured, the one still growing, still groping. Our father seemed to recognize, also, that this entity, called into being, must go on to its destined end, driving its host along with it, pitiless, ruinous. And it all seemed to be too much for our father. He pulled the evening paper towards him, newly-folded from the stationer's, and, nosing straight into the middle pages let out an exclamation.

"Hello!" he cried, "here's our Anda—with Royalty!"

Robert and I went to look. Sure enough, there was a photograph of our lovely sister with Mr. Maccabeus and, standing between them, was the visiting monarch of one of the smaller continental kingdoms. The occasion was the purchase of one of Claude's pictures by the cultured king, and the caption ran to the effect that His Majesty had not only asked for the distinguished artist to be presented to him, but also the model who had made the picture possible. It seemed that the artist and his protegee were in London, and the gossip column on another page devoted three-quarters of its space to describing Anda's beauty, popularity, and the high circles in which, with Mr. Maccabeus, she was now moving.

"Think of her hob-nobbing with Royalty!" said our father softly. He put the paper down, and a look of fond pride and regret came into his face.

"Well," he said stoutly, "she was made for better things than this place. She left home and now she moves with Royalty! I don't grudge her this success, I'm as proud as can be, only ... I wish ... I wish she had not left home in such circumstances that she cannot write and tell us herself about this pretty event ... I wish we did not have to hear of her successes second-hand through the gossip columns of an uncaring newspaper!"

Neither Steve nor our mother showed by so much as the stirring of a hair that they had heard or appreciated the glory that had fallen on Anda Valley.

I began to clear away the supper-things. Even the good news about Anda (from whom I had not heard for a long time, and had not seen for even longer now that she and Mr. Maccabeus were spending most of their time in London), could not hush my grief at what had overtaken Steve. What haunted me most was the thought of the fourteen-year-old threshing about in the streets, as he had done, cold and proud, confident of no mercy or solution, and arriving at those terrible conclusions. But it was going on all the time—everywhere. My thoughts flew out to all in the world who, that night, were listening, as my brother had done, to the taunting words of tyrants—to men and women in the clutches of blackmailers; prisoners in cells, controlled by bullying warders; little boys in boarding schools caught by sadistic seniors; hungry curs watching with terrified eyes their masters undoing their belts. My heart contracted with pity for them all.

"It's infernal, infernal! I can't bear it," I thought. It was a long time since I had been so cast down. But an unkind day, such as this, was not to end without some bit of magic. Riveted in those forlorn thoughts, I began to prepare for the washing-up, and as I went into the scullery, all the small attendant circumstances, and the delicious personalities of common kitchen things began quietly to assert themselves, asking to be recognized and valued, offering their own consolations—coming to the rescue.

The candle in the tin candlestick on the window ledge above the sink, wagged joyfully in a little draught from the backdoor; the candlestick of tin shone like a candlestick of silver; the candle flame was like a little rose set against the damson black night looking in through the uncurtained window. The dripping tap on the enamel basin sounded like a springtime bird cheeping, and the kettle, riding the azure circlet of lighted gas on the stove, gave off sounds of importance and pride. Stale water in the enamel bowl had a metallic lustre, giving an impression of a tarn high in the hills. High lights and prisms from the candle caught plates, the sides of cups, and the slopped tea in the saucers. There to be seen were the grease and tomato seeds and vinegar stains on the plates, resolving themselves into whimsical landscapes under the concentrated gaze of some bland potatoes that had not been used at the midday dinner. And all the pots and pans on shelves ranged round, glinted and smirked and leaned forwards in the friendliest way in the world. While a fired-glass dish of stewed shrivelled apples, also left over from dinner, seemed, in this humble metamorphosis after the pride of the orchardbough, to possess a helplessness, an inanimate pathos, before which my own sadness began to recede. I could not be overwhelmed by circumstances amid the awarenesses stored in this jovial inanimate little world.

"All right," I said to them, "all right. It's enough. You've lit the light!"

And so they had! They had flung me head first out of circumstantial misery into an immensity that seemed to dwarf eternity itself!

What a fool you are, I said to myself, as I rattled the crockery. Can't you see the amazing simplification of affairs, by living as though *you are not living at all!* The misery and the pain cannot be escaped, cannot be alleviated, but only *one* of your many, many *selves* suffers, you fool! The kitchen things have helped you to push the hordes of other selves into that vast liberating land which, year after year, you have been creating; making illimitable. The tragedy of life is not the tragedies! The catastrophe, you fool, would be if you had only developed *one* of your selves, and this *alone* had to meet the horrors and anguish of circumstance.

I could have laughed aloud. I had got back my feeling, lost only fleetingly, of the magic of life everywhere, at any time.

In the following days, no one said a word to Steve about his getting a job. It became his wont to leave the house with Robert and me in a morning, part from us outside the library where I worked, and remain away the whole day. He never returned till late or early nightfall. How he fared during those absent hours no one knew, and he did not offer to tell. Certainly he did not seem put out, hungry, or neglected, though where he was getting his food was a mystery. He now wore an air of casual endurance more awful than if he had fretted in all sincerity.

October came with lengthening evenings. One night, so late that our father had returned from the tavern and was sitting all in a mop and mow over his supper, Steve strolled in with an especial air of well-being.

He dropped into a chair and said to me:

"Oh, Laura, you should see how the mill-windows are shining in the dark streets! That is just what you like! They must be working a late shift. The effect is quite magical!"

Our mother leaned across to Robert and said, very confidentially:

"He's fourteen years old, he stays out till half-past eleven at night, and when he comes in all he can say is some fool thing to Laura about mill-windows! What d'you make of that?"

"I think it's a very sensible observation," said Robert. "It's a pity more people don't look at the lights shining in the dark night."

Baulked, she turned to our father, so much less of an ally now: "And what do you make of it?" she asked.

"I don't know'," he said, tiredly. "I don't know what to make of anything any more."

He stirred the orts on his plate with his fork, and meditated, frowning.

"A pity about you!" she sniffed.

She then addressed Steve directly:

"I wonder if it's asking too much of you to tell us just

where you have been till this time of night-to-night and every night—coming in with *that* look on your beastly little mug! Of course, boys your age could be made to speak—by the police. It'll be interesting to see just how far you will go before I think of bringing them in to you!"

"Oh," said Steve, amiably, "there's no mystery about where I've been. If you don't know it's because you've never troubled to ask. But, call in the police, by all means, any time you like. I should not be the only one who'd have to account for my actions. Anyway, I've brought off something besides the ability to see lights shining in the dark streets. I've brought off a thing that will make you see how right you were to invest in clever children for dividends in your old age—I've got a job at £2 a week!"

Even she was impressed. None of us, including our father, earned money like this. Robert, who was slowly rising in the counting-house of the firm where he had worked since he was fourteen, had recently had a rise to twenty-seven and six a week, and this, till now, had been the top wages in our family.

"What kind of a job is it?" asked our father.

Steve stood up and threw off his overcoat.

"You might give me a cup of tea, Laura," he said. Then, going to the table and seating himself beside his father, he said: "I'm on the stage, father. I'm on for ten minutes twice a night and two matinees a week. I sing a popular song, then I say to the audience: 'Dear ladies, dear gentlemen, do you believe in fairies—'cos I'm one': and I vanish through a trapdoor! Two pounds a week for nonsense like that! It's a shame to take the money!"

"Don't worry," replied our mother harshly. "You won't

be taking it. There's no child of mine going on the stage in all that sin and shame—not while I'm alive!"

Steve went on talking to his father as though no one else had spoken:

"I start rehearsals next week and will be paid thirty shillings a week till the show goes on—in December. It's a sort of revue-pantomime, pretty awful, but the money's useful, don't you think!"

"There's no child of mine going on the stage while I'm alive," repeated our mother like a sort of dreary Greek chorus.

"I thought she'd say that," said Steve to our father, jovially. "And she doesn't disappoint a person! Of course, I shan't stand it! I took the precaution on the way home of finding myself a lodging. I warned the landlady I might even return to-night if my unnatural mother objected too much to my turning an honest penny!"

Our mother gasped and gasped again. And then our father brought upon her a frontal attack, the most devastating of all his career. He stood up against the table and, leaning on the palms of his hands, he said in a loud anguished voice:

"All the children are leaving home! Going ... one by one ... soon there'll be none left!"

He turned to our mother.

"They're leaving," he said, "because of you! But we must stop the children leaving," he declared strongly. "We, and especially you, must treat them differently. Something has gone so wrong in this home that maybe it's too late to do anything to make amends. But we are going to try—*you* are going to try. The children ... are ... going ... one ... by ... one ... years and years before children need leave their home. We shan't let them. We must beg their pardon!"

He looked down at his youngest.

"Don't go away, my boy," he said with dignity.

"No, father," said Steve, looking rather stupefied. But he quickly recovered himself and said sharply:

"But, of course, I shall go on with my job, my precious job that my Greek reading so fittingly qualified me for! Do sit down, father, you are standing in my light! We, in this house, cannot afford to throw away wages of two pounds a week. Good heavens—what's that?"

We all looked round: a new noise was coming to us, a humorous, burbling noise. For the very first time we saw— our mother—weeping! Through non-usage the machinery of her tears creaked, and our reaction had no familiar way of receiving her outburst, either. We all looked away in case we should burst out—laughing.

Our father, who was now sitting peacefully beside his son, and even had his hand on Steve's shoulder, said to me:

"Laura, go in the scullery and see can you find me half a raw onion to have with the cheese. And isn't there something for this boy's supper? If there's nothing in the house, run to the fish-and-chip shop and get him a big paperful of something."

Our mother, realizing that no one was impressed by her drama, gave a loud wounded gasp and made for the stairs.

I gave our father and Steve their supper, and presently, the others having all gone to bed, Steve and I were left alone downstairs.

"Shall you ... shall you mind it very much, dear?" I asked him.

"No, not a bit," he replied. "I don't mind anything. God, but I'm tired. Do you know, Laura, even to get this mean little job I've had to hang about agents' offices for days.

And be servile to 'em, you know, and spread all my charms before them!"

He looked suddenly old and drained. He had closed his dispirited eyes. I remembered how wonderfully he had been attracted by the Hellenic emphasis on the peace and happiness of the *good choice*, and how now his dallyings in those pleasant fields might well never have taken place. The pride and light of his august dreams were all quenched, and he hadn't enough resilience to recover; his fervour was changing to apathy and finally there would be nothing. I went and clutched him by the front of his shirt.

"Is everything *all right?*" I asked roughly.

He opened his eyes and, upglancing at me, he permitted himself a slow smile.

"Oh, it's all right, it's all right! Nothing has been lost that anyone wanted or cared for! It was Larry Passagno got me my job. He's not bad. Not your style, Laura, but good enough for me. He's looked after me a bit. Bought me my lunches and teas. It's where I've been loafing all these days—in his place—he's a theatrical agent. Have you ever seen Passagno, Laura? Well, of course, you have not. He's pitch-black, half Spanish or something. He wears a dark jumper-thing over his trousers, and ear-rings—these flash! I don't suppose his sort ever walked into your library and asked you for something to read. He says reading is a terrible waste of time. He says everybody reads too much, everybody thinks too much. The only way to live, he says, without shoving your head in the gas-oven, is never never to think!"

"Why, that's all right," I said, "that's capital—if you don't know *how* to think!"

"You may have it your way for me! I would not argue

with you for a million! No, even though what you say seems awful fudge to me! But this Larry has been extraordinarily kind to me. If all the ordinary decent human feelings had not been filched from me (and I did try not to get too stony, yes, I did, but no matter) I might have cried some times at the things he has done for me. I talk like some old man, don't I? I always did! I *am* an old man! But Passagno thinks I'm a touching little bastard! Oh, the lies he told to get me this job! It comes to me entirely without my merit. He said I'd been on the stage since I was born, and that I came of a distinguished theatrical family! Oh, very theatrical, don't you think, Laura? But just think, and I give you leave to laugh heartily at this part, Passagno has bought me a dress suit for my ... my act, and a new overcoat and shoes: they're at his office."

"It saddens me to think of you depending on such a man," I said. "You. really can't accept presents like that, Steve."

"Can't I? If anyone is fool enough to be kind to me, I follow that up! And perhaps I *deserve* such presents, perhaps I've earned them. But don't you take me up on that! Those eyes of yours stare at me like a frightened horse! You see, ah, you see too much—you always did! Do not question me, Laura, for I shall always take care to prevent you from knowing the worst! What is *inferred* is best! Hush!"

He laid his arm across my shoulders in some passing hurlyburly of affection, then left me abruptly and sat down. He threw off some rakish, ruminating looks. It was plain to see, in his case, at least, that the innocence of the heart was burnt down once and for all. Dark, new forces in his life now were rapidly rising.

"Passagno, poor ass, is fond of me, don't you know, Laura! Haven't I told you that. You must try to understand. Often he says, blubbering even (it rather thrills me to see tears trailing down that sad ugly face of his), 'If you were my brother, Steve,' he says, 'I could not love you more!' That's just the way he talks! Lays out his motive before a person with the most appalling sincerity. Oh, he's brought me on! At first when he did things for me, I used to look amazed for no one but you ever did anything for me before. he, mistaking my surprise for gratitude, used to shrug and say hurriedly:

'Oh, well, you can pay me back some day—when you've got it!'

'But,' I'd say, 'when I've got "it", I shall want "it" for something more important than paying you or anyone else back.'

Then he laughed and said I'd be certain to make my way in the world because I had got the right idea."

"I'll tell you a thing," I said, dropping into a chair beside him, "there's nothing right about any of this."

"Very likely not," he answered cheerfully. "But it'll do for me. My only worry will be to cope with Passagno's awful fidelity!"

And so it came about that this boy who ought to have spent his youth in old college libraries browsing in the Classics while elm trees looked in through emblazoned windows, playing cricket on long summer evenings and talking with his peers—this darling of the gods stood night after night singing "Everything is Peaches Down in Georgia" for two pounds a week.

He wasn't an expert at it. Sometimes his audiences were rough with him, but not often. For if his singing voice was sentimental and thin, and his act a shabby sort of an affair altogether, his face was like an angel's, and he had about him some undefinable air of quality that hypnotized the louts who came to listen.

It was not long, of course, before the faithful Larry Passagno was dismissed, and a remarkable number of admirers of the worst type never failed to attend him— and were welcomed. He liked his friends to be his mental inferiors: this gave Steve power; and their praise and gaping were needed for his purposes. On them he used his jocund knavery, his whips and scorpions, and they, being so peculiarly constituted as to give off some suggestion of being only half-incarnated, they liked his robust cruelty.

By the time Steve was eighteen he was earning five pounds a week, and faithfully and expensively going straight to the devil.

It was when he was eighteen, nervous and cruel—an uncompromising, dangerous youth, that Steve said to me:

"Laura, to try the terrible charm of one's unknown fate, I'm going to go into straight plays and become a real actor! Yes, indeed—the star-turn!"

Chapter IV

*"Like a pilgrim who has no goal, but who does not
journey in vain."*

KAREL CAPEK

THE stars have no notion of what goes on in a beehive,
nor has a person an inkling of what destiny is preparing
from hour to hour.

No one could have foreseen that when my brother Steve
joined the town's repertory company at thirty shillings a week
for walking-on parts, he would rise from that to be a great
actor. The walking-on parts speedily became minor roles,
and soon he was playing lead all the time. He used to say:

"When I am acting, my real self comes out—the self I
might have been, had things been different. I only come to
life, I only am myself when I am on the stage. When all is
done, the paste diamond shines brighter than the real stone,
and only the mock sunshine lasts for ever!"

By then he was nineteen, and he looked thirty. He
wasn't very tall, was thin and elegant, and still his amazing
face looked back on the world unspoiled by the nether acts
of his life.

Women now scarcely gave him a minute's peace. They would do anything for this beautiful young man who unsmilingly ogled them. When he was in debt, and he was never out of debt, he let them do what they would for him, flinging out his commands with the arrogant ardour of a barbarian prince. He despised all women, but he saw no reason why he should not use them, offend and humiliate them to the top of his bent.

Robert, Steve, and I now kept the home running between us. Our, mother had given up her morning work in her brother's picture gallery; as for our father, he could no longer work but sat at home all day, a quiet invalid. Two things he resolutely refused to do; he would not consult a doctor and he would not move from the street. We now had the means for a better house, but he clung to the place where he had brought home his bride, and where his children had been born. An unhappy little house, but home for all that, and he would not be parted from it. When we tried to persuade him, he would say:

"But I shan't last a long time, you know. Let us stay here till I go. After that, why, you can move where you want. But stay here while I'm here, eh?"

And I, fearing that if we forced him to change, new surroundings would hasten his death, prevailed upon the boys to bear with the street.

We heard much of Anda, not from her letters—she no longer wrote to me—but through the newspapers and society magazines that I used to scan in the library for news and views of her. She moved in the highest circles in the land now. Her beauty was one of the wonders of London, Paris, and New York.

As for Robert, he still had his job in the counting-house,

a more senior position than before with a salary of £180 a year; this enabled him to buy the books he wanted, attend series of lectures and generally indulge his bent for history.

And though no startling change had taken place in my occupation either, a very dramatic alteration had come about in my personal appearance.

I was now twenty-one, and a few days after that particular birthday my dark hair all turned a brilliant grey in the course of a single week. It was so eerie having all that strange hair blowing about my shoulders, that I had it all cut off like a boy's—shorn and bright-silvered—and I looked, Robert said, like one of those quaint little figures that one sees hovering in the corners of Middle Ages stained glass windows.

I had a very pale, heart-shaped face, with large dark eyes. So I had to do something about all that pallor surmounted by silver, and I began to paint my mouth a bright red like fruit.

"Enchanting thing!" Steve was always saying to me after this metamorphosis. "Before, you were· completely unremarkable—at any rate, as far as your phiz went! But, now, I don't know anyone who looks so beautiful, so unusually beautiful!"

When my hair first changed colour, Steve had turned to our mother and said:

"You see what you have done now! You have caused your daughter's hair to turn white in her young youth!"

She, getting less noisy now but not a whit more amenable, looked at him carefully, and though she said harsh words in answer, she knew how out of reach he was, and always had been since that night she told him he must leave school; in that hour she cracked the vessel for all time, and had never since been able to make sound or filling. She said:

"That's enough from you! Don't you cast stones! Everyone

in this town knows what you are since you went on the stage! You are every limb of a dirty dog!"

He, laughing, said to her:

"Yes, indeed, and that is more of your handiwork, too, by God!"

Then, tucking my arm through his, he bent and whispered in my ear:

"Come up to my room. I have bought a new record for you—to celebrate about your hair!"

He had of late months indulged his deep love for music. He had bought a good portable gramophone, and every week bought something new to play on it.

So we went upstairs, and the music he played to me was Debussy's "Girl With the Flaxen Hair."

"Of course," said Steve, looking at me very intently, as had become his wont, "your hair isn't flaxen—but this is the nearest I could get to it. Oh, how different, how different you do look, Laura. You are become as a charming stranger to me, with all the dear familiarity of what you were before the change!"

"Well, never mind about that now," I said. "Let me thank you for this record. And will you play me now one of those sweet sad piano pieces by MacDowell: they evoke for me, somehow, quieter moments in the drawing-room of the Duchesse de Guermantes!"

"Proust, eh?" said Steve. "If I leave off reading Voltaire and Jonathan Swift, I myself sometimes have a session with Oriane or Miss Albertine!"

"You do?" I said. "Are any of *your* girls like Albertine?"

"*My* girls," he said, looking up in a surprised way from where he was changing the records. "*I* haven't got any girls!"

"But you are surrounded by them!"

"What of it! This country is surrounded by water! I tell you, not one of them has ever, will ever find the way to my secure and—unhappy heart!"

He said this lightly and permitted himself one of his rare smiles.

"All that is purest idiocy," I said.

"It may be," he retorted," but we shall not go into that—it isn't a bit important."

"I'll tell you a thing," I said, lighting a cigarette, "it is more than important for you to find someone who will smash a way into that secure and unhappy heart: leave lonely independence for such stoics as can make of it a proud and glittering achievement. You were made to give and to receive love. Give it, before it is too late!"

"Before it is too late for what, Laura?"

"To bring out the best in you. Oh, you must have tenderness in you, Steve, it must be there!"

"Yes," he said, lifting thought-charged eyes to look at me. "I have got tenderness."

"Then why not give it—show it to someone. Why don't you let someone draw near to you? You frighten and insult everyone away!"

"I suppose," he said, down-glancing at the shining disc he had just fitted into place, "you care for me a little, Laura?"

"Of course," I replied, impatiently. "You know it. But that is quite different!"

"It will do for me," he said. "Now, Laura, do stop talking, and listen. I've broken my two MacDowell records, I hit somebody with them. But here—here is something better. It is only little, this, but it is one of Rachmaninof's best."

He sat down beside me to listen to "The Rock."

Meantime, I thought: why does he watch me, so intently,

so coldly? Does he want me to help him? But how? Why doesn't he say? He won't let me come near him. He won't let anyone near him. There was that little actress, Myra—Myra Penn—she would have been so good for him! But he threw her over. They say his treatment of her was terrible—terrible. Her brother tried to kill him! Where will it all end? He won't let me help him—yet how much he helps me! Most of all it is to escape the misery his own unhappiness causes me that I seek in every waking hour the oblivion that lies in my "little nothings."

Life was my life. But the fervour of this love of life *for its own sake*, this secret happiness did not breed non-consciousness of the needs and sorrows of one's co-monarchs of the earth. You cannot love trees and ignore men. To devise some way of not being ravished by the suffering at large does not mean that one strives to become cold and non-feeling; but in order to go on living at all in face of the horrors of man's cruelty to man—and, worse still, to helpless, innocent animals—there has to be some means of not becoming engulfed and perishing of pity.

One does not forget people and their absurdities, kingliness, iniquity, sorrow, and goodness. Of all creeds and nationalities they are thrilling, every one, and it is an unspeakable pleasure to speculate upon them. Still less does one forget what is happening to one's own relations, and the disaster Steve seemed to be heading for was a thing that would have wrecked me, too, had I not had something with which to fight against it, some system of thought to stand between unhappiness and me, some coming to terms with the one Self who stood above all my other selves.

And then, of course, there always was our mother to

think into nothingness, to forget her utterly, to lose sight of her even as she stood raging before one, and that not by going out of the room, not by flying a thousand miles away, but by sinking into myself, deep far down, under the layers of it and the years of it—the memories, the embracings of stones and sunny roofs and static cloud—down, down to the bottom of my labyrinthine strong retreat where there was peace beyond telling and a sense of permanence. beyond a world where everything else must break and end.

With Robert and Steve well beyond her reach, our mother hoped, at least, to invade and defeat me. She disliked me equally as much as she disliked Steve: this had grown with the years, and her realization of the airy, wordless bond between my youngest brother and me.

One rainy Sunday afternoon, I was sitting on a stool enjoying a little fire that I had raised in the grate. I was carried away. I was floating in a vague this-worldly and other-worldly tide of lonely, delicious thinkingness, into which I had been idly and romantically tipped by the azure flames pouring from an old boot which had been waiting to be burnt. Our mother must have asked me something and I did not hear. The next minute she came behind me and gave me a push that sent me with my two hands into the fire.

"The next time," she said, "you answer when you are spoken to."

Both my hands were injured. I could not help but give off a few cries, and in the middle of it all my brother Steve came in. At once he hurried to me.

"What's all this about? How did this happen?" he asked me. I shook my head, but our mother, to hurt him, said:

"She wouldn't answer when she was spoken to; so I

gave her a push to see if there was any life in her! But she is so stupid, she fell into the fire. She needn't have; it was her own carelessness!"

"Had I been in," he said, hurrying to the drawer to get bandages, "and seen you do it, I'd have killed you!"

"Ho-ho!" she began, "murder, now, is it! Don't you talk to your mother that way. It was an accident, I tell you."

He began dressing my hands with the utmost tenderness.

"Talk to you!" he said to her. "Talk! Oh, by Christ, I should not have talked. I'd have killed you."

As he bent over me, he was grinding his teeth, and breathing furiously. His face had gone deathly white.

She stood watching us, muttering to herself.

It was so much of a glaring asylum kind of a scene, and my hands hurt so miserably, I could not suppress a groan.

"I'm just doing this for now, my darling," Steve said to me. "Then I'm taking you to the hospital. They'll stop the pain. Try and hold on for a few minutes longer. Do you wish to give her in charge?"

"Oh, no, no," I cried. "It was an accident—as she said. Oh let us get away quickly, quickly, Steve."

He threw one of his own coats about my shoulders, and we went out into the rain.

"Ah, don't cry, don't cry," he implored me. "I'll do anything ... anything! I'll take you away. Let us go now, at once, this afternoon."

He stopped in the street and took me into his arms. His eyes were half shut with tears. I leaned against him very wearily.

"We couldn't leave our father to her," I said, shuddering. "He's ill. I must wait. But after ... after ... why, then I shall go with you."

I looked up and saw the rain shining on the slates of the house-roofs. Above them clouds like great grey whales moved solemnly across the sky. I drew in a breath of the mild, damp air. I caught in it some vague promise of the soaking wild woods and plashy meadows where the cattle would be standing sheltering under good-natured trees, of rude tides of red hawthorn blossom rustling against wet palings, and frogs a-squat under the drumming burdock leaves. Peace suddenly arrived to banish fretful anxiety. Against the background of the rainy roofs and the extension of this downpour to every imaginative aspect, this matter of wounded hands was lifted out of its hot, ruttish, slatternly kind of drama and took on a queer, touching kind of dignity, a cool seemliness, some essence of not having been *in vain*. And, restored, I saw what a fool I had been to make so much of the incident.

Before God, I said to myself, you are the fool of the world! And did you think it a catastrophe? And did you think it was the end of the world? Is all that you've been building nothing but a bit of a tent-thing that the first strong wind shall lift off your shivering pelt? Bah! You'd bring derision from the stones on the road and the bricks in the wall. Haven't you learnt yet that the secret is to plunge into yourself not to rush out of yourself—you fool! Stand still to meet violence. Answer the shout with silence. The stunt is to be like a leaf yielding and merging with every wind, to be a piece of seaweed that surrenders time without end to the wave, that never breaks or disintegrates because untold strength lies in its very willingness to be submerged!

And Steve, dashing away the tears that were pouring out of his own eyes, said:

"It's coming all right for you, isn't it? Isn't it, Laura?

I can see that you have thought of something that makes things better! Something always impresses *you* out of shock and sorrow!"

"It is all right," I said, beginning to move on again. "You should forgive me, Steve, and try not to upset yourself over my silly weeping. She didn't mean it. I was a fool to cry out. It took me by surprise—that's all!"

But he still cried.

"Dear boy," I said, "this isn't like you! You seem to ignore the brigand role you have chosen for yourself! Where is all your tough urbanity, my dear?"

"That's for the world! When it comes to seeing you in pain, well, I can't bear it. Oh, Laura! Oh, hell! I always tried not to cry because I knew once I started I should never stop!"

I drew him into the arcade we were passing, I put my arms round him.

"There," I said, "cry all you want; you've never cried enough. You've never had anywhere to cry but against me, you've never had any real love except mine. You always succeeded with me for I understand best the bravery of your hampered life, and the hidden sweetness of your disappointed heart."

His hot mourning eyes winked against my cheek, and then he remembered about my hands, hailed a taxi since we had now arrived in streets where they plied, and in next to no time I was feeling comfortable and eased as a competent nurse bound up my hands.

Hovering anxiously, Steve said to her:

"Will there be ... any scars?"

"No," she smiled, "not a one! She's had a lucky escape!"

Once in the streets again, Steve looked in his purse. He had a pound. So we went to the best tea-shop in the town and had a splendid meal, while an orchestra played selections of music as passionately vulgar as "Madame Butterfly" and "Cavalleria Rusticana".

Other incidents of sufficient drama threw my brother and me together more and more closely as time passed.

His stage triumphs were incessant. Starting from the time when he had had his first big part as Ralph, the apprentice, in the "Knight of the Burning Pestle," his fame had gone the length of the country.

London engagements now kept him away from home for long periods at a time. He was always urging me to go to London with him, and dearly as I longed to go there, our father now was a chronic invalid, depending upon me rather than upon our mother; it would have been unthinkable to desert him.

So when Steve said:

"Look, Laura, it's four o'clock in the afternoon! Throw something into a suitcase and you and I will escape from idiots and criminals for ever on the midnight express," I used to refuse.

"Will you tell me why?" he'd say.

"When our father has gone, then I'll leave also. Till then have patience and wait—as I must."

"But," Steve would cry, and shake me by the shoulders till my teeth rattled, "you're simply sacrificing your youth to a sick old man. This is no life for you!"

"What do you mean?" I asked him, and indeed such expressions meant nothing to me. Why that mad rushing out after Appearance when Reality is at home? Why this passion for showing one's face here, there, and everywhere, for "getting somewhere" and "being someone," when the most triumphant life in the world can be lived in a prison cell, in a slum room, in a sick bed if a person has only grasped that sweet success and lasting happiness can be achieved by making importance of one's own self not in relation to the world but in total premeditated receptiveness to the earth and to life.

This cult has no formula, no rhetoric, no literalness: x cannot represent it. It is sly and vague and insubstantial; it is not vain, but it is very proud. It flourishes in the implacable loneliness of every human mind, but is not hostile to the crowd. And though it is not orthodox it is holy. It has not been consecrated, but it is deeply religious. It is fleeting but eternal. Self-concentration, not selfishness, is necessary for it, and it brings about self-forgetfulness. The intellect would reject it, but the weary heart and nerves joyfully receive it as a balm covering all frustration and every disappointment of expectation.

While I had been thinking this, Steve had been glaring at me.

"Isn't it wonderful!"—he appealed to an invisible audience, "she doesn't know what I mean—and I really believe she does not know. Expressions like *time* and *youth* and so on have no meaning for her! She lives and works in some dimension where we cannot follow her, where she thinks us all out of her existence!"

"What do you think I hold back from London for?" I said. "For heroism? You're a fool! I see our father now when he is old and ill as a little child—as the children we once were. I see him abandoned, as we were, to our mother—alone! Remembering all that, do you think I could go away and leave him—to her?"

"But what about me?" Steve shouted, thrusting that strange, thrilling face of his into mine. "Where do I come in? Have I always got to stay in this stew simply because you won't budge?"

"You can go immediately, if not before!" I replied. "What's all this about? Stay here *because* of me?"

"And who'd see after you if I left?" he asked bitterly. "Could I think of you left to her? You've got no one."

"No," I said, "I've got no one. And I never will have anyone except fleetingly. And, as a matter of fact, that goes for everyone who lives—right from the start! There'll only ever be me! And that's how I like it! You think you see after me, do you? Let me tell you, my dear boy, I don't need you or anyone for five minutes of your staying, for five seconds of your thought!"

"I know that," he interrupted curtly.

"I should like to finish my sentence," I said. "There is nothing for you to do but to see after yourself. And it's going to be a full time job for you with your flash-in-the-pan ideas of honour to steer clear to the end, without wrecking. I'm not leaping off for a sermon—everybody talks too much—but if you want to make me happy, and it seems as though you do, go away, go to London and stay there. *Be* something, *find* something, find someone, for God's sake, if not for your own or mine. You owe yourself a thing or two!"

"No," he declared, frowning, "I shall not leave you. It suits me to be where you are. I like your tempo, Laura, I always did, simply because I don't know what tempo *it is!*"

So for another three years, until he was twenty-two years old, remain with me he did though, to his chagrin, his everlasting, unforgettable performances as King Lear and Hamlet, would keep him in London for long periods at a time. Then he would assert himself, insist on appearing in our town's repertory theatre, and the critics—now at his feet—

travelled up from London in pursuit. The more sentimental of them would gush and declare that he stayed in the North from feelings of loyalty to the town and its repertory theatre that first put him on the road to imperishable fame.

Those in Steve's circle laughed themselves sick over the idea of his having loyalty to anything. He did not improve as he grew older.

"The way that cad takes on!" I'd hear the other actors say when I was back-stage—often the case when Steve was in our town. And they would look at my brother very malevolently.

Often he got threatening letters from fathers and husbands. He told me himself that the biggest proportion of his huge salary went to keep professional blackmailers quiet. His life and eccentricities were an open scandal.

Once he got a present by post. When he untied the wrappings he found a large egg in a box of straw.

"Only an egg," he said. "Now, why? How silly!"

He put it down carelessly on the edge of the table. It fell down on to the floor and smashed. A little dead snake rolled out. It was a reptile's egg!

"Oh, a pity it didn't hatch out and live," said Steve, pitching the present on to the fire. "A snake makes a nice pet! No difficulties about picketing for it—you can park a snake anywhere! And be its poison fang removed, it can even come to be endearing. But I know who sent this. It's a gesture from a fellow who has got the extraordinary notion that I ruined his sister!"

He sat down and looked solemnly at Robert and me.

"Good Lord!" said our elder brother, shocked. "Is that really the way you go on? All they say about you is true, then?"

"Very likely," said Steve.

"Well," continued Robert," you'll have to stop somewhere. Why don't you marry and settle down? Heaps of women would jump at the chance. My God, I've seen them queuing for you at the stage door—all that rabid *wanting* makes me feel positively sick!"

"It would," said Steve.

"Yes, but look here, why not marry some decent girl and concentrate simply on your career? It must offend your taste, surely, going about putting girls in the family way!"

Steve was sitting there, winking-eyed.

"Putting girls in the family way?" he echoed, faintly. "My amazement is strong! Where do you get hold of that? My dear fellow, I'm no snapper-up of trifles of virtue! Not only have I no surplusage of Nilotic fecundity but I'm absolutely incapable of doing such good work for the community! That fact cannot be too widely known! But, I beg of you—continue; your harangue is unexampled!"

Robert became angry and red.

"No," he said, going back to his work. "You're just a cad!"

"Well, I'm sorry you won't go on," said Steve. "I was hoping you would come to the part when you begin to hit off your own virtues—your dependability, your decency, your chastity—in short, your excruciating dullness, my dear Robbie."

"I'd rather be dull than unpleasant," Robert mumbled.

And so they would continue to despise at one another.

Of course, Steve didn't go round putting young women in the family way—his girls were too fly for that—nor was it true that he was incapable of it, that was just his pose. He did far worse to his dotes. He destroyed their beliefs for them. His immorality was of a quite special order. So far from guiding his girls to his naked bed, he never allowed them near him. He couldn't bear women, still less love or make love to them.

But during this year, his twenty-second, he was invited to play in America. He was away a year, and during that time our father died of the tuberculosis which, it turned out, had all these years been devouring him.

As our father had so steadfastly refused to leave the street, Robert and I fixed up the house as pleasantly as we could for him. We had electricity installed, bought comfortable furniture, decent curtains and carpets. We bought him hundreds of the detective novels he loved, and a picture or two of the kind he could live with—one filled with the sunshine of Vincent Van Gogh, and a merry street scene of Manet.

Towards the end of his life, he used to stare at those sunny fields of Van Gogh, and he would say:

"You know something, Laura. I'm *in* that picture, I'm there!"

When he became so ill that he could not get up any more, our mother used to frighten him so much, he could not bear her near him, so for the time being, I gave up my job in the library and stayed at home to nurse him.

To keep him amused, the doctor had inserted a length of tubing into his side which drained his lung of its fluid into a pail. This caused our father considerable pain.

"Side's hurting you, is it?" snapped our doctor. "Well, *I'm* hurting all over!" which, as our father said, remaining humorous to the end, was as much a consolation as a sooty poker in a sore eye!

A few days before his death, he said:

"Laura, dear, d'you think I shall get another chance where I am going?"

"Another chance for what?" I asked, busily drying his toes, for I had just given him his blanket-bath; his feet, so thin because of illness, were like long white wafers, and they made his toe-nails have an air of being ashamed of themselves, for they remained sturdily as they had always been—like those common little brown shells which the tide leaves behind on the seashore.

"Why, Laura, you've grown up now—you've all grown up with talent and beauty and everything—children such as your mother and I never deserved, and you can see at last the sort of parents God Almighty provided you with: the parents at no time were so rosy! They were so wanting in virtue and, above all, in tenderness, that your sister ran away from home, and your brother Steve hates us. It was wrong to have taken him away from that school. As things have turned out, he's made more of a name for himself than, perhaps, he would have done had he gone on to college. But that's only surface, only surface. Perhaps it would have been better for him not to have made such a name, not to have been such a success! It's been achieved through renunciation—a renunciation he had to make before the time for that sort of thing was ripe! It was too much to ask him to bear with; he didn't bear with it, Laura, he went bad. Oh, I don't mean the lad steals or murders, but he's *bad*; for he believes in nothing. That's not his fault—it's ours. At the time I said he should not leave school, I never wanted him so battered and humiliated—but, I did nothing about it. I'm a weak character, Laura, this world's been too much for me. There are people like that, and for us death is a picnic!"

A look of anticipation came into his weary rakish blue eyes.

"Death takes us away from things that bothered us,

things we never could cope with. Only—I'd like—wherever it is I'm going—I'd like to have four little children again, like you four that I had here, especially a little boy like Steve; and I'd like to show that I could serve them better, at any rate, than I ever served my own children here. That's what I mean by another chance. D'you think I'll be given it? D'you think it'll be fixed for me like I said?"

"I shouldn't wonder," I replied," if you want it very much. We all make our own heaven before we reach it! But, dear, wherever we're all going, we're going to *rest*, not to begin struggling all over again! It is going to be ... a picnic!"

"Aye, but before the picnic comes on, haven't you got to do something to earn it? Eh, Laura?"

He was looking beyond the room and me. He seemed to be seeing the montage of his breakneck life in streaming tints: within this term he was seeing the total, the curded experiences, disorderly encounters, pavement reelings, many hours of fright and greed and grossness—wet through, scorched through—snatching, yearning, the lit window always passed, quick short landings on the plains of happiness then whisked off immediately back to the old loveless round—spent, chagrined, constantly threatened, exceptionally downtrodden, incurably hopeful and foolish; no ease, no pay—swag sometimes; prying, nervous, derided, a disfigured unpardonable travesty; the possession of nothing—yet a reaping. For there shone from those blue eyes of his in the startlingly marked face, the invincible light of a higher truth that seemed to say, in his words:

"I'm not passed up! I never had the zest squashed out of me quite! I've not been afraid to walk alone with my loneliness. The forlornest day has had something in it for me, by God, it has, though it seldom came to me from human kind. I learnt lessons from the green grass when I saw it struggling up in the heart of the town, and I got courage from watching shabby cocky little horses with running eyes bullied on the streets, from alley-cats with no homes, wandering about desperate, looking for a snug to have their kittens in, and from listening to the pounding wind when I flung out of the tavern at nights! I've betrayed myself on most everything, but not the core, not *what you're born with.* I've kept that safe, untouched. I've seen the sun many a time when it wasn't shining. I've overcome a world whose one aim was to overcome me!"

None of this he spoke aloud, but he said it to me. I knew, I understood, for it was that wisdom he had passed on to me.

Of no personal beauty himself he had given two of his children an exquisite loveliness. An ignorant man, with a notion of history so telescoped it seemed to him but a few generations ago since William the Conqueror was burning and clouting the Saxons into submission, he had fathered a boy who was to be an historian of the first rank. A timid man he had, withal, found the refuge against a broken heart through an inarticulate, elemental recognition of the poetical overtones of things and this—he had transmitted to me. I seized his hand:

"Yes," I said, "the picnic needs to be earned and, you have earned it. Never fear. You have earned it many times over. I know. The children are grown up, as you say, but that doesn't mean we can see only the shortcomings. We can see many things that, perhaps, even you can't see. And we see that you have earned your picnic. You—and everyone. We're *all* so much better than we ever suspect. We'd all like to have done better than we did, and that's what the tally will be taken on—not what we've done but what we'd like to have done."

"You're a jewel of a girl, Laura," he said, smiling. "You've got the human touch! You're a great comfort to me, and always were. You're the thinker—the others are clever and lovely, but you are great, without any noise. It strikes me it's not the children who have to learn, but the parents. They should help one another, children and parents, for we're all children really, all blundering learners. Isn't it a pity that you can't begin life with what you know when you come to the end of it!"

Our mother came bustling in with milk on tray. He shut his eyes against her.

"What's he been saying?" she demanded of me with angry suspicion. As I didn't answer, she went on:

"You must not take any notice of what he's saying now. His mind's going!"

She went out. Our father opened his eyes and smiled.

"We know, Laura," he said, softly, "we know!"

During the morning of the following day, about eleven o'clock, our father died. Robert was at his office, and our mother had gone shopping. The sun was streaming across his bed like a splendid river. I was standing by the window with a cup of coffee he had asked for, waiting for him to open his eyes. In the radiant sunlight the street below had taken on magnificence. Everywhere there seemed a feeling of good happening.

Our father opened his eyes. He stretched out his long thin hands and dabbled them in the stream of light flowing across his bed.

"Oh, it's nice!, it's very nice!" he said, with a sigh of content. "It's only like dropping asleep, after all," he said, closing his eyes for the last time. A few seconds later he stopped breathing; his big hands still lay in the sunlight looking as though broken away from the useless sticks of wrists.

I sat down beside him for a few minutes.

You're not here, I thought, but you haven't gone.

I laid my hand across his eyes; and for me our father's life took on great nobility. The fact that he had *lived* the years allotted him, though in this mean street and without *seeming* success or beauty or strength, rose and demanded new recognition in its own right, seen in this moment of his simple, happy death.

Indeed, the life of everyone, be they never so unimportant or criminal, seemed suddenly stupendous and brave, entrancing in its incomprehensibility—eminently worthwhile, having real purpose and tender glory.

Our mother came stamping into the happy sunny room.

"Asleep, is he?" she sniffed. "Wish I could sleep!"

She went and looked down at him.

"He seems very still. He ... Oh, he's dead!" she cried.

She stood there aghast. She had a look of trying to remember what the rule ought to be now. She was tugging at the strings of wont and usage to determine what she should do now. Suddenly she had it. She began to weep loudly.

"He's gone," she blubbered. "Oh, it's horrible, horrible! I can't bear it!" and she clattered away down the stairs.

I looked gayly at our father on the bed—*on the bed*—had he been alive I should have thought of him as *in bed*. And then I went down to attend to the strange woman who had found that happy mortal event frightening and horrible.

"You must see to everything," she said, as soon as I appeared. "You must go to the undertaker's and see to the insurance. I can't have anything to do with any of that. My nerves wouldn't stand it. Oh, it's a nice lookout for me! I shall have a breakdown! Oh, why did this have to happen to me? Oh, the trouble I've had in my life! There aren't many women had to undergo as much as I have."

Well, don't upset yourself about it," I said. "Have a cup of tea."

"Yes," she said, "I will. I deserve one!"

A few weeks after our father was buried, a motor car drew up outside our house one Saturday afternoon. Out of it stepped a tall lady wearing a green hat with a wide brim, and a huge fur coat. With her came an ugly man, equally as tall, but four or five times as stout.

Thump went the door-knocker. Wondering, I went to open to them, while my brother Robert and our mother speculated on the identity of our callers. They turned out to be my sister Anda and her husband, the Earl of Cassiobury.

Yes, Anda had married an earl, a fabulously wealthy man; that's what Cassiobury was famous for—his riches.

I could not help but recall that day on the tram, when we were children, and Steve had said to the young tram guard:

"She isn't going to marry anyone less than an earl!"

Excited question and answer flew about our living-room kitchen. I had never seen our mother so animated. She turned to Anda's husband enthusiastically, and said:

"Well! I never thought Anda would turn out as well as this!"

Anda gave our mother the strangest look, while her husband, not understanding, lifted his eyebrows.

"She means," said Anda to him, "she never thought I should marry into the aristocracy!"

"Oh," said he, "Anda herself is pure aristocracy!"

He beamed at our mother implying that, of course, since *she* was the mother of his prize …

"She was a wild lot when she was younger," our mother told him. "I had great trouble to rear her, but I can see she has grown out of that. Laws! She could not have done better for herself!"

Robert and I looked at one another surreptitiously, and the corners of our mouths went down with sly smiling. We were thinking: No, indeed, this beautiful sister of ours, bred up in a mean house in a still meaner street, could not have done anything more interesting; it was from such properties scattered up and down the large towns of the country that the Earl of Cassiobury drew his millions. Anda and he were related: she was one of his products, one of the fairest flowers sprung from his muck-heaps. Whether this had ever struck *him*, it would be difficult to say and even harder to find out. But probably he had never thought of such things, bred up as he was in traditions that made thinking deeply about anything, let alone about the nasty hurly-burly of poverty, highly unsuitable as a pursuit for gentlemen.

As I made afternoon tea and handed round queen-cakes, I saw how simple and sublimely uncomplicated real evil is. It does not shriek aloud; its face is eminently respectable, it even says its prayers and draws attention to its virtue! For true evil quite simply is—stupidity and ignorance, and the two most evil persons I was ever to know were now sitting amiably before me, nibbling cake and sipping tea—our mother and Anda's husband!

When I went into the scullery for more water Anda followed me.

"What about Mr. Maccabeus?" I whispered.

"I came to tell you," she said in a low voice. "He died

two years ago—in Paris. It … he … well, you know how I loved him. Since he went nothing has been the same for me. Cassiobury came, he asked me to marry him. Nothing mattered much—so I did."

"Aren't you happy with him, then?"

"Laura, I could never be happy with anyone after Claude, but Cassiobury will do. I suppose there must be *someone* to help you to get through life. We're going to have children, as well, and they'll help. We're going to have a lot of children, it's my idea. They will remind me of Claude. Odd, isn't it, that the one who never was a person's lover is the only lover! I'm going back to them now; I don't want to say any more else I shall break down and Cassiobury would wonder. He's very very kind, Laura. Hush!"

But this was undoubtedly the happiest day of our mother's life. She could not stop smiles of joy from chasing across her face as she reflected on the status of her—son-in-law! She kept looking at Anda with the nearest approach to fondness we had ever seen. All, all was forgiven.

As for Anda she kept commenting now on two things, one with regret, the other with enthusiasm—our father's death and my changed hair.

"I do wish I had been … in time," she said sadly, thinking about our father.

"Oh, never mind," cried our mother, gaily. "What's gone is gone. The dead are dead. You can't bring 'em back."

"People don't die," I said, softly, looking at Anda, "unless you want them to."

She smiled at me, and seemed glad to change the subject to the colour of my hair.

"Why," she exclaimed, "before, you were nothing, but now—you are lovely! Isn't she Luce?"

Luce, her husband (whose proper name was Lucian), said: "Yes, indeed, she is lovely. You're an amazing family." He turned to Robert.

"And what does this young man do?"

The young man told him.

"Ah," said Luce, "we must change that. We must change everything!"

From then on till late in the night details of the changing of everything were discussed and finally settled.

Our mother was to be whisked away to a wonderful house in the country with hens and other livestock and gardeners and grooms to boss to her heart's content.

Robert was never to go back to his office. It was the University of Cambridge for him now; he was to go there and study History for ever! He sat dazed with his good fortune.

"We shall not be able to do anything for Steve," said Anda. "He wouldn't let us. We went to see him in London, Laura, just after we were married, when he was playing Hamlet. Did he tell you?"

"No," I said, surprised, "he never mentioned it."

"He wouldn't!" she said with mingled irritation and regret. "We went round to his dressing-room after the show. I sent in a note, but he refused to see me. We were told afterwards that he was too drunk to see anyone!"

"The beast!" said our mother, all her old rage and dislike of him boiling up at this treatment of an Earl.

"He never drinks," I said to Anda. "You may take my word for that. He has many shortcomings, but drink isn't one of them. No, the plain fact would be—he wouldn't want to see you!"

"I suppose not," said Anda. "We never hit it off. In London

we used to hear the strangest stories about his pursuits. Luce and I would be much too tame for him. On Sunday nights he used to appear in those entertainments where oldtime Greeks with leaves on their heads flap about on the stage giving off unremitting wails. And, Oh, the tales we heard of what went on back-stage afterwards!"

"Who cares about him?" demanded our mother. "Forget him. It doesn't matter what happens to him! The devil looks after his own."

I was thinking of Steve acting in those Greek plays, and I was remembering much. Aloud, I said:

"Steve is the possessor of no more nasty traits than anyone in this room. His may be more open than ours— most sewerage runs underground. So we won't, I think, have any more to say about his failings. Instead, I will thank you very much, Anda, for the many many suggestions you have thrown out for my welfare. But the fact is, I intend to stay here in this house and wait for Steve to come back from America. We always planned that we should go to London together if anything happened to our father, and now—there is nothing to detain me."

Then I must have a very large cheque. Anda insisted upon it. She claimed to be starting a new fashion. Instead of receiving wedding presents, she was giving them. And I must not refuse a cheque.

I smiled faintly, but nothing could have induced me to take a cheque from Cassiobury. I liked him for Anda's sake, but I did not want anything from him.

"Oh, never mind her!" said our mother. "She's like Steve. They hang out together—those two, and there's something not right about them!"

She regarded me with a kind of baleful majesty on this, the most triumphant day of her life. The earl said:

"We must leave Laura and Steve to choose for themselves. We have only their good at heart! Perhaps it seems now that they lack nothing, but if they ever should—why, they have only to call upon us. I may say that Steve doesn't seem to me to need help from anyone: I have never in all my life seen acting to equal his. And as for Laura ..."

But before he could bring out what he had been meaning to say, I asked him:

"At the Greek plays did Steve ... speak his lines in Greek?"

"I don't know, my dear," he replied. "Anda and I never went to hear them: she couldn't stand that sort of thing and, to say the truth, neither could I! But I'm told he did speak in the original!"

I wondered what Steve had been thinking when he spoke Greek again. His acting, tinged by those thoughts, must have been something to see!

Soon afterwards, this well-intentioned pair made their departure.

Within a short time our mother had gone to her country house in Shropshire, and Robert had departed to a tutor preparatory to entering the University.

Meantime, I waited at home for my brother Steve. All this while, of course, he had not written a line. He never wrote to me when he went away, and the only time I asked him about this, his retort had been:

"Well, you see, my dear girl, when it comes to writing to you, there are so many words I may not write down, it seems useless of me to write at all."

"I'm not afraid of bad language," I said.

"Who is speaking of bad language?" he replied.

The weeks went by. It was during this time I had to live to myself, that I strengthened for everlasting my own private art of life, which was nothing but to extend to the limit the union of my mind with any town shower of rain, the wind on the walls, thunder and lightning—ephemeral but eternal things tenanted as they are by essences from a world other than this.

And, in the very act of lifting eyes to stars, or drawing the winey wind into lungs, a person's life is thrillingly amplified by participating in strange, subtle pangs and rumours of the expectations and raptures of all who've ever gazed on stars, or breathed deep of the wind, ever since men could breathe at all. How time-defeating this is! How we do enter into mysterious harmony with the inarticulate grandeur of the thoughts of the monolithic men, *not dispersed by words*, and therefore grown into entities which we may pick up in these delicious contemplations of ours.

I found my way of living easier and easier the more I threw off subjugation to preconceived notions of life and living, and reverted back to impressions and reflexes of my earliest childhood, reverted back to the sexless, neutral human tablet I was then, free and abandoned for the writing of vague and unco-ordinated sensations. The invocation of these impressions were daily events, by the assertion of some bygone moment in the sunny window reflected on the door knob, the *look* of candlelight on the scullery wall, coal-dust, the handle of the bread knife, the python in the hot glass cage in the zoo, aspects of moonlight and water, the taste of marmalade, the furthest lamp at the end of the pier shining lonelily to the silent sea, the magic letters "Violin and Mandolin Strings Sold Here": these were some of the hundreds and hundreds of little ribbon paths all leading to that One road, a dark lonely tempest-road, but the only road along which the Secret Rose is to be found softly and mystically blooming in the savage dark. These things, *by themselves*, without words or books or philosophies or sermons contained, for me, the truest wisdom and the noblest intimations of eternity.

Oh, there were no diversions. Our father's sufferings over, our mother's rages removed, I was at liberty to enlarge the harvest of those furrows I had been compelled to plough by those two very vicissitudes. There was nothing to interfere at all with my imaginative contemplation; I knew a happiness entire, in large and undivided life.

Then came the day when *his* taxi drew up outside the door.

Swiftly he came into the house, putting out his arms to me.

"Hasn't it been long—this time?" he said, sharply, drawing me to him. His bold, hungering eyes plunged into mine. "It was nearly too long. I must see you from time to time for my good. This long time in America has made me realize more than ever how much I depend on you, Laura, for my feeling that life is warm."

"I hope I may never fail you," I said, touched.

"You couldn't fail anybody, and you will not fail me. Do you know, when I was in New York I made a vow, and that to ensure, somehow, that you will not die before me!"

"Oh, how absurd you are," I said, smiling. "No one can make arrangements like that—except God!"

He laid his hand across my eyes, and said softly:

"Then I must do God's job for Him—that would be a change, don't you know, for they say I usually do the devil's for him! Indeed, an American lady of my acquaintance went so far as to say that I *was* the devil. Think of that, Laura!"

His head had fallen upon my shoulder. His big shaggy travelling coat smelt of the Cunard liner, and cigars and women's perfume, the sea and trains and travelling. It was all there. I sniffed it eagerly.

"Where are all the people?" he asked, going to take his coat off. "But never mind. Don't bother to inform me. What do I care! Just tell me what you have been doing, Laura. Are you well? You look most marvellous to me. It is luck, the others being out. I've got you to myself, Just as I pictured and hoped on the way back to you."

His eyes were alight with the rapturous welcome he had for me.

"America seems to have made you more affectionate," I said, pleased. Perhaps he had met someone to love at last. But the next second he said:

"Only to you, Laura, only to you. Oh, you must be with me the next time I have to go away."

"Yes," I replied. "I will."

"You will? You mean …?"

He came and sat down beside me on the sofa, taking my hand eagerly. He had been away a year and in appearance had changed, the face having become more overwrought and arresting, the eyes more sad and cavernous, the character in the crystallization of experience, more bland and unfathomable. Now more than ever his own identity seemed to be swallowed up in his amazing powers of constantly impersonating other people on the stage.

I told him of events while he had been away. He listened in silence—he always had been a good listener, even though so often he had had to listen to his own doom. Perhaps that was why he was so good at listening: there really is nothing to say when all that a person wanted has been taken away. But this time, at least, he was hearing news that pleased him.

"Oh, my God, isn't all this *magnificent*!" he brought out. He looked at me with shining eyes. He made little inarticulate exclamations of pleasure.

"To lose the lot at one go! To have all the obstacles taken away at once! Why, I could almost believe in God!"

"It all depends what you mean by God!" I said, smiling.

"Well, what do you mean?" he asked.

"God?" I said, "why God *is* any patient old corporation tree choked in the cement of city streets, but showing forth so bravely, so beautifully in the spring, and God *is* the grass on the waste land beside the factory, and the town sparrow born of dust and a little dew!"

"That can't be right," he said.

"Why not?"

"Why—well, *it's too much, it's too simple!*"

"Yes," I said, "that's how it goes—too much and too simple!"

"Never mind," he cried, gaily. "What does matter is that the people have all gone and I've got you to myself. I must keep on saying it to myself so as to try and understand the luck of it. They've gone—every one!"

"You might, at least, have said a kind word about our father."

"Why, Laura, why?" he asked, instantly. "Why kind words now when I never spoke them in his lifetime. Nor he to me!"

"He did his best. Life and us and our mother were all too much for him."

"Our mother, especially," he said. "Oh, to think, to

think, Laura, of not having to see her ever again! And Anda—married to an earl! But earls are easy fish to catch in your net if you have Anda's looks—or even mine! Try the same earl if you're pock-marked or squint out of your eyes and see what you get!"

"Another thing," I said, "our father often and often spoke kindly to you when he was alive. And before he died, he told me many things about himself and you and all of us that will make me love him always. Try to love him, also, Steve!"

"Oh, I will, I will," he said. "I will try to love anyone you say, Laura. But never mind, never mind about all that now. The thing that is burning me is—there was once talk of you coming away with me: and now you can, you can! Don't you know what? We'll go to London immediately. Oh, how many many times I have said that to you, and always you refused. But now, *now* you do not refuse. Now you can come with me!"

He looked round the kitchen with a warm wolfish expression on his face. He said, exuberantly:

"You will let me look after things for us now, won't you? As I always wanted to? It won't be dull, I promise you. I've got a new long London contract beginning this autumn— Shakespeare all the time—my King Lear, Laura, that tears the hearts out of people who never before realized they had hearts! We'll find us a nice house to live in! You shall choose it, and I'll fill it with everything fine that the world can produce! There'll be interesting people for you to meet. And how you'll love London! I can just imagine you—and *it!* So you will come with me, Laura?"

"Shall we get on?" I said.

"Why, of course not, Laura," he said, surprised. "Who said we were saints and angels? We shall quarrel, of course, as we always have done. You will try to make me better, and I shall try to make you worse! We shall have our ups and downs like all people who live together, but when we have quarrelled how sweet it will be to make it up again!"

He suddenly bent and gave me one of his little kisses in the palm of my hand.

"No man ever had a little sister like you—so independent, so unaffected, so gay! Oh, Laura, say you will come with your poor Steve! Dear, will you do this for me?"

"I'll go with you," I said, "of course."

And I thought wryly of how my time of freedom was over, and now I must face and fight against all that in Steve would militate against my own beguiling cult. Without rancour, I saw him symbolized as the world battling against the clod of earth that I saw as myself. I saw his impious spirituality seeking to undermine my holy elementalism: that I also saw him with pity and love did not make the coming conflict seem any easier. And if I flinched from the by and by, I was also exhilarated, too. The stimulant, after all, lies in never allowing one's self to get *too cosy*. By God, I thought, exultantly, I shall go through with it: whatever is to be *will* be, but I shall hew out the time to practise my personal way of living.

While I was musing like this, it suddenly came over me with the quietness and nonchalance of the profoundest truth, that it was now *too late* for Steve or anyone to destroy me. I had had time, through habit, to make my secret wayfaring the most dominant thing in my life.

"And I shall stay with you," I continued to my brother, "until you meet someone who will live with you under rather different circumstances." ·

"What are you talking about?"

"Why, some day you'll marry. I should not stay with you and your wife!"

"How your mind does run forwards," he said.

"It's a pity yours does not, too," I retorted.

"The present and the passing show have always done for me," he said. "But that's quite enough about the future. The point is, you'll come to London with me—now. Laura, let's you and me go out right now and have some dinner. I'll tell you about New York. You're dying to know, I can tell."

We drove to one of the town's big restaurants, one of those glittering palatial places outside which we had often stood and gaped, as children. Now here we were entering and conducting ourselves as though we had never been used to anything different.

And yet, as I sat there, leaving Steve to order the wine and the dinner, I was still that ragged child whose nose wanted wiping, whose stockings were on the descend, who marvelled at everything, at the rich food and the waiters, the array of cutlery at each side of my plate, at the glittering glasses and the sparkling wine chugging into them from the crusted bottle. So heart-whole did I resurrect that ignorant joyful little child again, that I touched my brother on the sleeve, and said:

"What are all these knives and forks for? What am I supposed to do with this long array of cutlery?"

He, entering into what he supposed a game, replied, making a helpful paraphrase on a line from "Alice in Wonderland":

"Oh, Laura, begin with those immediately to your hand; work your way straight through to those at the rim of the plate—then stop! Because the dinner will have stopped!"

He began to tell me about New York. As always, he had been the success of the generation, the toast of the town.

"Did you like your American audiences?" I asked.

"Oh, audiences are the same the world over—earnest or drivelling, men in the geometry of evening dress, the women packed as tightly in the stalls as delicate Bordeaux pigeons in market boxes—people waiting to be wrung out by us actors. But, perhaps, in America, where everything is a little more raw than in the suave old world, the actor gets more zest to stand on the emotions of the audience, for that's what an actor does, you know, he stamps on the aggressive, straining hearts of his audience, like vine-treaders press the wine from the grapes!"

It seemed that towards the end of his year on Broadway, Steve had appeared in a fantastic, brilliant play called "Cuchulain at Trinity" by—Bernard McCann.

Bernard McCann. When he said that name my heart stood still. All the restaurant ran light and glory. Bernard McCann—this One who, beyond all, wrote, and lived as I lived. Across the mists of my early adolescence I saw again his vehement signature.

"What's the matter with you?" asked Steve, stopping in his narrative. "Have you seen someone you know? Who are you welcoming?"

"No," I said, "it's all right. I'm thinking. I'm seeing the places and people with you!"

In New York Steve had acted with Oriel McCann, Bernard's wife. He mentioned this casually.

"I imagine she must be marvellous," I said.

"Marvellous?" he repeated. "Good God, no! She is nowhere attractive to me. But it can be said of her in passing that she is the only woman I have ever known who matched my insult with return insult, who has endured every indignity from me, to whom I have shown every means of causing dislike—yet she still *loves* me! I cannot put her from me. Yet she isn't the kind who lays herself open to be taken by surprise: she tells me that before I came along she had had no misgivings; she had been rather a faithless woman but had never demanded fidelity from others, not even the appearance of it. 'God send the old days back again,' I said, when she came out with that, for she led me a terrible time. She must have a maternal fixation on me, Laura. I am twenty-three, in case you do not know it, Laura, and she is ten years older!"

"And …?" I began, but could not go on. I had meant to ask him where Bernard McCann came in on all this.

"Yes?" he said.

"Nothing."

"Well," he said, "there it is! I thanked my stars in more ways than one when my ship sailed for England; she was one of the ways! I had an awful time with her, Laura, just before I left. She implored me to let her divorce McCann, and marry her. Of course, I would not hear of such fantastic nonsense! I do not wish to be encumbered with any woman. Marry them, what for? That seems to be a catastrophe of real merit! I have no feelings for women, Laura, not even *those* feelings a man gets for a woman—I set cold reason to conquer all that, a long time ago. I loathe the fair sex so much I could not bear to be dependent on them even for *that!* And there's your answer to your trying to get me safely married down! Does this sound splenetic? It's meant to be! It's unexorcisable in me—and nobody's fault but our mother's. You understand, of course. So this fervent little Mrs. McCann got nothing from me. Besides, I have nothing against her husband. The fellow has great depths of imagination, and is not unattractive in himself. He's about forty years old now, and impressed me, who am not easily impressed, as the most brilliant lunatic I had ever met. You would like him, Laura!"

"Would I?" I said, faintly.

"Yes, and her, too, very likely. Naturally, the woman McCann married had *something* in her. But she wearied me! She slew my interest almost as soon as she kindled it, by becoming far too interested in me! Ah, it's as well not to take on introspectively at such times! It's as well to doff the hat to the ashes of romance and admit that quicksilver gets out of hand if tenanted in space too large for it! You hope to do better next time: But, Oh, Oh, it's what you never have that's the best, it's what you can't find that's so alluring!"

At last I managed to say:

"Did … *he* mind about her being in love with you?"

"Who, Bernard? Oh, good lord, he didn't mind a bit. He's got other things on his mind. No doubt Oriel (isn't that a silly name) did the same to him as to me. She burns you out all in one—there's nothing left but ashes. But, you see, *she* goes on burning—a flame trying to kindle ashes. Do you get the uselessness of it, Laura? Of course, with his wife hanging round my neck, it meant I could not be in Bernard's society as much as, perhaps, I should have liked. He's a fascinator, all right! He is a big, burly man, not unhandsome in a rugged fashion, and, do you know, he is the very stillest man I ever met. The stillness of a … a volcano, I suppose. Before Oriel and I became so entangled, he invited me to his house one night. He read us some of his works. Indeed, he has an amazing, golden voice—with an Irish accent, too. I could have listened to him reading that stuff of his, and some of the poems of Willie Yeats and James Stephens for a long time. It was his voice! What has a man like that to worry about a woman for? He has got enough. What did he care whether Oriel was hanging upside down from the Woolworth building or behaving herself quietly at home? I believe he hardly noticed her infatuation for me. Men like that seem, don't you know, Laura, curiously aloof and detached from the rest of mankind, and yet are intensely noticing and *of* mankind at large. They may come to England some time, then you shall see for yourself. If it's left to her, they'll be here on the next boat. Oh, what a terrible thing *fidelity* can be, Laura!

"I can't fathom Bernard. I don't know about him. *You* would know at once! Yes, you would! Come to think of it, he's the only person I ever met beside yourself, who had got hold of something—I know not what—but something I myself would be the better for possessing. The only thing I do know about it is—it's given you both the amazing faculty of finding delight in sheer moony mazy nothing at all! Either you and McCann are mad, or the rest of the world is insane and you the only wise two alive I subscribe to the latter view. That's why I cling to you, Laura, with all my faith and bones. That's why I'm nothing without you! And tonight is our night, yes, and tomorrow and tomorrow— we're going away for ever! Laura—" he raised his glass, "to our darling unknown fate!"

Chapter V

*"Why should knowledge of the world make people worldly?
It ought to do the exact opposite."*
GEORGE SANTAYANA

JUST as, in my childhood, I had packed every sort of magic into the words "Violin and Mandolin Strings Sold Here," so when I first went to live in London, the essence of all those teeming new impressions was concentrated into the words "Aerated Bread Company" to be seen written above the cake-terraced windows of many a teashop. Into those ordinary words my spirit flung its new raptures, and they came to be for me the whole charter of the city.

The means to be used are the means at immediate disposal, and so it came about that two sets of shop signs had the mysterious power of overthrowing for me the barricades which civilization sets up round matter, and plunged me into full unity with the lurking-everywhere secret of primeval being. They were passwords to that part of my mind that had been alive before I was, that had been alive before there was any life on this earth—this Outer mind that ravished me constantly with the endless procession of its miracles.

I never got over the sheer delight of simply walking in a London street.

This is London, I would think: this is Me *in London!* And my glee knew no bounds.

A thing that delighted me very much was the presence of trees in so many of the streets. And there was the thrill of the London grass. I saw it everywhere, in every kind of desperate nook and cranny, and my heart melted. Knives and stones didn't stop it. It's hungry—town grass—like the town dispossessed. If they gave over sweeping London, in a year it would belong to the grass. If they didn't watch out the whole world would be grass. If they didn't watch out the whole world would belong to the dispossessed.

Grass of the towns! It was a noble sight to see.

My best time for walking in the streets of London was at nights when my brother was in the theatre. But when once midnight has struck, metropolitan nocturne can be a frightening catch! Then it is the London of George Cruickshank. It leers: it is grotesque. The pressure of darkness brings on all manner of excursions to cause alarm.

The coffee-stall keeper falls heavily down behind his barricade of jam tarts and sausage rolls, and a deft violent hand robs the till.

Characters emerge from basements for basement behaviour. Waxworks, museums, and any large deserted buildings locked up for the night, become places of assignment for elementals and bad shades to plot harm to you.

Cats creep on egg-shells. A knee-high tide of headlights swishes through Hyde Park; comes a head-on collision between two cars.

There's a suicide off Blackfriars Bridge. "Sweet Themes runne softly ..."

What goes on in rooms has an extension into the street. In the dark night the hand reaches for a gun, a rosary, a dear shoulder, and the portent of murder, prayer, and love surges into the silent, waiting street.

Old odd poets are back. Verlaine, square-jowl, Pan-mask, is standing once more in the shadows of a Soho street. Arthur Rimbaud knocks big red hands together at the night.

You might meet, too, Kit Marlowe, by some river stairs. On him would hang a short brocade coat with fur crossing on his chest. Ear-rings shine in his ears; there is some phosphorescent quality in his thin vulpine bearded face.

"I'm going your way as well as you," the whisper might arrow to any woman.

No use to say:

"But you didn't like women! You couldn't even create a good woman-character in your plays! You liked men of power! You were treacherous. You ... it says that you 'attempted sudden and privy injuries to men.'"

And still that shade would walk beside you! This sort of stunt is sometimes more than a person can cope with.

Then there were certain London characters who gave me much to speculate upon.

There was a thin old woman who sang in the streets, hideously, exquisitely ugly. One long tooth had a solus position between her big pink lips. I would hunt her out and go and give her an alms just to be able to gaze entranced into that white flabby face, vile in its meek nightmare blankness, and hear that special one-tooth voice of hers saying, ingratiatingly:

"Thank yer, me darling!"

It used to thrill me with horror, a thrill that would oddly have increased if, under her bonnet, I could also have known that she was *bald*. I would picture the foulness of lying on this thin unwashed lugubrious little figure, of her arms stretched up round a person's, neck, of what it would be like to press one's own mouth to that white wobbly face, and I would entrance myself with horror.

And a fruiterer's assistant, besides, aged forty years or beyond it, in whose stout figure, thin spindle legs, pretty rosy face and raven locks, I saw a reversion to that eighteenth-century type which figures so much in Rowlandson prints as lecherous milkmaids and alley drabs, gave me pleasure to see. I would go and buy a pineapple or a paper-poke of little apples that I did not want, simply to be able to gape at her and from her person see the whole montage of night life in Drury on towards 1750: a cut-throat, prodigiously bawdy, merry scene, with lights leering in the houses of ill-fame, and smoky lamps on iron arms shooting from pawnbroking establishments, gaming-parlours, and dram-shops. Through her I would hear full-bloodied calls from pie-men and whores, and see many well set-up scoundrels of both sexes, prig-pockets, gamesters, fruit-girls of the streets, pimps, assassins and apprentices on the loose, run and reel down the flagged way. Above all, a hand is flung over a lute. A voice sings out a madrigal.

Moreover, there was a broad elderly prostitute whom I used to see at night, dressed very respectably like some man's excellent mother; she had sandy hair in a tidy bundle under her flat black hat, and she wore gloves. That she always wore gloves devastated me. A prostitute with gloves on! My roving eye would travel to her big feet in their black woollen stockings and carefully polished flat-heeled shoes, her skirt of decent length, and the travesty she was vastly intrigued me. I would hand her two-and-six for having stared at her so. It used to vex her, however, that I would never go home with her.

"Come on, do," she would say. "I'd like to make a friend of you, you funny little carcase. Don't let's stand here on this windy corner. You come along 'ome with me. Nice flat—nothing posh or comfortable, but decent, you know. I'll make some toast! Then you can talk to me, and I'll talk to you. I'll open your pretty eyes! I'll educate you, little heart I I'm special! I'm the one boys come to when they want to feel *safe*!"

Shem, being instructed in the Cabbala by the angel Japhiel, could not have been more rapt than I, listening to her.

But I'd decline her invitation and go off, saying over and over:

"She'd make toast—*toast!*"

Would she make it with those gloves on? Would she make love with gloves on?

In London Steve found us a small Queen Anne cottage in Hampstead, that stared with all its might across the windy heath. We had two gardens, a strip at the front, and a long wild one at the back with a tangly old pear and a peach tree.

What a thing the heath was! To my town-eyes it seemed like the *country* smack in front of the street door, and this was enchanting. No train journey to get to trees, ponds, and grassy delights—all a person had to do was to open the street door, and there was the heath rising so steeply, so greenly, sheer from the tarmac, with seagulls in the winter squealing like ungreased wheels, landing, skidding and reeling about as though they had flown leagues without once alighting. What a pleasure was this beautiful fittingness of the country beginning at the very doorstep, this looking straight from one's own windows upon trees standing motionless as green bottles in the pellucid evening light, which seemed as though the character of all the yellow plums in the world, the buttercups and the gold, had yielded the finest air-spun mimosa light, winnowed and sweet enough to entice tongues out of heads to taste!

"Why do you stand staring across the heath?" my brother, coming upon me, would ask.

I'd break off my exhaustive communion with the heath to say:

"Well, there is a secret in a nutshell, a sea-shell, and all that is enclosed, but the greatest secret of all is in open windy space."

"I must try and discover that," he would answer. "Ah, if I could only fathom you, I should be easy, you know. I, should think no more about you, you know. And I'd be glad!"

He would stand beside me, brooding. He detested the heath on a sunny day. He mistrusted open smiling country, just as people with free, easy manners and pleasant outward forms made him askance, he suspecting the chilled heart under the sunny face. What he preferred, though it ever caught his heart away, was a twilight over the heath of dark cold gleams, and a high, hoarse wind, when the sky above the treetops was watery silver, and the trees themselves were staggering under the belt of the rising sap; when any white stone received a four-fold intensity of its pallor; when the sky and the earth seemed to turn their backs on the world of men, giving nothing and asking nothing.

He also liked to stand with me and watch the people. We would see our neighbours coming home, turning into the gates that led to their houses which, with some shabbiness but an eighteenth-century aplomb, faced the wild land. All the front doors were differently painted. There was the black door with the gold facings, the royal blue, the olive green, the cyclamen. But the white door with the Chinese crimson hieroglyphic under the fanlight opened to our home. The significance of that red dart was "Serenity."

The people, our neighbours, came off the streets where they had been nobodies, leavened into the common uncaring crowd, and the minute they opened their little garden gates you could see the change that took place in their natures. They would walk upright, dart assured looks upon their aconites, tread more firmly, for as span as they entered on their own property the people assumed the roles which they saw themselves playing, in their span, against the waltzing pistons of life and time.

I used to stare with the greatest interest at our little group of everyday human propositions, and speculate upon how far their Homeric, Faustian, or Proustian conceptions of the universe were heightened or collapsed by that day's aspect of the heath.

The people trod, dreaming of girls, cash, or the shape of things to come, their hide-bound routes streaming steadily away to perdition or paradise.

Were they happy the heath heightened their bliss. Were they upstart and vain it made a nose at them. Had they done wrong it judged them sullenly. Were they betrayed it announced, a-grin: "But I am still here!" If they were sorrowful, it unfolded a grief far more ancient and majestic.

To be sure, though its bigness slipped into us all, the heath was never subordinate to us. There always remained something withheld, some mystery focussed in the tussocks of tangled grass, in the twinkling leaves, in the whirr of wings for ever.

The heath had been there long before we had lived. It

would be there long after we were dead. There is something impressive about such implacable continuity, and it is in the nature of people to care about being in association with something greater than themselves.

It was something for us to dwell upon as we floundered, confused and tired, through the surplusage of our affairs, that when we were dead the heath would still be magical under the burnt-sugar light of the misty November moon, would stand up in the pulsing amber light of summer afternoons, and coil unspeakably terrible in every midnight instant.

This ancient slab of humped land covered with scrub, scattered swan-haunted ponds, fidgeting grass, a little wood crushed with convulsions from the eighteenth century, left unmolested on the shoulders of London, watched and heard the people, and, in the depths of their well-guarded personalities, it took the soundings. It heard cries that never came out of their mouths, and, knowing how much more than themselves they all really are, it threw off messages to their uncharted consciousness that prompted them to their own salvation or gave them the one shove needful to cast them over the precipice.

I always felt its attentiveness to my own affairs as I watched its vivid complexion.

And of our humility, cupidity, misery, glee, love, lies and ecstasies, the heath took some toll, storing it up, giving it back again in haunting on an unsuspected future day. In this way, some aspect of itself suggesting a happy mouth, some strained parched look on an albinoed kind of day, a rapacious tongue of snow, some soft, far, early radiance, some bundle of gaunt weeds, a declension of burning autumn willows, some sour green moon arriving among tatters of fuchsia sunset cloud, a message of unearthly threat as the day was ending, would evoke for us an incident passed, celebrating once and for all the defeat of mathematically-recorded Time.

Steve and I took great pleasure in furnishing our home. We installed droll prints by Rowlandson of bawdy-house bullies and street drabs in leather stays on the wainscoted walls of the hall The panelling went right over the ceiling, swart, living, leathery timber that, remembering the lost green wild wood, gave off crackles and creaks, till at times on windy nights, I would be so caught up in raving forest-consciousness that it was imperative for me to dip my hands into the flaring pansies of the hall coal fire to establish house-sense once more. I never doubted that there was a sorceress in that ceiling.

The staircase was like a cinnamon giant kneeling with arms raised worshipfully under a tall stained-glass window that spangled the giant with a flurry of mimosa-coloured trees and vermilion stars on towards the late afternoon when the sun, never forgetful of the least of its duties, threw in a genial if reserved ray through the window which, in all the previous hours, had steadily been gathering itself together for the approach of this glory.

On each side of the fireplace, two low brocaded chairs crouched like assassins. These were friends to none. A person never sat in them without some sensation of being imminently hugged to death.

One week Steve would inform our callers that the chairs had belonged to the Sforza family; another time he would forget what had gone before, and they heard that Lucrezia Borgia had sat plotting in them. If one of his infatuated friends took Steve to task about this deviation, he would say brightly:

"But I don't mean to be a liar! I am merely anxious to

make life like the tinker's drunk bitch—endlessly diverting! That's why my dates are never plumb-line, and sometimes my values are frightfully mixed! I am also apt greatly to change my mind. Thus, if I remark an eighteenth-century mask in the map of your face, the chances are next time we meet I shall tell you that you remind me of a King Charles's spaniel! All this means that you have to be careful with me, unless you wish to be left wandering and angry behind. When you know me, you will be careful!"

Certainly those little chairs held a Renaissance lodgment of hooded alarm.

As for the rest of our hall furniture, there was a table as tall as a hussar cluttered with contemporary periodicals steadily accumulating, and on the mantelpiece stood a basalt clock beside a pot-bellied article of Battersea enamel. The clock had a sweet chime and an old gentleman who whisked out and stood bitterly at attention while the hour rang.

There were also, of course, such things as plants in pots, and daylight, and the diamond gleams in bovine bits of coal in the scuttle, and smoke, draughts, and dust—all part of the livingness of this hall, identifying themselves with events, gathering about themselves extensions of moods, and best of all, communicating their own private personalities.

Opening off the hall was a passage to the kitchen, a diningroom, and a room full of books and four armchairs where Steve and I sat together late at nights after he came home from the theatre.

Upstairs were his and my bedrooms, and two spare rooms, one of which Steve had converted into a bathroom.

His bedroom was cluttered with odd precious trifles such as: a record of Sarah Bernhardt's voice when she was old—a high passionate clattering voice, bringing the dead famed one vividly back into the room—and he had a thigh-bone that was said to be the thigh-bone of Charlemagne. This was the sort of thing he went in for: he was lost without a flourish.

My own room had nothing in it but books, a bed, and a William Morris wallpaper—dark-wine background with bright scattered sprays.

We kept no servant as it was too much of a pleasure to me to care for our little home to relinquish it to a cool stranger. Besides, I should not have known how to treat a servant. As it was, I always addressed tramps as "Sir," which made them guffaw.

But there is nothing to compare with the magic of living in a *little* house, especially if you live in it quietly and alone. With Steve peace had to be snatched. All his admirers found their way to our home—actors, actresses, and every sort of the tempting worthless person he was in the habit of whistling to his side. Steve liked to be the centre of the oddest schemes, and picked up the kind of characters who would not deny his wishes.

That propensity to choose shady or unlawful characters for companions which, as a child, had led him to make friends with a prostitute, now brought him into contact with people so strange that before we had been living in London a year, it was intimated to him in a friendly, roundabout way, that Scotland Yard was taking some interest in the places he frequented and the friends that hung on his arm. This quietened him somewhat, but then he brought his associates home. People came to our house with long hair, no hair, good living legs, excellent wooden legs, with glass eyes, wall eyes, angel faces, rodent faces, cheeks ravaged by paint, cheeks ravaged by disease. There were girls like boys: boys like their grandmothers. Some sombre Great

Ones bearded like Frenchmen, goats, or kings on playing cards. Flaring gusts and eddies of people, everyone well-off, irregular, bird-brain and pleased with themselves, all more or less directly related by the sex thrust. And all unhappy.

Listening to their conversation, I couldn't discover them showing any clarity of mind, any determination, stability, or conscience. Everything was madly uncertain. Certainties were worn down by bright, immediately irrefutable talk.

There was a whirl of pleasure to try and find what was lost, in some cases, what they had never had, the old nobility and decency of the generations. They climbed the steeps only to fall back into the mud, again and again, until they stopped rising.

Everyone laughed and talked at the tops of their voices. Harsh, strident, unhappy. Steve was very successful with them. It was easy. All you did, you commented friendlily on the obvious, even enlarged upon it. The people liked this, it could not upset them, or make them think.

I, saddened, would remember that this was chiefly going on in dining-and drawing rooms the world over, and it was a huge success.

We definitely need a deluge, something mad and strange, I said to myself, something to knock us out of this pitiful nothingness. Anything is better than this.

The men, if they were not buffoons, were sadists, while the women were in the habit of visiting expensive psycho-analysts to be put through their paces in order to stir up the subconscious and bring to light all manner of occurrences that mercifully had been forgotten. And so, having reaped up, one time or another, such an arsenal of horrors they were now more or less unbalanced, I could not help thinking to myself:

"Thank God, we shall not be judged on the subconscious!"

But Steve had a mania for people like these, for probing and ogling, for hovering and dropping depth charges, for frightening and making suggestions to assault the imagination; for he was enthralled by a notion of the heart being a palimpsest of human variations upon the seven deadly sins, with the thin, eerie tracing of the first childhood sin discernible under the heavy scorings of adult crimes, strata below strata, retreat within retreat, layers of it, a lifetime of it.

He knew of nothing more engrossing than this pursuit, this satisfaction he derived from taking the top of things.

"It leaves me ensorcerized in the dark," he declared to me once, looking with narrowed, exultant eyes. "So suspect it is, so dozy, so rapturous, so vomiting! I've known some scenes all right, scenes without validity or reason, but blazing with colour!"

Tirelessly and gravely malicious, he liked to listen, to prompt, to record mentally, to brood. He never used any thing on the people but themselves: it was a. devastating flail, especially when he so intensely set at naught the power of the human will to rise above the human instinct for erring.

Smiles would make little events on his face as he would launch his humiliating or offensive attack. He cracked the whip, it was his notion of a good time, and he was a specialist at it. There was mutiny, of course, for many of his friends were spirited people. But mutiny was just what Steve liked. To set the whole company flaring with feelings of hatred and revenge.

And nobody could get back at him. Smiling and ruthless, he would say:

"But *I* have nothing to declare!"

There was little to be done with a man who did not respect even his *own* humanity.

I had thought that with the street and our mother's presence removed, he would find some kind of happiness, but he was as chagrined as ever—perpetually boiling over with his own themes—a desperate, fanciful, unmanageable, unhappy creature for whom nothing came about as he would. He nagged and reproached and quarrelled. Not that anyone could keep up with him: any argument freshened his brains wonderfully and caused him to discover points in his own favour that had not previously occurred to him. He could only be won over by patience and suggestion, and sometimes by a vein of diabolical fun.

Only once did Anda and Robert come to visit us. Robert was spending a vacation with her at her earl's Warwickshire castle, and they had come up to town on a shopping expedition for her first baby. Both chatted happily to us of their achievements—Anda spoke of her child, and Robert of his university life. His choice integrated mind was now showing forth and he had already published a history of Greece for children wherein he had not merely gilded a few plums such as the Trojan war and Alexander's exploits, but he had got down to the drudgery of the Peloponnesian wars, his reward being the interest of half the schools in the country. This book brought him his first renown as an historian.

Their visit, of course, was a disaster. In next to no time Steve was violently quarrelling with them, and they left, deeply offended. Thereafter when I saw them it was by appointment in restaurants or in one of the many Mayfair houses where Anda was received. Time and time again they urged me to leave our outrageous brother, but in those days there was no compelling reason for me to do so.

Besides, if they said he was bad, he was also often sad. There was always some element of weeping about him, even when he was laughing most loudly in some wild jollity or stood after the triumph of a performance crushed with attentions from an adoring mob.

His personal beauty was now a little dispersed by the rigours of maturity, and something had come into his features that seemed convulsive and withheld. His expression now was more nervous and audacious, and the eyes gleamed more ferociously, lit by no content but a kind of desperate glee in the mangling dance of his life. What was particularly engaging about his face was that when amusement came to him, as it did so seldom, his smile flickered through the bones and eyes before ever it reached his mouth. I believe he had what is called a "skin short," and this contributed to his appearance of passionate, unearthly fragility.

All about him was something imperial, abrupt, and mischievous. He had only to appear on the stage, or enter a room, and the people were for him without question. He was, as always, slim in build, but he was a giant in presence.

He now was never without finger-rings that fizzed in the light, an eye-glass like a soap-bubble shooting from his cheek, and other affectations including a choice of two hundred walking-sticks.

For the most part he was unflustered and unscrupulous. He possessed a curious kind of hither-thither cleverness that enabled him to bluff through most situations, but he shied away from thought for its own sake as though afraid of coming face to face with himself.

It was sad and curious to see how he never threw off what had been done to him by our mother. He was imperious because he still expected to be judged and derided, even now, when he stood on top of the world. As a child he was never allowed to believe that anything he ever said was lucid, worthy, or important, never allowed any feelings of well-being, or left with thoughts of comfort and encouragement. So he still gazed round with wonderful airy looks after he had made an utterance, expecting scoffing and denial—and equipped to deal with it, too. As for feelings of happiness, these had been so furiously driven out of him that nothing could really bring them to him now.

At nights when he and I sat together, following the departure of the crowd, he often threw his favourite act for me, in which he was Oedipus and Hamlet and Dante all in one. He acted, acted all the time, filling his life full of needless complications, exaggerating everything. He would whip up a desperate situation out of nothing at all. He was fantastically clever at this. He looked at things with eyes that saw twice as much as was there, but he never looked on the shining form, only the brackish petrified underside.

If I became impatient, as I sometimes did, a first-class row blew up.

"It comes as a shock to me when you are scorching and angry," he'd declare sharply. "The familiar reels—like when one catches one's amigo in the arms of some other person, or like seeing a bishop in his pelt!"

Then he would lean forward and say, wonderingly:

"But how can you hurt me now? When I was a child, a child, moreover, who was cheated in his parents, our fond mother dashed me to pieces, so, being nothing, I am strong! You cannot wound me—there is nothing of me to have feelings. I am disintegrated, strong, already dead! You stare, do you? And well you might! I've never known solidarity or peace. I'm what loneliness and neglect lead to! Life's tragedy is not warfare, or monetary pressure—it's the absence of love when one is a child!"

Thus launched, he would go on and on, accusing me of not caring for him, not being interested in him till, worn out, I'd say:

"Well, then, mend it, mend it altogether. Let us live apart!"

That would bring him up with a start.

"You can't mean that," he would say.

"I mean it very sincerely," I'd answer, longing for peace and to be by myself. "I have some patience, I believe, but you'd wear out a saint! You had a bad time once, but you were plentifully equipped to get over it. The secret is—you didn't want to! No one is poor unless they *want* to be. Your mind and your thoughts always were your own, and private thoughts are the riches—or the ashes. You talk about your tragic fate, but you enjoy being tragic, you revel in the pride of the forsaken! What an inflated idiot you are, after all! You thrill over what you call being 'misunderstood,' 'treated badly'. You aren't treated badly, and have not been for years now, except by yourself. You've had time to get over it, instead of concentrating on a poor pinchbeck attempt to get back at life for what you've never taken the trouble to accept from life. Your endless battery is not a sign of real strength, but a proof of weakness and defeat—defeat because what is lacking is lacking to you through your own fault.

"The majority of people have sorrow and ill-luck, many worse than yours. The very fact, the very fact that you are not at this moment a patient with cancer in a hospital bed, or a rabbit caught in a snare, ought to be enough to give you a glimmering of happiness! We're all brow-beaten by sorrow, statistics, and science that believes nothing, but what keeps us going is a vague, vegetable expectancy. Daft the whole world may be, but that is better than being doused.

We are all built to rise above everything, including the positive element of evil with which we are born. Disaster sharpens the wits, and this being so, helps people to find that compensation which is everywhere, everywhere! Often there's nothing left except *life*, and often that's the first time you begin *to live!*"

"Magnificent," he applauded, wryly, "only there is no compensation *anywhere!* There is no compensation! No, not even in your clear eyes and your sweet face. You do not compensate me though often I long to come and kneel to you, to ask you to forgive me in the name of all I've ever wronged. You make me wish to arrive at some sudden fusion of honour—to make amends! There are times when you startle out of me an instinct for good, when you give me relief from myself, when I can hardly look at you with balance. Every word you said just now is true, I am sure, but they come too late for me, I am walled in by my own iniquity and, really, it doesn't matter what happens to second-raters like me!"

"You're not speaking lines on the stage now," I cut in, cruelly. "Like everyone else, you talk too much. Oh, how it enrages me that any human being should represent himself as a second-rater and, worse—accept this—live down to it! How little you know or understand, after all, you who are so clever. You, who wish to possess all humanity have never learnt to possess yourself! You are so proud of the way you are damning yourself, so proud and so enthralled by what you call your evil! But don't you forget it's a hair's breadth between good and evil. Don't you forget that infinite Goodness was crucified *between* two thieves! It's all in the mind, your mind! Heaven is no far-off shining shop where everything is free, and hell isn't a subterranean furnace. *You* make 'em. You! Everyone for themselves! Nothing is *there* that you don't *already know about!*

"God! It's bad enough that you hate everyone, but it's worse that you hate yourself most of all. How can you love anyone if you detest yourself!"

"I love you, Laura," he said, quietly. "I detest myself!"

"If you love me," I said, wearily, "show it—by trying to love yourself a little, also."

"But I can't bear to have only myself," he protested, "I'm afraid of missing something."

"You're missing yourself!"

"Selfish—all that concentration on self! I recoil from myself. I have something more interesting on hand than to harangue my immortal soul—if any! I want an ideal cause!"

"Well, you've got it—yourself. We ought to try and know ourselves—the rest will follow."

How difficult it was, I thought, to propose that people should love their own souls. They love everything about themselves except their souls. Unloved is to go uncared for.

"Is anyone such a decent turn-out that it is worthwhile knowing themselves?" demanded Steve.

"By what standards do you reckon a person decent or not?" I put in., "We ought to know ourselves because we cannot know anybody else alive. If we don't love and respect ourselves how can we love and respect other people and find interest in their doings? We're all lost and ask questions because we neglect the endless miracle of ourselves and our relationship to the daily wonders going on all round us!"

"Your words change all my life!" exclaimed Steve, sarcastic and sad.

I went away from him to the window, dispirited. Seeing his positive, frowning doubt, I thought:

There must be something mad or wrong about this fact of my wanting nothing but my own heart and mind at liberty between the earth and sky, flowing in harmony with the old cosmic forces emanating from trees and straws and feathers and mud, intangible, yet the only reality for me, the only way in which I can get over the sorrow and rage in the world of men, in the world of animals. It means that in my secret heart I have no need of anybody, and no change or circumstance can affect me. The only thing that brings me utter misery is the time when I cannot say that I have kept faith with myself. And the time when my love for my brother avails us nothing—as now.

"Help me," I implored the heath, humble and afraid.

But out on the heath in the half-light, the wind had got hold of a little tottering tree and was trying to pull it up by its hair. Still I looked and waited.

"Have you nothing for me?" I wondered.

But the heath had: as I looked, the moon clouted a way for itself out of immense slabs of cloud. It was a new moon, a lonely bent pod like a peanut which nightly would swell till it had become a full radiant rondure. This moon hailed me, and I saluted it.

Down below, like handfuls of gleaming yellow rice, the lights of London were quietly winking, and a crimson tremolo rose with intense passion above a building. A chime escaped from a spire. The wind went in flight over the trees like a grey goose. Moonbeams on the dewy wet roofs gave a blue eerie light of the consistency of sea-shells, looking as though it could be scraped off with a knife. Fluctuant islands of lilac light flared round the moon and went out. The spell of the night was balm and renewal to me.

I turned back to my glooming brother, and I kissed him, hard, on the mouth.

"If there's nothing else, there's always my love," I said.

He drew me against him with rough despair.

"Your love! Your love!" he murmured. "It's the 'music at midnight' to me. Oh, don't ever detest me; never be far off, my darling. Have patience yet."

I did have patience, and I did not leave him—not then.

The tragedy was that he did not want to change. He didn't want real happiness at all. He refused to know what real happiness was. He wanted it to arrive to him permanently through pleasure. To look for happiness within himself would have been too much trouble. And yet, he had spent the whole of his life in endless, torturing effort looking for the illusion of happiness and not finding even that.

Some evenings he would be altogether different, and after the play would sit till far on into the morning, while I read to him the letters of Charles Lamb or William Cowper, or from the works of his favourites—Swift and William Hazlitt.

"I am so charmed with you, Laura, for persuading me to read again, or at least, to listen to you reading," he would say. I used to read to him sitting at his feet, with the book on his knee, and my arm round his waist. I read to him passages from Hindu scripture, from the Bhagavadgita; he couldn't bear the Christian Bible, he would say:

"The old testament is a fearful book, Laura, with all those wars and strange love affairs and the most diabolical feelings of hatred. As for its image of Jehovah, this is unequalled anywhere in literature for spite and idiocy!"

"Don't go judging God on the old testament, Stephen Valley," I retorted.

"It's no wonder Jesus had to come and put the old testament on the market," said he, unabashed.

"Well, you cynical loon," I said; "*tell* God, tell *Him* that the old testament bores you! You ought to know that God often works without the Bible, and often without any orthodox religion. It comes down to this—everyone makes their own image of God, and in that form alone they shall see Him at the last. If the Bible doesn't help you—help yourself!"

Steve also developed a fondness for readings from Rousseau's "Confessions," and Landor's "Imaginary Conversations." When I had read a bit, he would say:

"Now we will think about that!" I'd lean my head on his knee, he would stroke my hair, and some peace would steal into the room.

Then I'd resume the reading till we became so mazy with various philosophies we'd open the house door and charge across the heath in the melodious wild wind. The dark was intense, but we were night-individuals and could find our way in the dark. The wind thumped the floor of the high heath, the flying boughs roared and sang. The wind had broken the surface of the ponds into many hundreds of porpoise backs. A shore lamp or two sent canary-coloured gleams across the black whipped-up water. We'd climb over the fence into Ken Wood where the wind was shut out among the mighty trees. There we would find a seat and huddle down together.

At such times Steve would recall our childhood days—and not always the bad times. He would confide some bygone delight to me. He would remember the lights from passing horse-drawn carts—how they had wheeled across the ceiling. The light would start slowly in a corner, mount steadily across the ceiling then, with a triumphant flash, disappear smack against the opposite wall.

This performance with the cart-light was accompanied by a delightful rhythmical slapping-down of horses' feet, as though they were treading in a mixture of cream and stones.

Prompted by a sense of adventure, Steve would follow the horses much further than this. All from his bed, he would see their progress along the streets, the big veins standing out on their bodies, their heads bowed and nodding as if in eternal agreement with a ghost-horse that persistently argued at their side; and on their legs were bunches of shaggy hair which made them look as though they were wearing Wild West trousers.

At last the driver would growl out a final "whoa there," he would climb down from the cart with some quite friendly remark such as:

"Come on, you bloody, lazy bastard!" and begin to take the old warm brown horse with the blonde mane and tail, out of the shafts.

Having thus satisfactorily seen the horse nid-nod into the dusty, golden stable, the little boy would turn his attention upon the bare room in which he lay.

The ragged piece of carpet beside the bed was a dolphin swimming vainly about in a cold stony sea. He leant down and said something consoling to it.

Then he laid his head flat on the bed, tunnelled up the pillow like an igloo, and from there he looked out across leagues and leagues of glittering snow under the Northern Lights, and saw the reindeer running across the foot of the bed.

His ear might itch. He would insert a finger, forgetting the irritation at once in the invention that his ear was a dark staircase, leading up to a wonderful castle within his own head, gaily thronged, brilliantly lit—gas *and* electricity. He wanted his finger to gain admission to these delights; but the finger could go no further. Regretfully, he withdrew it.

These things Steve would remember with pleasure. When his voice had died, the little wood asserted itself over us. Now it seemed to be full of incorporeal images from the eighteenth century, standing off on the upper air, abstruse presences riding by, and perilous airs and catches of the bygone age were to be heard in the leaves.

In no time the ghosts had transported me back to a London of narrow streets, of coffee-houses, of men in periwigs and square-toed shoes stooping to enter sedan chairs. The mercer went to look at the bill for the night's play where it was stuck on the post, and shouted something humiliating after a passing negro servant.

I saw a seafaring man with a square, varnished hat and pigtail go by with a parrot that screeched:

"Up the devil! The old gal's died of Purples and Spotted Fever!"

The fop came staggering from a gaming-house. He had just lost his inheritance at Ombre. He fell over on his high heels into the gutter, to the mirth of two scurvy beggars under an arcade.

Old London cries arrowed faintly down the streets:

"Buy my Small Coals!" "Twelve Pence a Peck, Oysters!" "Buy a Rat-Trap!"

And then, heigh ho, I was caught up in a great press of shadowy forms and whirled to the scene of a public execution. High storms of laughter burst from the terrible crowd as the blubbering victim was hauled on to the platform.

I tried to escape from the hot mad reeking scene and

could not. A hand took my neck in a vice and forced me to look to the end of the hanged one's struggles.

I came to, and found that although I was back in the twentieth century, my brother's arm tightly round my neck, my feelings were still quivering, still bewilderingly mingled with that open jeering brutality of a bygone era.

"You've been dreaming, darling," Steve comforted me. "What is it, what's troubling you? You're here—here with me, and no harm can come to you."

The darkness, then, before the dawn, was so intense, the eyes looked at nothing. This is an afraid thing for eyes to do, and I'd suggest a move out of the boiling dark of the wood to watch the coming of the morning from the open heath.

The light would begin to break over the tree-tops, and the dome of St. Paul's would be the first to announce the presence of the city below. One by one the white spires, the turrets and towers glinted into sight, robbed of solidity by distance and the silver-strawberry light of the dawn, and they looked part of a fabulous city that had been let down from the sky, a visionary city such as Blake or Thomas Traherne might have seen.

"These are the good times," Steve would say, his face haggard and stern in the thin new light. Then he would add, with all tenderness:

"You know how I love you? All the time, all the time! There would be nothing at all in any day for me if you were not in it. I never cease to value you, even when I am being abominable! Oh, you have done me good, nothing but good!"

Between his love and his bitter quarrels, caught up in our imperious and altogether entangling household that fluctuated between the dotty and the divine, I might have come near to real unhappiness if it had not been for my inner scheme of things that received so tremendous an impetus from all the London impressions.

I wandered, about, spying out the scene from beneath a shady hat, seeing buildings, citizens, the blanched stone spires against dove-grey and lavender skies, and old courts housing many a Dantesque secret, as though on the first day of an unspoiled world. Mystery, wistfulness, and the old poetic romance of things were everywhere—in a quiet piece of waste land over in Islington no less than in a shabby little shop in a side street with "Harbour Lighting" over the window. The shop *sold that!* If I went in would they serve me with six pennyworth?

Then the waterfront scene beside the Thames would take full possession of me. As I stared at the river, I would become a disembodied stream of consciousness flowing with the water over rusty kettles and corpses, under the greenness of trailing weeds and blue of the sky; under bridges bearing outrageous traffic thunder, past wax candles shining in lone shanty windows at nights. I *was* the river guffawing against the Wapping stairs, rasping hoarsely in the links of anchor chains, making entreaties against the greasy sides of oceangoing liners, barking under the arches, slapping the rumps of long flat boats carrying hay and coal. I *was* the river, knowing the waterway straight from Wapping to the quays in Paris. Aha—I am this river: this river is better to me than any living person. But I would realize how far I had stepped out of myself and struggle for my own identity. If someone came and spoke to me—a stranger, say, asking a direction—before I had had time to *get back*, arrested between dimensions, as it were, only half there, and, consequently, somewhat at a loss, I'd look at the person as though he were the half-witted one and not I.

Another place where my thoughts poured steeply was Fleet Street, where the old taverns are squeezed between the large modern newspaper offices. Down Fleet Street flowed a stream of stars broken away from the minds of those who haunted the thoroughfare in other times—stars from the minds of Charles Dickens, Coleridge, Wordsworth, Charles Lamb, the Gordon rioters, the tender Oliver Goldsmith, the beetling Dr Johnson, Addison and Steele, Swift, the parson poets of the seventeenth century, Ben Jonson, Marlowe, and Shakespeare himself. But the stream did not stop there; it took from the thoughts of Chaucer and King Alfred pondering on his translation of Boethius, and on back to the time of the Roman occupation when those who walked in Fleet Street walked in a wild country lane that led to the west gate of the town with the ugly face of the god Lud leering down; the thoughts of those who had hastened to get within the walls for safety out of the night, returned to me, so that I knew their fear of the wolves and boars ranging the misty country, and their fear of the evil dead lying enclosed within the ivory pins of their shrouds in the vast cemetery upon which, one day, the cathedral of St. Paul's was to rise. I felt disturbed and rich in the force invading my willing consciousness. And my mind in the mind of the dreaming dead who inherit the earth for ever, I would be confused and unable to answer when a modern policeman would touch me solicitously on the arm saying, "Aren't you well, miss, you don't look well!"

There was no doubt I had many and many a place for my communings, for drawing a peace beyond understanding into all my heart and mind.

Once, after a particularly blasting encounter with Steve, I went out and presently found myself in the Charing Cross Road. There I saw outside a contraceptives store, a thin, blackened tree, a little stranger to fresh air, an estrayent from the forest, strangled in a few pitiful inches of greasy, nonnourishing dirt—the whole of London standing on its straining heart. In spite of all this, its branches were running with brave red beads of buds. The stoicism of this tree, its unquenchable life-force, the patient joy it gave off from some remote triumph, transcending its staggering handicaps, brought the tears to my eyes.

All at once my mind opened like a fan of fire on the uncertainties and fears of my life. All my fettered impulses were freed by the indomitable force of that tree's spirit, and my own liberated soul rushed into a harmony of ineffable sweetness with the life-feeling of the tree. There came to me an intimation of immortality so compelling, I could hardly contain myself. A storm of highest hope and happiness took possession of me. I had risen above the absurd, diminished creature who had listened so wretchedly to Steve's ranting. I saw that I was not earth-bound. The world, I felt, belonged to me, because the essence of its purpose, beauty, and mystery was caught in my own heart-strings for ever.

Standing in the roar of the London traffic, before the shop that doled out shillingsworths of sterility, beside the humble, formidable tree, I was never before so keenly aware of how everyone who lives is mighty. From beginning to end we miss nothing, share all. We *were* before we began. We all have been in the dust of the Athens of Socrates: we stood in the crowd at Calvary, and we read Elephantis with Tiberius on Capri. We were with Cormac Mac Art and the old hero kings in their winged battles; we slept in the straw with the cattle in the Middle Ages and sat in the ear of the great Schoolmen. We drank the warm blood of an ox, we were burnt at the stake as witches. We were the smoke that darted against the beams of the Mermaid Tavern, and we were "touched" by Queen Anne against the "evil." We were the star that looked in when they took the death mask of Keats, and we sailed with Nelson for Trafalgar. We were the genii in the gems of Regency architecture, we froze to death in the Crimea, and we saw the angels of Mons. We have *been* of saints, of devils. We are more, much more than ourselves.

We are nothing. We are great. We are associated with the smoke going up home and factory chimneys, with the fruit on the trees and dim planets travelling in limitless space, with the fungus on the ocean floor, and with all those things that have collected about themselves so rich an affinity with charity and sorrow and necessity—the bakehouse, the surgical knife, the street lamp, coins, salt, symphonies—all things. Escaping nothing. Infinitely potent.

This is not fancy. This is reality. Everything on earth is magnificent, purposeful, and ultimately wise; nothing is unrelated; one harmony binds all. What has been taken away is returned a hundredfold. Every time is the time to come to perfection.

And I wanted to say to the uncaring crowd surging past me:

"It isn't what comes to you that matters, and it isn't what you know. My dear friends—it's what you *believe!*"

It had been a rare encounter, this; it had been like the whole of life in one moment; it had been perfection.

But now Steve and I had been in London together for two years, and the wranglings, eccentricities, love and happiness of that time were like an interval between two major acts—our childhood and our later destiny.

One morning Steve was flicking over his letters and suddenly he picked one out with an exclamation. Soon he said:

"It's from Bernard McCann. He's coming to London with his newest play, he asks me to have the lead with ... damn, Oh damn, with Oriel! Never mind! I shall enjoy this. I told you I liked his work. Ah, Laura, this pleases me. They are leaving New York next month. Now, now things will begin to happen!"

Chapter VI

"If a man urge me to tell wherefore I loved him, I feel it cannot be expressed but by answering: Because it was he, because it was myself."

JOHN FLORIO

BUT, after all, it was Oriel McCann who came alone from America in the late summer. Bernard was too ill to travel, and she came on his behalf with a commission for Steve not only to act in the new play, but to produce it.

Rehearsals of "The Woman in the Moon," Bernard's play, were soon in full swing. The play was a tragic fantasy, and took such a hold of me that I often sat alone in the vast, deserted auditorium to watch and listen.

Of course, right from the minute of Oriel landing in England, she and my brother took up the threads of their web where they had left off spinning it across the sea in America. Not that Steve would agree to set up housekeeping with her—but he graciously allowed her to be at our house every night and day; with this Oriel had to be satisfied.

To me, at any rate, she was a wonderfully glamorous woman. Her shining black hair cascaded to her shoulders, and her eyes, looking out like frosty blue flowers were fringed with marvellous thick lashes; these eyes were violet-shadowed in a way exclusive to persons with a long-extended malaise, but, be it remarked, Oriel was as strong as a horse. Her narrow face was cleverly never painted, off the stage, save for the pimpernel of her mouth. It was a strongly beautiful face, and it seemed to have come from the dark, to have been alight in roots, and to be a little askance now in the full glare of daylight.

The figure drooped a little, like a tree that too many winds have tugged, the whole creature having romance, a private magic, some wine-drenched kind of glamour peculiar to no one in the world but herself. At the same time, Oriel gave off something unhappy and tricked, something stern and wondering without a central essential fixation.

And she had what I think is always extraordinarily challenging to see, a very small waist with breasts like blown roses.

She came of an aristocratic English family—people who had been born simply to inherit. She had been placed on her rich plot and told never to handle a spade, as it would all come to her anyway from unseen labour in the dark. This happened.

Oriel was not poor in money, and she was kind after her fashion: she desired the good of the community provided she herself was not called upon to make any unusual contribution towards that end.

She was dashing and moody, and, to persons .who captured her interest, she could be extravagantly affable; she successfully imparted an air that for them alone she had unbent so delightfully.

Others found her bad-mannered, treacherous, and vain.

She was a bundle of nerves, greeds, and strange discernments, with rare times of yielding sweetness.

She was in love with my brother past all reasoning; that was plain, otherwise how could she have borne with him. For he treated his lady disgracefully. Most of the time he showed her that contemptuous curiosity he invariably displayed towards persons who loved and admired him. Usually he succeeded in annihilating what they felt for him by the most offensive analysis of their passion, but there was no shaking Oriel off, even though it was Steve's habit to listen and to look at her with grave and incredulous attention; poor thing, this was one of her greatest trials—that he persistently treated her as though she were either a corpse or a lunatic!

I used to wonder when I saw (with the curious thrill it always gave me) their two heads together gleaming black and gold, what there was in it for him, apart from the satisfaction he got from tormenting her, and I could only conclude that in this woman, ten years older than he was—seasoned, indulgent, exciting—he was looking for, without any thought of sex, the mother-love he had missed and would feel the need of to the end of his days.

But there was her side of it, too. She had no notion of standing in any such role to the fascinating young man. She was out for all the things women usually want—homage, admiration, possessiveness, respect and the most abandoned sensuality, all in one.

I don't know. There was something charming and pitiful about that passionate Oriel. I cared for her very much, right from the start, and there could have been the most delightful friendship between us had things been different. As it was, she kept me at a distance. She would not even allow my homage to her art, for she was a distinguished actress.

"Oh, do not praise me," she would cry, when she and Steve came back to our cottage, their nerves on edge after a strenuous rehearsal, and I sought to give her unction.

"Think yourself honoured that Laura praises you," Steve would say angrily. "This luminous girl is no ordinary person, I can tell you!"

"I recognize that," replied Oriel, tartly, "and, indeed, it would be difficult not to when you say it over and over again to me, like a litany."

And she shot me a look from under her lashes that was not a kind look.

"Perhaps I do not like the way you say that," put in Steve, softly. "Perhaps I ought to make it conditional upon your coming here that you treat my sister, *my sister*," he repeated, grinding his teeth, "with respect."

And she—she loved him so much, she even agreed to say to me then:

"Oh—forget what I said just now. Don't remember it against me!"

She turned to him:

"You are no ordinary man, but we must treat you as though you are! Kiss me!"

She got her face all ready for his kiss, then found she wasn't going to get one, after all. His simple, brutal rejection of her gifts was a lasting misery to her. I once heard her say to him:

"Of course, you are like most men to-day—you're all eunuchs or descendants of the Encolpius tribe!"

He laughed:

"It is wilful in you to say so, and many a man would be only too willing to give you the lie. Doubtless you speak out of the arrogance of the misunderstood, but you are difficult, too, you know, Oriel, so melancholy, bored, and restless, so always asking violent questions and worse—expecting answers! You're like an arrow that has never been shot, or a bird that failed to go to Africa at migration time!"

"You're right," said Oriel.

Well, there was no doubt that Oriel detested me. If we were in the house alone together, she would speak of her real feelings towards me.

"You and I will always get on very well on the strict understanding that I dislike you very much. I see through you, Laura, Oh, so clearly! I understand all your artful little ways—that hold you have over your brother. Oh, I see through your little game, my dear girl!"

Fascinated, I went to her. It always enthralled me to be told that a person *disliked* me. In the clarity of their hate I saw pictures of myself, aspects of myself to remember if ever I got vain.

"Have I got a 'little game'?" I asked her. "I have, but I doubt if you have recognized it. Certainly it has nothing to do with my brother except in so far as it helps me not to be made unhappy by him. But tell me about my 'little game'—as you see it."

"Don't come near me," she said. "I should really like to kill you! 'Tell me about my game!' Oh—that sort of talk *is* your game! That weighing up of every single little thing. That pretence that everything is important and matters— even lighting the fire or sweeping the floor. You make wonders of such things—as though they mattered. I can't tell you how I detest you—your enthusiasms, and your brutal, absolute unselfconsciousness! Steve thinks you've got hold of something—he thinks there is reality in your pretence— not that he knows what you're talking about, and neither do you. You've fooled him beautifully! Why, I … even I … listening to you, sometimes, I almost think that life is *real!* You're a born spoofer! You're so like Bernard. I detest in you the identical things I loathed in him—things that made me stop loving him as soon as I knew his … inhumanity. You're inhuman, too. You both ought to go about labelled 'Danger de mort.' No wonder, after all, that you attract Steve, who's got a stone where a heart should be. Ah, well, it was my fate always to be bound to people who were foreigners to ordinary decent human pleasures!"

She lit a cigarette. Self-pity crept into her eyes. She looked at me with intense curiosity:

"I suppose you're a kind of young witch—you and your dark smoky eyes—and that strange, strange hair! Yes, there are times when you have the power to make even me feel that I am not just a mere accident! Perhaps that's why I dislike you so much—just in case, in case there is something in what you say!"

"Well, you are not an accident," I said. "There's much more about you than that."

"Yes? Designed with love and care and intended for heavenly mansions? Oh, it's an old story, and rather touching, too—this extra-terrestrial rubbish! Meantime, however, there is this sickening earth to be endured!"

I, to whom "this sickening earth" was inexhaustible and miraculous, I was speechless.

"Oh, how tired I am of myself," she continued, "and the sameness of people and everything. My colours are all blurred. I wish, you know, that you were different. I wish you were human, not a strange, unfeeling kind of creature like a mermaid or a cold little fish coming up, elusive and silver, from the depths of green water! How you would suit

Bernard McCann. He's unfeeling, too, exactly like you. But if you were decent and comfortable I ... I ... could have made of you a friend, a dear friend. I could do with an ally, I could, not only to deal with your brother, but to help me with ... everything. There must be something more in life than I've had out of it. I've had nothing. Nothing! Only pleasure."

And, determined to agonize for a larger outlook, she continued vehemently:

"And even I, who believe in nothing, occasionally get a terrible feeling that life is only lent and some time must be handed back to ... *someone!* What shall I say, having used my life so ill? Drifted from affair to affair, soiling steadily! You, and other people, have a way of understanding these things that completely passes me by. Some necessary focus is lost to me. Everything ends in pain and ugliness for me. Wrinkles will soon begin to go about my face! When will be wise? Or happy? To think that I shall die—come to the end—with nothing resolved!"

I, drifting upon an inner stream of vague, happy thought, turned to my brother's friend with civil concern:

"Things needn't mean sorrow to you—unless you let them. What do you want, Oriel?"

"I want to be happy," she declared, throwing herself into a chair where she lounged, open-bloused, her fine, insolent eyes fixed on me. "You ask me what I want, *you*! But you are just the person who stands between me and happiness! You have got all my lover's heart! He really thinks of no one but you. He is bound to you by memories and shared experiences that have gone so deep—such was the nature of your life together—that no other woman has a chance of making much with him. He loves you so much it is impossible for him to think of another woman at all."

Sorrowfully she glanced down at her hungry, angry breasts.

"Will you believe me," I said, "when I tell you that I have asked Steve, times without number, to leave me and go to you? Do you think I should mind? I would not. I have no need of him or any man. You say I am inhuman—perhaps I am. I learned to live without any expectations, that's all!"

"Then—*you* leave him," she said, eagerly. "Since he will not leave you—you go. At least give me a chance of *failing*. I haven't even that bitterness! I have nothing. But I might have something, if you go away!"

"And what do you think would happen then?" I said. "You know very well. He would, as he has threatened so often, follow me wherever I went. It would not make things better for you—it would make them worse. He would break with you altogether knowing well that because of you I had gone away. It would wreck Bernard's play, and make matters a thousand times worse. Try to be patient, Oriel, with him and with me. Something will happen to straighten everything out, you'll see. Meantime, help him—don't goad him. He only thinks of me as a person who is always there in case of being wanted. It is nothing but that. He thinks of me as he did when we were children—as the only barrier between himself and harm. When he was little he depended upon me, as many an urchin depends upon an older sister. So—try to understand. Think about him—even more than you do. Love him—even more than you do. Someone like you could change him utterly—and for the better. You don't know how I always dreamed of him finding someone who would make up to him for all his real and imaginary wrongs. Very real and terrible injustice was done to him once, but now his happiness is chiefly his own fault. Nevertheless, no matter how you or I may feel impatient with his imagined setbacks and let-downs, he believes with the utmost sincerity that life is cheating him, and therefore life *is* cheating him. Oh, I have waited long and long for someone who should come and raise him from this slop of self-pity into the better, wider air of his own true self. Why should you not do this for him, Oriel?"

"Why not me? I can answer that immediately and briefly—because of *you!* Because you are always, *always* in his thoughts, because you always will stand between him and any woman who might save him. He has not only to be saved from himself, he is also to be saved from you!"

"Well, you could do it," I replied. "I believe in you, I have faith in you."

"No doubt you are trying to be kind," she said. "But I dislike you so much I can't trust you. You have too much power. And I am too unhappy!"

I should have liked to say roundly to her: You've no business to be unhappy. Not with a face as lovely as yours! You might have been born as ugly as sin! Persons with as much beauty and health and talent as you ought to be ashamed to be unhappy. Given all those good things, what more should you ask of life that you yourself do not make and put into it? What you *are*, you give off into the world-stream, so either add to happiness or add to unhappiness. The people who fidget for happiness are just the ones to miss its nearness, the *immediacy* of the thing.

But this is the sort of a statement to weary the listener, and suddenly Oriel said in a pellmell of spite:

"It occurs to me that since you always seem assured and happy, why don't you let me into the wonderful secret."

"Well," I said," I daresay happiness will come at you when

you least expect it. Happiness is a battle—against yourself! It's a fight between one's master-Self and all one's other whimpering, incorrigible, scolding, yelping, grumbling, frightened, sick, and sad *other* selves. If a person (and this has nothing to do with academic qualifications but is something anyone can accomplish) will try to control the thoughts that come clamouring for admission at the gate of his own mind (and no thought can enter unless admitted), then he can overcome anything, for the whole of happiness *is* contemplation—the *harboured thought*! Nothing is but what is thought to be! We can't escape sickness and sorrow and disappointments, but we can escape *from* them!"

"Well," she said, "go on!"

"But it must irritate you, Oriel! If a person is unhappy, it's a mistake to listen to another's method of achieving happiness!"

"Tell me about this happiness," she insisted.

"Oh," I said laughing, "you make such a business of it. Don't you know, Oriel, there's a lot in simply saying, 'Now at this moment I will be happy, I am happy'—standing on the neck of circumstance, as it were, asserting yourself over what has come to you. The very fact that at this moment you and I are not being crushed to death under an omnibus, or trapped in a burning house, is enough to give us some happiness. I'm being lurid on purpose! One has to be *excessive*. You have to insist on being yourself to the full drama and pride of the thing. And, then, if you search, you know, you'll always find, if not one thing then something else. Remember about Paracelsus? He tried to find the Elixir of Life and discovered laudanum!"

"God! This one-to-one conversation is apt to lift the hatches off the more insistent aspects of truth!" grumbled

Oriel. "There ought to be more of us! Then what you say would be more ... er ... dispersed! It's because you might just be right that I dislike you. It's for the same reason that Steve adores you! Listen, you haven't lived long enough to know so much!"

But, of course, I knew nothing. I only knew that people talked too much about happiness. That's why, no doubt, they don't find it—as though it could be found, anyway, all waiting to be picked up like a sack of coals. Often they don't even know *what* happiness is. They think it is a lot of smiles and perpetual good news. But it is underlined with unseen tears!

I had turned away from her to the heath, to the land enfolded in a rich green rug of grass under the pink haze from the sundown. A thin long line of birds were streaming home.

Seeds and wind and soil-tremors. Earth everlasting! "Keep clean—be as fruit—earn life!"

In that minute a released stream of pent magic rushed into my mind, soaring upwards like a fountain of stars, bridging this dimension and another. What splendour lies in these exquisite memories in cockle shells: damson bloom shaking over old walls; sea-sand pocked by the toes of gulls; prismatic colours in petrol pools on the road; the spangled web on the briar; ferny patterns of rain on smooth stone pilasters; the heath when its tints were those of an old tapestry, dishevelled green, cool sorrel, glitter of water; wind pleating on ponds; a diffusion of larch green light in far evening skies; the fresh smell of newly-ironed silk; designs traced by dust, and smoke, and leaking gutters!

Jubilantly, I stretched; then turned to Oriel, and said:

"Oh, Oriel, let us be friendly to one another when life is so short and so very sweet!"

"You're fooled to the hilt!" she replied, crossly. "Life isn't worth living! Think of me with that brother of yours, always bitter, always wrangling! He and I are wonderful examples of life's loveliness!"

"I flag as well," I said. "I *live* with Steve. It is no easier for me than for you. Things are often on the verge of getting too much for me. Why not? The amiable smiling sister of the great actor, Stephen Valley, has to cope with the genius in his off-moments! Nearly all his moments are off-ones! I have, doubtless, the capacity for being hurt as well as the rest of you! But I escape from you all, from the demands and moods of my brother, from your dislike, from such of his friends who take it upon themselves to be 'in love' with me—from all of you I can escape, yes, and remain in your midst."

"Tell me about that," she said, mockingly. "I am interested in you. My God, I should think I am! I'd give anything to find what Steve finds in you! Tell me what refires you when the common crowd gets too much for you."

"More of your leading questions, Oriel! Oh, Lord! I feel like a little blue herring sailing through unknown, dangerous waters! It always is dangerous to make definite statements! The best things are said when they're only half-said!"

"Never mind! Tell me what makes life exciting for you. How do you get away from people, from us?"

"I get away from you," I said, "by nothing but by meditative inaction. I simply shut you out of my thoughts by a constant wonder in those mighty affairs that you clever ones take for granted. I slough my skin! I don't mutiny, I accept. The smallest, or seeming-smallest thing refires me, if you really want to know. Any old ramshackle bush on the heath, any drop of milk on a lower lip, a fly! When I think of that admirable, minute chassis set so cunningly upon those jointed threads that serve a fly for legs, I haven't room to think of anything else! Yes, I give myself up to wondering about the mystery of things, and the kindliness and hostility and aloofness of things—moor and meadow potencies—the character of an old wharf and a green springtime wood—life and death poignancies, the uneasy beating of the world-heart and the all-peaceful all-pervading beating of the earth-heart—that secret nobility at the heart of all things.

"I only want to speculate, I don't want to *know*! It would be dull to know everything. Besides, if we *knew*, we might be outraged, not being equipped to bear it! Let's have recognition, but could we stand complete accomplishment?

"You think that the charm of life lies in its being unknowable? But that is what terrifies me!"

"Oh, Oriel, there must be some mystery! We and our part-discoveries, our common notions of nature, the universe and all—*what* certainties can we arrive at? Why should we want certainties? Appearances are amazing. Inferences are marvellous. Imagination is all! This half of a moon staggering up so wildly is enough for me to think you, Oriel, and everyone, right out of existence! I don't suppose there is any virtue in this, but Oh—how it suits me!"

"What will you say next, you terrible girl! You're mad, after all. That half of a moon! Any old bush on the heath! Any old fly! How morbid you are! It's only words, mad, morbid words! I have small doubt you don't always believe what you say, but are left lonely and affrighted, like anyone else. A bush and a fly are small things, they don't matter."

I looked down at a little fleet of red-polled weeds, nodding exuberantly, at the side of the garden path.

Oh, the tremendous importance, the greatness of *little* things! Aloud, I said:

"Yes, indeed, I do get frightened. I can be as miserable and frightened as anyone, but I don't let myself *remain* so! I can only state from my own experience, and nothing is the same for any pair of people: but I find happiness and pride in *myself!*"

"Me and myself, eh! It sounds like a first-class recipe for neurosis! Besides, how boring to come face to face with one's self!" Oriel retorted.

"I don't mean introspection—a descent of self into selfishness, I meant expansion, the sharing of one's self with the earth!"

"Oh, what fatigue, Laura!" she cried.

Well, there it was. She didn't want to find what had to be found if she wanted a change into reality: she didn't want to find her inner self. And certainly it is no lark to find one's self. You have to go out from the fastness of old assured things, from friends and love and possessions. You often have to lose everything to find all.

I gave her a cigarette. Shaking the flame off the end of the match, I said to this beautiful glum woman:

"Shall we drop the subject. Clearly I am talking unthinkable nonsense to you."

"Yes, but I should really like to believe in your nonsense, not because I think you are admirable, but because whatever you have got hold of goes down so well with Steve!"

"Steve doesn't agree with a word I say. Don't you know that? All that I've said to you. I've said to him, at his own request, many a time. Don't you know?"

"Oh, he never discusses you with me," she said resentfully. "He rather feels that I am not fit to breathe the same air as his wonderful sister! He surrounds you with some suggestion of an Arthurian dream! Lovely for him, so tedious for me!"

"That's only his pose," I said.

"Well, are you advocating a cult of self as a way to happiness."

"Yes, but not selfishness which is completely useless. I only mean the intensification of that wonder and pride in just being alive at all. There is much glory in simple things, drinking of tea, stooping down to tie shoelaces, to feel shoes on, to feel feet in shoes—feet walking! The thing is to do everything with all one's heart and being. But I am not one who can comb up a tirade that will carry people away, as you stage-folk can. Life is exciting for me because every hour comes to me as though I were a stranger to all that it can bring, as though I'd *never seen anything before*, not a rose or a pinch of salt or a window-pane!"

"So you begin the wonderful day—every day. And what do you find? It's raining—for a start—I'll be bound!"

"Right you are, it's raining! There's a lot to find in rain that never has been discovered before. Am I too enthusiastic about things? Well, I am, and I don't trouble not to be. No one is enthusiastic enough!"

I had a sudden pang of pity for all who, like Oriel, found life so wanting. And what could one do for such people—even at their own request? They did not deeply wish to change.

It's queer, I thought, how easy it is to find persons who are strung to one's pitch of blood sensuality, persons who favour one's most secret whims on the matter, but one almost never finds anyone tuned to the supersensuousness of one's mind. There is hardly a man or a woman who will stand beside one and enjoy a downpour of rain, or the perilous journey of a snail across a dock leaf, who will enjoy with one the conscious delicious surprise of being *able* to draw air into the lungs. And here I got a whiff of that quite special early morning air that has lain on the open dewy faces of kingcups, on the drenched green moss round old wells, and on the cool little heads of birds in tenements of trembling leaves.

"I should like to be pleased with what you say," Oriel broke in, "because there is a lighthearted and atrocious sincerity about you! Yet, how stupid you are I You talk about flies and trees and things, but you have no proof even that they exist. Who says anything is here? Who says anything exists?"

"Perhaps they don't for you, but I am simple enough to believe the evidence of my five senses: I think they were not given to me merely for a joke!"

"You are curiously unenlightened," she said, "if you really believe that you *see* an object! You see only its displacement in space!"

"That's what you see," I replied, "but I, who cannot bear abstract ideas, know no better than to believe that my five senses affirm for me the actuality of sticks and stones and tastes of wine and milk. You go your enlightened road and are wretched. I go my idiotic way and am sublimely happy!"

"Yes, and even your happiness is only an illusion," she said. "I don't like illusions! I don't understand when a fellow brings half a zoo out of a top-hat. I like to hear how it's done!"

"Why choose to question it when it is so very excellent to see?"

"I will question, I always will: I yearn for some *finality!*"

"There is none," I said.

"There will have to be, some time, for me and all who, like me, are bound by reason—negating reason, maybe, but there it is! I feel sometimes as though I am only half-incarnated," she went on, now thoroughly determined to malign herself. "I feel a slut!"

"Oh, for God's sake, Oriel, why do you lead yourself such a dance?" I asked, worn out. "Why are you so unjust to yourself, so unjust to life? We're all sluts and failures. We're all murderers, bloody sadists, oppressors of the poor and defrauders of our dearest. We're all kings and saints and heroes, as well! *It's all there*—in the mind. But, don't you see, *it is what we release that we live by!*"

She sat brooding. Then she snapped:

"Well, if you're enthusiastic for nothing but rain and blades of grass when I .am enthusiastic to hear about real life, I don't know that I wish you to continue. The way of living that suits you would only mean deliberate mortification of the flesh to me! I end this conversation on the note I began it—I detest you, Laura!"

"Leave the house at once, Oriel," cried Steve, suddenly striding into our midst from the gathering shadows. Heaven knows how long he had been there, or how much he had heard.

"Leave our house," he repeated to Oriel. "No one, no one shall speak to my sister like that!"

"Your *sister*!" she said, undismayed by his haughty consternation.

"Oh, don't quarrel," I intervened, wearily. "You didn't hear what went before, Steve. You don't know what I said to her. Little wonder she detests me. I can hold my own. All this spite and fury over nothing! Oriel, will you sing to us?"

For what held both Steve and me spellbound in Oriel was the singing voice she had, low and sweet, like a child's, seeming to demand of its hearers a reply to a question that had no answer.

"Oh, God," fumed Steve, "I don't want to hear her sing! It only makes me wish that I, and especially Oriel, had never been born!"

"I congratulate you on your wincing candour," said Oriel to him.

"Well, I should like some music," I said, "do sing to us, Oriel."

"Sing, then," he snarled, looking with fury into the beautiful sulky face staring out from its down-falling almost blue hair.

"Sing then!" she repeated in a passion. "What do you think I am! Flung about like a rag between the two of you! What sort of people are you? And what kind of an idiot would I be to obey you?"

"You can either give us the only pleasure of which you're capable, or leave," said Steve, dry and merciless. "To begin with, you are here only at your own invitation, and you would not be here if you did not like it. Everyone must pay for what they like. And I expect you to sing!"

"You do, eh? You know what I think?" she asked, abruptly.

"I am not in your confidence," he said.

"I think that one day someone is going to usher you out of this world rather sooner than you expected!"

Oriel left.

He came and sat down beside me, his eyes shining in the dusk. He said:

"It's nice, very nice of her, to have thought of that! But what had she been saying to you? I will not have you upset!"

"I am far more likely to have upset her," I answered. "What will you have for supper?"

"I don't want any. God! What a rubbishy article Oriel is!

Don't you find she drains you, wears you out? I shall send her packing, for it is time that I did!"

"And upset the play just when it is due to open? You know she would walk out of that, too, if you make her walk out of your life."

"And do you imagine for a single instant that I care what happens to the play—or to her?" he demanded, incredulously.

"Perhaps not," I said, "but I care intensely what happens to Bernard McCann and his works!"

"*You* do?" he said, doubtfully. "Why? Why do *you* care?"

Realizing what danger there was in allowing him to have the slightest suspicion that I cared for anyone but himself, I warded off his enquiry.

"I know nothing about him except what you have told me. You spoke of him so well—and it's highly unusual in you to speak well of anyone'—that I could not fail to be impressed. You even said you admired him, and now when you are in charge of his affairs, you want to let him down!"

"Oh, well," he said, "I expect I shall stand his wife till he reaches this country. He has already left New York, and ought to be here for the opening night. He'll know how to manage Oriel. He'd let her walk out of the play."

"Well, let *him* let her! Not you," I said, going to the kitchen, for if he didn't want his supper, I was in acute need of mine.

One morning, a week later, I was sitting alone in the auditorium, watching the rehearsal, and the drone of the voices, the steady wrangling, sent me off to sleep.

I wakened to find all the auditorium lights blazing, and the entire company standing round me.

"What's all this about?" I asked, sleepily, stretching. "Is the play going on down here now—in the stalls?"

"That's it," said Oriel. "And you are the sleepy-headed heroine! How good our play must be when it drives even you to sleep! But, there, I'm not going to quarrel with you." She turned to the others. "Laura and I are firm friends. It's a good thing to be friends with Laura, I can tell you!"

"It must be," said one of the young actresses. "She is the only one who can manage that mad devil of a brother of hers!"

"Laura can do anything with me, as well," said the comedian, a fashionable fellow with two strips of bright grey hair growing down his jaws as though glued there, in handsome contrast to the rest of his head which was still jet black. "Every time I see Laura," he resumed, "I ask her to marry me. I'll ask her now, and you shall hear the answer I always hear: Laura, will you marry me?"

"No," I said smiling, to a round of applause.

"You see?" said the comedian.

"Well, what are you surprised for?" put in my brother, looking heartily pleased. "·Laura has no need of people—especially people like you. Oh, but I'm forgetting. Laura, my dear, today for the first time there is one in our midst whom you will find engaging and good. May I present to you the author of our great play—Bernard McCann."

Out of the faces came one face. With my heart in my eyes I looked into Bernard McCann's dark-skinned ardent face in which steadfast dark blue eyes dwelt like the blossoming extensions of his rare mind. He had a mass of smoky black hair, and a strangely tilted, humorous, tender mouth. His expression was one of benign thoughtfulness. His hands were very beautiful, with the longest thumbs I had ever seen, with strong delicate fingers. He was a big burly man, about forty-two years old, dressed untidily in grey, with a rustcoloured tie wrenched into a tight knot on his brilliantly white shirt.

All about him was an air of heroic contact, of "other places," the quiet splendour of one who knew life so intimately he had already ceased to be a part of circumstance.

As he came to me, it was like the best of my life coming back to me as a whole gift. He held out his hand for mine.

"Laura," he said, and raised my hand to his lips.

"Oh gallant, gallant!" applauded Steve. "How quiet they are, yet, perhaps, there is more in this meeting for them than any of us will ever know!"

"And perhaps you are right," said Bernard, releasing my hand and smiling for the first time.

During the next few days, I saw him in the theatre several times, never to speak to, but always to remark his intent gaze upon me.

On the morning of the final dress rehearsal—the play would open that night—I was sitting watching the blazing stage, head on my arms in the dark stalls, when someone came and sat down beside me.

"Only Bernard," came the unforgettable voice. "I know it's Laura who is sitting there like a gleam in the dark—Laura Valley, about whom I have heard so much!"

I looked into his face. His eyes were on the stage, but as soon as he felt my gaze, he looked down at me and the corners of his mouth went up with smiling.

"You and I," he said, "ought to know one another better— the sooner the better! Nothing could be more interesting to me than to talk with the sister of that brilliant devil on the stage there."

"Let us talk, then," I suggested.

"But not here, Laura. How could I shine for you, as I wish to do, with all that drivel going on."

"That … drivel is *your* play!""

"Well may you say so!"

"Yes, but it isn't drivel. It's perfect loveliness—like all your work!"

"So you've read some of it?"

"Read all of it."

"My dear Laura, it's very amiable of you to say so!"

"I was sixteen when I first opened your books," I said.

"We are old friends, then!"

"More than that!"

"Laura! Really?"

"I *live* by what *you* live by."

He had taken my hand.

"We must go out and find a place for talk and coffee! Laura—shall we?"

"But it's the dress-rehearsal!"

"Damn that! Let us go—at once."

We did not, however, go to the nearby restaurant, but in his car we rode into the autumn sunshine to a little cafe beside Putney Heath, with chairs and tables in a garden.

Shall we get on, I wondered. What horror, if I make him angry, as I very well might, in the first four minutes!

Our coffee came.

"Oh, this is so nice, Laura," he said; "this is better than a parcel of stage people monkey-chattering! That golden wolf, your brother, will keep them in order! Meantime here am I with Laura—who lives by what I live by! Upon my soul, what do you mean by that, dear girl?"

I told him.

We talked till a waiter came and asked us if we wanted lunch for it was past one o'clock.

"Eh?" said Bernard. "Lunch? What's he talking about?"

"You've been here two hours," said the man. "Don't you want your lunch?"

"Yes, but not here, thank you," said Bernard, jumping up, and taking me by the hand. "Come Laura. Let us go on. This unnoticed flight of the hours is due to nothing but the fact of two strangers finding themselves so astoundingly *already known* to one another, so compellingly close to one another, that no such thing as separation could ever happen to them hereafter!"

We got into the car again. He turned in a westerly direction.

"Where are we going?" I asked.

"I don't know," he said, "the country somewhere, if I can find it! I don't know my way about England much. But it doesn't matter to me where we go as long as I can go on listening to you talking, little sweet. I've never, no never in all my life met anyone like you. I've never met a girl who said that the only sin against the Holy Ghost was—*not* to be happy! By that you don't mean, do you, that one must force one's self to be happy?"

"No," I answered. "One can't avoid times of anxiety and sadness, but these arrive because of *circumstance*, never because of life! And though such times come to everyone, they needn't remain and dominate everything."

We were driving through treed lanes, with a wind sweeping into the car from apple gardens and broom. Burning leaves fell down in a slow hail from the autumn trees. I stopped flowing out to this loved man and changed the current of my life-feeling to mingle with the dusty honey-coloured horizon, the azure smoke winding up from cottage roofs, a clutch of young geese under a spindle tree, the violet gleam on the turned heavy earth, the verge of the autumn woods—a riot of carmine and peppermint green.

"I'm looking for a quiet place for our lunch," said Bernard. "Are you hungry, darling girl?"

"I am," I replied, returning to him.

"So am I," he said, "but hungry most of all for the talk you talk. I think this little inn will do us handsomely!"

A brilliant crimson creeper ran out like fire from the brown looped velvet of the inn's thatched roof. They gave us our lunch indoors because rain promised.

I was enthralled in feelings of magic event; Bernard was all that I wished. He was so *real*; for him I became alive with all my being, whereas with other people only a part of me had been animated.

Over our meal, he said:

"Steve used to talk to me about you when we were in New York. He told me that I was the only one he had ever met who reminded him at all of you."

"He said as much of you to me," I retorted.

"So I was always interested in you," he went on. "Always! But you are better than the best of my expectations! I always dreamed of a girl like you, giving immediate promise of mind, as well as having personal beauty: a girl to make everything different, joyful, and important, a girl limned excitingly with unreality! I have all this in you! Right from the minute I saw you—it was a week ago—asleep with your shining head on your arms, like a seagull in the dusk, you've made my heart pound! But more than all this I find ... I find that you took my words to yourself and you not only understood them—you lived them. And so, don't you see, you gave yourself to me?"

"But what have you not given to me?" I answered, looking away from him to the window. "You made everything possible. You *made* me! Once I needed a gigantic sunset, a whole symphony, the black stars on a red Cretan pitcher to set me on my way. But now, because of you, let music be mute and the sun screened, for any grey sky, any ladybird on a marguerite, any weed by the road makes non-being *Becoming* for me! Here I am, you gave to me and you made me—and, isn't it wonderful"

"You can't imagine," he said, "what you are doing to me."

It had begun to rain;

"Let's get out," he said, suddenly; from the expression on his face, his mind seemed to have gone off on a little spree among the rainy leaves in the garden. He put his hand on my shoulder, but he had forgotten me.

At the end of our silent exploration of this unknown garden we came to a long alley covered right over with a green creeper that was turning crimson. Here we stood, elated, having no doubt of one another, exquisitely attuned. Here in the aromatic damp air, in the green gloom, with the rain pattering softly all about us, he said:

"Should you think me mad if I told you ... if I told you ... that from the moment of seeing you, I loved you, my darling one."

I did not answer, struggling as I was in seas of wonder, breathless with amaze at this instant knock-down love. Here, indeed, was an experience that would last through life and time.

"You cannot believe how I love you," he went on. Then

he said, looking down at the red bricks of the alley floor, "Do you love me?"

He raised his head abruptly. He saw my eyes. With a soft exclamation, he drew me to him.

"From the time I set eyes on you," he said, "I longed to do this—to take you in my arms."

"Oh, God," I said into his ear, "how good it is to be a girl standing among leaves in the rain, in the arms of a man like you, Bernard. I had not dreamed of anything so perfectly lovely. How charming and lovable you are: you make me rejoice! I want just to lean against you, and say nothing, for you know I love you. I want just to be glad and silent."

And he, who had refrained from kissing till then, slowly and with infinite tenderness, with a strange kind of finality and zest, he found my mouth.

The surrounding leaves, packed, gummed with spiders' webs, breathing so musically in the rain, gazed impassively back at us, and the Place endowed the Enactment with its own private spirit, and in the strength of this the moment was made enduring out of all proportion to its human effort.

"Say it again," he proposed, "tell me that you love me!"

"If I tell you that I love you," I answered, "such words could not open your heart or understanding ever so little to what I really feel for you, and have done since I was a girl of sixteen. I could never hope to give you the least notion of what your words have conveyed to me."

"Oh, the light of paradise to you, Laura! And why did I never know!" he lamented, his lips brushing my hair.

"How could you have known?" I laughed.

"By God, to think ... to think that we might never have met! Laura, now that I have found you, you must never go away again!"

"Even if I do," I said, "I shall not have *gone*. This is real; we can hold love for ever, even if you and I should never meet again after this hour."

"I haven't got as far as that yet," he said, smiling. "I want you beside me—always—from now on. Oh, Laura, what are we going to do about ... us?"

"Why," I said, "love one another."

"Yes, yes," he cried, "but won't you come and live under the same roof with me, my dearest? Oh, how that thrills me—to think of you under the same roof with me! You know, don't you, that Oriel and I ... we have not been in love for years now, nor have we met except in connection with stage affairs since your brother was in America above two years ago. Oriel left me for Steve, I don't blame her! So, won't you let me share everything with you? One of the British actors has lent me his house in St. John's Wood for all the time I am in this country. It's a little house, Laura, very little, a doll's house. What could be better than a girl like you in a doll's house with me! Say you will come to me. Come—please, dear—come. What a feast you are! You are beautiful, you know; not only does your sweet face evoke for me all kinds of imaginative raptures, but the way you *think* enthralls me. You reconcile a good many things that fall just short of my faculties. I can't do without you. Not now, my imponderable girl. Laura, it's a misery for a man to part from his girl at night, and go a separate way. Must that happen to us? Let it not! We must have sleep and the night together. We must have sleep together!"

I had loved this amiable, romancy man so long, without any thought of ever meeting him, and now the idea of going to live with him, was *too much*. As though Socrates or Shakespeare invited one to perpetual life with them!

"You are silent, my dearest girl! What are you thinking? Does it come to you with misgiving that it's all too sudden, too soon? Do you think that, after all, you do not love me enough?"

"I think that I love you too much," I said.

"And I understand that, too," he replied, giving me light, soft kisses all over my face. "I understand very well. For, you see, I don't expect to find in you awarenesses and wiles of physical love, since you have always lived and thought in terms of a humanism that has, by some miracle, transcended sex, sublimated it, before ever aware of it. People *are* what they have made themselves. They have made themselves *what* they have thought, and in you I find the most lovely, reflecting spirit I have ever encountered. Could I think of wanting to destroy you? All I ask is—be near me, always."

"Oh, the gain your understanding is to me!" I exclaimed. "I was always too busy trying to recapture the *whole attitude* my childhood to bother about anything else—to *imagine* fact as it came to me, to find magic in reality, and delight in the mystery of ordinary things. The older I get, Bernard, and the more discoveries I make, I only find that I *knew* them *already* as a child."

"You don't have to look for the way back to the childhood world," he said, "you have never left it."

"Well," I continued, "I always had enough work and enough dreams to keep my inclinations free of uneasy moiling, and when it came to love, to thinking of *you* and love, it has been a profound and unsubstantial rapture down the years. I never dreamt that we should ever meet, but now that we have, and now that we love, before that love's appeal and necessity I will yield with all my nature."

"You are ready," he said, "for your fine integrity to be so dispersed, so grandly *wasted*—in love?"

"Nothing is wasted that came of love," I replied.

"There's one thing," he murmured, "we're both too romantic merely to be passionate!"

His hand went under my chin:

"I am a fool for you, my beauty," he said. "You make life seem so limitless. We writers need stimulants to give us the joy for our words. But you—you only need what you see. If you were blind you'd only need what you heard and felt—a rustle—a sunbeam upon your head. From dust and ashes you know, as none other, how to call up the brilliant phoenix. Your secret is, I believe, your humility; being humble, you can fuse. Only the humble possess the earth!"

"Say no more," I begged, "for, indeed, you make far too much of me. There is nothing praiseworthy about me: I'm as stupid and as selfish as anyone—probably more so. I have *no heart!*"

"I'm glad to hear you say so," declared Bernard. "I wince when I think of what has been done by people with a 'heart'! You have something much better my girl, you have—tenderness."

He looked at me with stormy delight.

"Do you say you will come to me now, at once?" he demanded. "Do you? Laura? Laura?"

"I'll come to you for as long as you want me," I said.

"Why, then, you're coming to me for good and all! And Laura, listen, we'll go back quietly now to the little house. All tomorrow the bell will ring, and the telephone. It'll be people for us! But we shall not answer!"

"Tonight is the first night of your play," I said. "The public will certainly expect a curtain from you, and the actors, besides, will feel a little ill-used if you are not there to help with your presence."

"Perish the thought," he said. "What do I care for plays and first-nights and other people when I've got you. It should be the full of the moon to-night. The moon will shine over the little town garden, and over you lying in my arms through the night-time! And then you talk about plays and first-nights!"

From the inn, I sent a telegram to Steve:

"Staying with a friend."

In the early twilight, Bernard and I went to the house in St. John's Wood. In that large walled garden surrounding it, the last of the dark gold light was draining up from the earth. The evening star was burning steadily in a sky of soft brushed violet. Lights from windows softly began to gleam in the London night. Standing there, a feeling of old far-off romantic things came to me from the beautiful pellmell of trees—red beech flaring beside the dark glittering green of high hollies, a trinity of thin streaming birches, and an immensely tall lime tree. Pears were hanging limply, lovelily against the old russet bricks.

I looked into Bernard's charming, thoughtful face, and, his personality invading all mine with sharpest romance, I said:

"How glad I am to be in your keeping!"

His tender smile came out.

"Why are you looking at me like that, Laura?"

"I am undressing you!"

"The devil you are!"

"Yes, but I'm not only taking off your nice suit of clothes, dear Bernard, but I'm stripping off your skin and blood, and I'm looking at your gravely beautiful skeleton. I am looking at and thinking about Bernard's bones. I am loving Bernard's inmost reality!"

"Well," he declared humorously, "you know more about me than I do! But there's one thing—if you can think of me stripped of all that the faithless world sees, and think of me in the true starkness that life sees—you love me as no one else has ever done—or will, again. What a tender little creature you are, so ardent, so searching! You're like a dream made flesh. You are a great mystery to me!"

He came to me, gazing violently, no kiss, only roughly stroking back my hair from my face. He said: "You have been calling me, I think, from the hour you were born. I've been journeying to you ever since. I've had to make many false starts, many mistakes, before I found you, but now, now you are here and I love you, Laura, I love you!"

Afterwards there was the delight of getting supper for the two of us, and kneeling on the hearth together with hands spread before the flying saffron flames, our minds chiming steadily together. The Chelsea porcelain gleamed in the firelight, and a sombre French tapestry flapped on the wall to the cool amaze of some framed prints by Hogarth and Canaletto.

As Bernard had thought, the moon when it rose later, was full. I turned out of his arms to gaze my fill at the witch light that urged every object to mystic strangeness. The lime-tree boughs dipped before the moon.

"The life of the lime is sweet," I murmured: "lovely and pleasant in the garden it ends its life as piano-keys. There is no death for the lime."

"There is one difference between us," said Bernard. "I wouldn't be able to lie and stare at those branches against the moon and be thrilled unless you were lying beside me, too, unless I loved you. Then, and only then can I say: with this tree and this girl, I could live for ever! All my life I needed to be in love with someone. I've written my works on love, and devil a line could I write without it!"

"There's no hint of that in your gnomic, haunting books," I said, "only an utter completeness in yourself."

"Yes, well, that's where my writing has overtaken my life. My works are more courageous than I am—so were Goethe's. You remember? All writing is an attempt to see life bravely and often one's thoughts will do better than one's poor shrinking flesh. So I always needed love. But you, in your simple sufficient life, you've never felt the need of any such building up. You are absolutely complete in yourself, needing nothing but yourself and the wonders of created things. I get the queerest unease thinking that by being in love with me you may destroy yourself."

"Were I merely *in love* with you, very likely I should destroy myself—and you. But, but, I love you, Bernard, my soul, and there's a whole world of difference in loving and being in love with you."

He answered:

"It would be a wonderful thing to have a feeling of permanency with a girl like you! I should like to say to you— Remain with me to the end of the world. But I will not say it, realizing as I do and must, that your stay with me will be brief. You notice I have no fear of losing your love, only dread of losing you. I'm not sad about this—no one could be with you and be sad, my dearest friend—I just want you to know that when the time comes for you to leave, I shall understand, even though I shall rebel! What tragedy could economics or politics or anything bring me in comparison with losing you!"

"Have you got some politics, Bernard, then?" I asked.

"Only in so far as a support of movements for the liberation of men."

"My idea of public good is simple, too," I said. "The people must have enough to eat, so that there shall be enough *thought!* Is that mad, perhaps?"

"That isn't mad," said Bernard, "that's magnificent!"

We talked on; his hand with the gold finger-ring was under my arm; it was difficult for me to believe that this melodious voice, making thrilling variations upon his love, was meant for me.

The moonlight faded. It would soon be morning. A beautiful silent brightness, charged with immeasurable strange potent, fell between us. He came first out of the vivid, intimate spell.

"Oh, my beauty, you try to remember happiness like this for ever!" he said, finding my mouth to kiss.

I answered:

"I hold you to me, dear Bernard of the white shoulder! And I pass to you in these kisses every joy I ever had, that I have now, and will have. I feel the warm soft skin that encloses your dear, radiant personality, I feel your heart beating against me, *your* heart, and I can just make out your shining eyes in the dark. This is all more wonderful to me than I can say. Here we are, and Oh, darling heart, let us worship the livingness of one another, our breathing together in this little room, and let us go to sleep thinking … thinking of us … being *us* for ever!"

With a murmured exclamation, he bound me tightly to him.

The sun was shining when we wakened. From the newspaper we saw that Bernard's play and my brother had been towering successes.

"And that's that," said Bernard, flinging the news-sheet away. "A woman comes here every morning, Laura, to tidy the place—I always had my meals out before you came, apart from cups of tea and odd snacks. But she will be positively invaluable in telling people that I have been suddenly tailed away to the North of England—or the North Pole—I give her leave to say what she likes. Come here to me, beloved girl, it's like a million years since I last kissed you!"

We stayed there without anyone knowing for three days, and then we decided to go back into the world for the shortest possible time to put certain affairs in order. Bernard had agents and theatre managers and distinguished friends to deal with, and I had—my brother, Steve.

The day I returned to Hampstead to collect some of my belongings and to break the news to him was heavy with pent rain. At five o'clock as I turned into the road beside the heath, heavy clouds, divided by long lanes of glaring silver, were gathering above the tree-tops the foliage of which had turned cindrous and blue. Eagerly I sniffed the moist, laden air, and sent my spirit roving free among those trees waiting for the downpour, and from them I gathered forces with which to meet the onslaught of the coming storm. I let myself into the cottage. Steve was in the sitting-room writing.

"Hello," I said, going to him at once. He got up, and seized my hands.

"And did you have a nice holiday?" he asked, savagely, "with a friend?"

"Oh, a heavenly time," I replied. "I ought to have given you more warning. But we arranged it all just on the minute."

"We?" he said.

"Well, you know who," I answered.

"Yes," he said. "I know. The two absences were too much of a coincidence not to have some connection. But now you are back, and I don't care what has gone before. I only know that I have missed you, and that life has been horrible without you."

"For three short days?"

"It was like three hundred years!"

Sighing, I went and sat down by the fire. He poured me out a cup of tea from the tray.

"You've taught me a lesson, you know," he said, dropping his hand on my shoulder. "Oh, such a lesson! For the first time since we came to London together, I have been without you. I don't care for that ever to happen again! I'm going to be different! You need not be nice to me as you were, but I shall be wonderful to you! I'm going to be different, different, and make you proud of me! You'll see."

"I'm proud of you already," I replied, "and you don't have to change your way of living to please me. Whatever you do, I am proud of you and love you."

He said enthusiastically, with a kind of sob in his voice:

"Oh, Laura, I'm so glad you're home—glad, glad, glad!"

I looked down.

"What is it?" he demanded. "Is anything the matter?"

"You make it difficult to tell."

"I don't mind what you say now that you are home again!"

"But I haven't come back to stay."

His smile went out.

"Laura! What do you mean? This is a mystery to be taken in hand at once!"

"I'm going ..." I began.

"I know," he interrupted with eager relief, "you're going

on a visit to Anda. You haven't been to see her for a long time! That's what it is! Well, you shall go, but not too soon, not just yet, Laura, eh?"

"I am going to live with Bernard," I said firmly.

He drew back a step.

"Ah, don't say that! Oh, God, what a thing! I'll not believe it! It's too … sudden! It has happened too quickly. Besides, I couldn't spare you to him!"

Desperately shaken, he backed away from me to the sofa where he threw himself down with an air of one who felt that he needed a little moment in which to marshal his twittering thoughts.

"As you know," I answered, "I am devoted to you, but this time I must choose for myself."

"You can't, you can't," he stormed. "I simply will not let you, Laura! Oh, this is monstrous! This is the sort of revelation that leads to headlines in the Sunday papers! A man simply does not expect to be told after two years that his life is to be broken up! And for Bernard McCann! I knew that you and he would hit it off, but I never dreamt … I never dreamt of *you* falling in love. Oh, I see it all! It's no use making too free with another man's wife! That man is nearly always bound to be vexed! He will even resent it! But what does my man do? My Bernard! He does nothing at all and he does it so vehemently as to condone the thing! That is how he is! What do you think of that, my little sister? I'll tell you what *I* think of it—I think he's glad that the brother took away the one obstacle that left him free to adore the little sister! Well, it's absurd! He's old enough to be your father!"

"That isn't true," I said, "and even if he were old enough

to be my *grand*father that wouldn't make the slightest difference!"

"And you don't *know* him! You can't possibly know him!" he cried, aghast, starting to his feet again.

"I don't want to *know* him," I replied; "I shall always be very well satisfied if I can know a little *of* him!"

"I will not allow my sister to go living with a man, like any girl of the town! You ... you're altogether outrageous!"

He turned a cold eye steadily upon me as if to drive home the terrific guilt of the thing.

"So is a sermon—coming "from you!" I said. "I am laughing at you, of course. And I must tell you, Steve, that I myself am my only judge in this matter. Your opinion and the opinion of other people count for nothing, for less than nothing!"

"Oh, Laura," he cried, anguished, "don't be like that, so ... so removed! I didn't mean to be officious. It's just that, well, damn my heart—I can't bear it that you should live with anyone but me!"

I was so locked and engrossed with Bernard in the secret places of our dreaming minds, that it came a little weary to me to send out any reconciling orientation to my brother. There seemed no validity in this scene, it seemed oft-told, a little ludicrous and dreary.

"But I shall be very happy where I am going," I said. "Doesn't that please you?"

He had been holding his eyes half-closed.

"Eh?" He lifted his head and looked at me haggardly. "Haven't you been happy here with me?" he asked.

"Yes, always."

"Well, then?"

"Happy—in spite of you!"

"I see. As bad as that, was it? Do you expect me to begin calling myself names, then? But I bear myself no ill will!"

He stood looking important, injured and, somehow, soiled. He moved across to the window. The trees on the heath beyond took on the sudden-seeming insistence of gallows.

"It's costing me a whole continent of effort to adjust this," he brought out. "I don't deny that you are the most devoted of sisters, and I have small right to complain. You packed all your enthusiasm into helping me to try and be happy. Now you transfer that undivided interest to another man! Why should I mind? But I have no sweetness or generosity in my nature, and I do mind! I mind desperately. You have done my heart to death! If anything too strange happens to me from now on, I should not be able to bear it!"

I didn't say anything. After a silence, he said:

"When are you thinking of ... going?"

"Now," I answered.

He turned round on me:

"You'll have to come back to me, you know," he said, roughly, completely entranced by the disaster he imagined had come to him. "Else I shall go under! You are absolutely necessary to me! Don't you know that you are my very own self—the self I might have been, had things been different—the self to whom I turn for such consolation and light as can reach me. It is my misfortune to love you to death! You see, you force out all my poverty. I have nothing. I am nothing—without you!"

I tried to treat this as lightly as possible.

"Oh, Steve, we are both deeply fond of one another, but I am not called upon, in the nature of things, to stay with you all my life. Don't you see, dear, dear. Steve, you are doomed to unhappiness if you rely on me or any other person *for* happiness. You are completely out of line in thinking of me as *your* other self! People can't belong like that. You have to ... to find your *own* self. We both know that from earliest days. And you and I are the sort of people who know we shall never have anything permanent or lasting, and that to *possess* is not to *own*! What comes to us is only lent as a fillip to dreams. And that's all we want. We are not dreary people to wish enchantment drawn out till the last of magic is drained and only a shabby husk left. Knowing the world as we do, having been deceived and exploited by it, the time has passed when its uncertainties can hurt us. We know enough to be like the stars in the proverb and make *no noise!*"

Steve laughed aloud and was not amused. Sudden sallies of incoherent words rose to his tongue. He looked demented. Suddenly he managed to say stiffly:

"I do not wish to do anything I should be ashamed of! I shall remain calm even though I hear that my goddamned day is over!"

He, having reached this semblance of composure, I hurried up to my room to pack. I dashed some things into a suitcase. He could send on my books and remaining belongings.

Ready to leave, I went running down the stairs, hesitating before going again into the sitting-room.

Now my brother was sitting under the window, with secret tears in his eyes, and he seemed to be expostulating with someone unseen as to his prospects.

"I've left some things behind," I said, "and all my books. You ... will send them to Bernard's house?"

But he got up and came to me.

"Don't go! Be pitiful! Don't leave me!" he cried. "Only an hour ago when you first came into the house, how glad and fortunate my life seemed! And now—why, the tears in my damned eyes are blurring everything—I can't even see you!"

One who pleads and weeps has insistence. I was caught away in such conflicting emotion that I groaned aloud. At that he seemed to come to himself. Struggling no longer he said, stern in his authority on the subject:

"All right, all right! I submit! The commotion within has hardened. It's been a star-turn! What a pity you had to do this to me on a day when you have done your hair a new way, and look more winsome than ever! So there's to be no one but Oriel for me! I've always tried to keep my head—from now on I needn't bother, and why should I? The imprisoned must break out—fermentation can't go on for ever! You can't do away with things by ignoring them! My humours, unexpressed, caged, mad, need no longer be contained. In a way, you free me by going: you free the zany and the assassin in me! A steady, secret stare often comes at me in the dusk: it used to make me terribly afraid. It was— myself! Now I shall no longer be afraid!"

"You are trying to think of everything to break me down!" I said, distractedly.

"No, no I am not," he said. "No! I want you to go, now! But I think, Laura, you would not have gone to keep McCann company had I not become entangled with his confounded wife! Subconsciously, I am sure, your main motive is to make up to him for the loss of his dear wife! Oh, Laura, Laura, I always tried not to think of you, to see you as a woman who would be *wanted* by men! Well, well! I hope to survive this!"

He folded me to him, almost leaning upon me, completely

unhinged. He was trembling and had closed his eyes above my head.

"Nothing is changed," I said. "You do not love one person less because you love somebody else!"

"You do love 'em less—you can't help it—that's the whole point," he threw out, wildly.

"It may be your point—it isn't mine," I answered. "Steve, dearest, nothing can alter what we have—our loving affection!"

"Bernard will alter it! You don't see that, but I can. I take the long view: more and more he will absorb you until soon—I shall be forgotten!"

"You look on the human heart as though it were one of your gramophone records!" I exclaimed," which can only play its one tune and then is done!"

"Oh, I wish you had never met him," he retorted. "God! To think ... to think it was *I* who brought you together—praising the one to the other, running from one to the other across two continents, so fond, so busy ... so busy—undermining myself!"

I tried something else.

"Why don't you make a great success of it now, with Oriel? I shall not be here to hinder. Have her to look after you. She can divorce Bernard, and you and she can marry."

"And you and Bernard marry, too, eh?" he said, softly, looking away from me.

"I was not thinking about that. Who knows whether Bernard and I would want to marry?"

Suddenly he laughed.

"Yes, 1 shall invite Oriel to come here. She shall come. Oh, yes! She always wanted to: But who will I turn to when I get into one of my frequent jams?" he demanded, furiously.

"You will turn to me, as you have always done," I said, peaceably. "Farewell, now, my darling!"

"Farewell, farewell! Now—I have no one to ... *glorify*!"

I went down the garden path beneath the fading hollyhock spires that rocked in the night breeze. At the gate, I turned. He was still standing at the door. With a pang, I saw the whole lustrous get-up of him, the caged sorrow. But he went in and kicked the door shut with a violent crash.

I looked across the heath over which the seeds of night were darkly blooming. A troubled orchestration convoluted between the stalks and the hidden stars; against the turmoil of the vast, agitated night, my own upset seemed very small and, at the same time took on more dignity and worth.

I stood and looked to where below the lights of London threw up a dusty fan of carnation-coloured light. Gradually I got the feeling of an effervescence having died down, of something flown, of sudden decorum and peace.

I walked a short way down the road bordering the heath, and I came to a little carmine fire glowing before a watchman's hut where the road was being repaired; hurricane lamps round the digging bowed and scraped before the draught—little silver-limned flames behind rose-glass lantern walls.

All at once the little scene threw up for me a tide of evocations—strawberries, crimson darts under moist green leaves in a garden; red shells on the white sands of some far-off shore; the dark theatre dotted with the dull red stars of live cigarettes.

And all earth seemed twice its amazing self, enhanced, coloured, and supercharged because of Bernard's spirit which, with me now, rejoiced and shared the thrill of these associations.

My life went into a tremendous blaze of happiness. People are not loved for themselves alone: they are much more than themselves, for good or ill. We love an individual and possess him through the universe. The love theme recurs in an endless symphony of sounds, sights, and touches.

And meantime, across the road, the heath, in the pitch dark, under sudden sallies of autumn leaves, with the long streams of sap running down into the earth, added another layer of human consciousness to the huge scarred old palimpsest it really was, drawn from this violent hour of farewell between my brother and myself, drawn, too, from these sweet indwellings of love.

The heath took in, elaborated, heightened, and grimly romanticized all that had come to pass. The new deposit slipped quietly up against the trunks of the trees, piled itself into grassy hollows, nothing lost, nothing wasted-the essence of it all psychically stored, to be absorbed again another day, another century, by any questing consciousness coming upon it, and recapturing these human sensations and experiences, in all their bitterness, sweetness, and brevity—all that had been loved and lost and learned—as it had been hundreds of years before we were dreamed of: as it would be again, hundreds of years after we were all forgotten.

Chapter VII

"For to fear death, Gentlemen, is nothing else than to think one is wise when one is not: for it is thinking one knows what one does not know."

PLATO

MY happiness in Bernard McCann never abated. The absolute of beauty came to me from his life and love. He provided a wonderful new impetus for my happy communings. I never loved him half so much as when I drew him with me into those vast, sylvan spaces that lay above and below the top crust of my thoughts.

The secret of a happy love is the same as the secret of every other kind of happiness: it resides in contemplation, an ineffable harmony of thought that is at once part of life and goes beyond life.

One of the high-lights of life with Bernard was the being left alone. Oh, how refreshing this was to me after Steve, who had never left me to myself, but poked and pried and interfered, trying, because he could not understand my way of living, to reduce me.

Never, in any way, did Bernard encroach on my inner

life, just as I never interfered with his. In the beginning he said:

"Never, never change for my sake, Laura, never be what you think I'd like you to be. Don't indulge my whims, but—Oh, how important this is—indulge *yours* to the top of your bent. If we let one another be what we were born to be, the familiarity of our days will never lessen our strangeness to one another—our *strangeness* that made our love!"

And because we allowed each other to be at peace in our separate inner lives, we were able to make each other radiantly happy in our life that was shared. We indulged one another's preferences no matter how extraordinary or outlandish they seemed, and by encouraging each other's selfishness in intensely personal matters,—we achieved the smoothest willing co-operation in things shared. Because we were so different we were *one*.

"You are my only good," he would say to me. "I never had so much assurance till you came. What you have brought me, my lady, is not only comfort and not only love: it's a thing I only had some time before you came, but now I have it for all time; you have given me a permanent heightening of that sense of joy in just being alive at all. This will never die. You've given me myself. You've let me have my own mind in loneliness entire, for you immolated everything that prevented me from enjoying the oddness of myself—the oddness of life. You've made me—out of myself! Ah, you are much more than your own excellence. What you have given off in your moods of joy and endurance, thrown off as airily and as prodigally as pollen, will live on after you, and be caught up by any seeker. One person could not use you up. Those little messages and currents you have started on their way will journey long after we are dead, my darling;

just as you and I picked up messages which others, long since gone, left behind of *their* little tremendous lives."

"But you have done as much for me—and more," said I.

"No, you only took from me what you yourself brought along."

Bernard and I had been together a year, and during all that time I constantly saw my brother, who had now developed a most menacing quietude when he was with me, though on the stage, the highly-wrought excellence of his acting was often more like a maniac's than a gifted interpreter's. The splendour and sadness of his "Hamlet" held his audiences paralysed as they watched his unique genius many a time pushed over the thin division into the searching authority of madness.

Right from the time I left him he had taken Oriel into the Hampstead cottage; and she became for him a reincarnation of our mother, the one who stood between him and his own way, the blade that had cut in two his life with me. Steadily, ceaselessly he blamed her for the upset of his days, and he set out in a whirl of contumely and revenge to make her wish that she had never been born.

How she bore with all of it, I do not know. She must have been crazy for him.

Steve often came to the house in St. John's Wood where Bernard and I lived in romantic beatitude. He was now acting in Shakespeare all the time, and did not appear in those plays of Bernard's which succeeded "Woman in the Moon." Oriel had also gone to be with Steve, and though she had deserted her husband's home and plays, she refused to desert his name and would not divorce him, as Steve, to my surprise, constantly exhorted her to do.

"Why, do you intend to marry her?" I asked him once.

"Certainly not," he replied, "but it would give you and Bernard the opportunity if you wanted to."

"As though you really wanted that," I scoffed.

"I don't want it, but you might," he said, shortly.

My first twelve months with Bernard were nearly over, when I had a long letter from Anda. Our mother had died. The way she had died was so at variance with the way in which she had lived that I was struck speechless at the peculiar rounding-off of that violent cruel life.

In her country retreat our mother had lived in great comfort, never ceasing to complain the while of the heartlessness and beastliness of her two children in London and the one at Cambridge. For London and university life were synonymous in her clouded mind with going straight to the devil.

For company, our mother had a mongrel dog called James, and it seemed that upon him she had unaccountably (for her) spent all that she was capable of releasing in the way of love. She had been taking him a walk, towards evening. They came to the wide pond where he was wont to have his swim, but on this evening what was his chagrin to find his domain invaded by two mysterious swans. Very angrily and very gamely, for he was a small dog and they were huge king swans, James swam out to them and began to dispute his exclusive rights to the pond.

In no time a terrible fight was raging in the dusk, with a new moon looking on. James, as was to be expected, speedily began to get the worst of the engagement between the powerful, outraged birds, who clouted him insensible and finally killed him.

But before the end, our mother, screaming and gesticulating on the bank, and finding that no one heard her cries for help in that lonely spot, plunged in to her dog's rescue. She could not swim, and the pond, shelving steeply towards the centre, soon accounted for her. The two corpses were taken from the water later that night.

There had been an inquest, and as she was to be buried within two or three days, Anda wanted to know if Steve and I would attend the funeral.

He flatly refused, and I had made arrangements to go, but was prevented by the strange feeling of deadly illness and weariness that for some weeks now had been attacking me from time to time. Neither to Bernard nor to Steve did I say anything about this, and just in case anything serious ailed me, I never went to a doctor, either.

So through indisposition I stayed at home the day our mother was buried. What she must have felt as she stood at the pond-side and saw her dog being done to death! What she must have felt when she entered the water and plunged beyond her depth!

All that desperate twilight struggle seemed to epitomize the difficulties she had strewn over other peoples' lives: her own end was like a symbol of what she had done to other people.

After this upset, Bernard's life and mine settled anew into peaceful happiness. He wrote constantly in those days, while I was out in my paradise of the London streets, and at nights, if there was not the theatre, we read and talked together, or entertained. Sometimes I sat to one of his artist friends—the catch being the silver head on the young shoulders.

In Bernard's warmth and wisdom, in his strength and charm and never-failing gentle kindness, and in the ecstasy of love that never lessened, my normally happy life was heightened to such a pitch, I used, often to wonder how I could go on living and bear it. And often he would take my face between his hands, and say:

"Each day I believe I love you as much as it is possible for any man to love a girl, and then you do or say something which so delights me, I am swept away on new tides of tenderness. You storm my heart till I am like to die with joy of you!"

Our love informed all our days with a magical fire; often when he came into the room I would have been glad for him to *go away*, for his presence was too much. I could, as I had done before I met him, have lived out my life to the end, loving him and never seeing him. But it had been my fate to meet him and be loved by him in return, and I tried to do bravely by the excess of joy the gods saw fit to give me. I always hoped never to be too small for my destiny.

And soon I was to hear the price demanded for a happiness entire, soon to test the worth and permanency of that happiness, its ability to continue when all normal reasons for happiness had gone.

Bernard, sitting on a high stool, and holding me against him, would hold court on entertaining evenings. The feeling of his masculine nearness in the crowd at such times was an extraordinary comfort to me because when I, to escape the herd, let my thoughts dwell on the nonchalant continuity of stars, the imponderable majesty of oceans and deserts and icefields, the relentless unreasoning life of lions and mountains and ants, the strangeness of criminals and idiots and everyone, the delight these things usually gave me would be shot, not often but sometimes, by an undercurrent of panic, and my soul would shrink, acutely uneasy before these great mysteries and its isolation, its withering ignorance. So at such times, when I, convinced of my paltriness and unworthiness, saw Bernard's human eyes shining with love and felt the kind arm across my breast, I was carried away by the great and unexpected honour of being singled out for his preference. His brilliance and warmth, reaching out to me so kindly, so strangely from the mystery of ail life, would restore and nourish me.

Once Steve was present when Bernard was holding me like this in our thronged room; Steve's face darkened at some jovial, affectionate remark Bernard made, and my brother, in his aberrated way fastened on this absurd thing.

"With the most attentive love, I always watched my sister's career," Steve said; "I always looked upon her as the greatest prize of my life, yet I don't remember ever showing her off as I would display a favourite hound, or the insides of a new motor car!"

"I am sorry to bring out all your spleen, my dear Steve," said Bernard, hugging me, "but I think that Laura and I understand one another. I think she sees something rather different from mere pride of possession in my enthusiasm for her!"

Steve lifted his high, arched eyebrows.

"I hope she does! It only gives me the kind of feeling a person gets looking into a lover's lighted bedroom window from a train!"

Steve's expression, remote, disdainful; unhappy, giving off some odd kind of a warning, struck old nameless fears into my heart. If only someone better and wiser than I had stood nearest to him, had lovingly bidden him, "Have patience, little saint," and even more tenderly explained so that he could have understood how a smiling renunciation is required some time of everyone who lives, and that ultimate fulfilment and triumph is the lot of those who submit with a willing heart, all, all would have been different.

I had done my best, but my best had not been good enough. Things had gone from bad to worse with him since I had left him.

Only once had I accepted Steve's invitation to go to one of his and Oriel's Sunday afternoon gatherings: it had been a wretched event.

"Oh, hello, you!" Oriel greeted me. It showed in her face what Steve was doing to her.

"Yes, you can look!" she said, with passionate resentment, finding my eyes upon her. "You and that brother of yours— you're not human people at all!"

"Oh, Oriel," I faltered, "I am so sorry!"

"You say that as though you *cared*," she said, looking at me with wonder. "As though what happened to me mattered—and mattered to *you!*"

"So it does," I replied. "It matters to me more than I can say!"

"The little saint, eh? You, who feel happy always, how can you be affected by the misery of others? You feel that the world belongs to you—don't you?"

"If I feel that the earth belongs to me," I replied slowly, "I also feel that I belong to the world; would to God that I could make everyone happy, but true happiness is too simple and too ample for people to accept. They think there must be a 'catch' in it somewhere."

"Ah—what do you know!" she said, contemptuously.

"Nothing," I answered, "that's just the trouble!"

"How is Bernard?" she demanded, roughly.

"Very well," I answered.

"And happy, too, I expect," she sneered.

"And happy, too!

"He would be!" she declared, ill-naturedly. "I said that you and he would get on very well because you are the two most selfish people I ever knew—always excepting your brother Steve. The only difference is that he is unhappy in his selfishness, but you two are happy!"

All this was being said quietly on the sofa.

"But, Oriel," I said, "may not a person take joy in a thing, just because it is *there*, because it is just what it was created, without thinking about its cause and effect and agonizing over it?"

"Not in this world," declared Oriel, "and not when there are persons in it like this one": Steve had come up to us and stood smirking coldly and maliciously at Oriel.

"My dear Laura," he said, seating himself on the sofa arm beside me, "I am so glad that you are come among this rabble! I want to have a few words with you. Oh, never mind *her*," he said, as I half-glanced at Oriel.

"No," she said," don't mind me, Laura. *He* doesn't!" Steve leaned across me to say fervently to her:

"Oh, how *tired* I am of you."

"And I of you!" she returned.

"Well, then, you know what to do."

"Yes," Oriel sighed," I know, but I can't!"

"Don't say that I hold you back," he cried.

"He's always violently on the defensive," said Oriel to me; "such a sign of ill-breeding!"

"But I've never pretended to be anything but ill-bred!" he laughed.

"What ... what beastly people you are!" said Oriel, looking at Steve and me in a way to wither us. "*You* everlastingly in the trenches of self-defence and spite, and Laura wallowing deep down, miles down in the strange mucks that bring her this wonderful, innocuous happiness of hers!"

"I imagine, yes, I imagine that Laura and I must seem beastly people to the folk on the heights like you," he said, reflectively, "the lucky, stony folk on the heights! Laura's naturalness is so complete, it is suspect to your kind. I often told her it was folly to cast pearls before swine! But we would not change with you, no, not for a million! And even in our depths, we are a cut *above* you."

Oriel said no more: she wept with hard, wide-open eyes.

"Hoo! You needn't be upset," said Steve to her." You have not caused yourself to think that you are any the less remarkable, you know."

She got up and went away.

"Well," said I, "after that scene of domestic bliss, perhaps you can call to mind what it was you had to say to me."

"It was to tell you how glad, glad I am to see you! So glad, that I never really meant to have a falling-out with Oriel! But, I can't help it! Every time we set eyes on each other we begin. We have got so used to it now, we can't leave off. It's as natural as breathing for us to abuse one another!"

"No," I said, "be honest! It isn't Oriel you abuse and make wretched—it's our mother! All that you ever felt against *her* you take out on Oriel."

He thought about this.

"I believe you're right," he remarked at last. "But, just the same," he ended, darkly, "Oriel, in her own right, is a tiresome devil!"

"She must find you the same!"

"So she does, but she knows the remedy. Oh, Laura, come and do something with me, for it is time that you did!"

"Why do you still depend on me?" I said. "You know, I am the only one of the family who has come to nothing. Anda is world famous for her beauty, and now, her title; you are one of the greatest actors in the world; and Robert is making a name for himself with his histories. While I, what am I—a ship that never looks for, or expects to find—a harbour."

Steve replied:

"Yes, and in saying that, you only emphasize how you, who are not world-famous, are in reality, the greatest success and the better one of us all. What you have got from life— the secret of an enduring happiness—is a higher achievement than any of us have reached with our art and beauty and learning. We, perhaps, have overcome the world: *you* ... have overcome *life*!"

The weeks went by. At last the strange ailment that had overtaken me, obliged me to decide upon medical advice. Now a pain would squirt up from my lungs and become embedded like a rusty star in each of my shoulders. Now, when I coughed, bright blood would quietly stream into my handkerchief. So, without telling Bernard, I went to an eminent chest-man. He made the necessary examination.

"Are you alone in the world?" he asked me, "or have you parents—a guardian?"

"I am—alone," I said. "Why do you ask? What is it?"

"Since you are alone," he said, "I think you ought to know the truth."

"I want to know the truth," I said." And, what's more, I can bear it. What ails me?"

"You've got tuberculosis," he replied.

"Oh," I mumbled, "I never had that before. How is it I get such a complaint?"

"I should say it's through self-neglect, or through some intensely creative kind of work you have been engaged in. Both your lungs are affected and, so badly, I'm afraid it has got to the incurable stage. Why, Oh why did you not come to me long before this? You must have had the symptoms a long time, even to the haemorrhages."

"Yes," I admitted, "but there was always something more important to take care of than my cough! I didn't come to you because I rather thought it was serious, and though it doesn't matter for me, there are ... certain persons ... I did not wish to have disturbed!"

"But I thought you said that you were alone!"

"So I am, but there are always other people in a person's life. So it's beyond a cure. Well, then, how long have I got?"

"I can't really say. It is a strange disease! Possibly ...if you go into a sanatorium where you will have every care—a year, perhaps. If you live as you are doing to the end, it would come sooner."

"I'll think it over," I said, and left.

How simple, how beautifully final it all was! I had been prepared for bad news, but not this. I was stupefied. I was caught, I was down. The complete anarchy of my bones and tissues overwhelmed me. I couldn't bear to go home to Bernard. I sat me down on a corporation bench to think.

Straightaway, my own soul seemed to have some questions to ask now that hints were flying of the near dissolving of its partnership with my body.

But, I said to this fretful voice, haven't I been of *any* use to you? You despise me—you make me feel that you abhor me, that I have disgraced you; but I made up to you, sometimes, for *everything*. Sometimes God said things to me in *italics* and, for a little time, at least, the way was clear. I never allowed you to become dulled or defeated by sophistry and science which would deny your very existence! You have never been browbeaten by reason; you and I always saw *above that!* We turned everything, everything to our own formidable imaginative ends! I let in extra light upon you, light that you could not have had but for the livingness and receptiveness of my senses. I have released into you streams of bird-song, lute-song, sunlight, earth-murmurs, treetremors; yes, yes, and love, "love most mighty and allbeguiling." Have you forgotten Bernard? Have you forgotten my brother, Steve? What is the use of your forgetting these things when I shall always remember them? Without my sly, whimsical mind you would have missed much. I have been of use to you. You needed my co-operation, always.

I paused, hunting for something else to say, but it seemed that, for the moment at least, either I had stunned my restless soul by saying so much, or it was pleased that I had said too little.

Now it was time to deal with my fears, and reach some purposeful outlook.

What if, after all these years, I had been cheating myself, and the armour wherein I had trusted would now fall to pieces at this time of supreme testing. Before the stony drama of an incurable disease, what was there to rise up and challenge it? Was the sweet song of life to end because of approaching death? No, no; and no again! But the thing to do was to find out what was troubling me. It wasn't death itself I feared; I who had loved life yet had always been prepared to die just on the minute, I had no cause to weep over death. Why, a person was incomplete without that

tender roundingoff: gates thrown open! a state of being ...
out of reach! wisdom at last where before there had been
only knowledge!

I certainly did not fear death, but I saw that I dreaded
the *dying* that went before, dreaded that, perhaps, actual pain
would not let me keep a cool front to the end. But how could
I know what this would be like *till it came*? When it came
it would not be half so bad as I had imagined it in prospect,
and, just as it would be a most drastic change, so would I
also be changed in order to meet it. A person nearly always
finds that he can bear cheerfully in reality what he quailed
at in imagination.

Besides, I thought of what had been happening to me
every day for such a long time—how the once-unconscious
happiness of earliest childhood kept coming back to me
through memory, recovered in every sort of sight and sound,
making every minute of the day so engrossing that I never
noticed what was taken away; I never noticed when my
health went; *I should not notice when I died!*

I remembered, too, that all the events of my life had only
been to me what my own mind had made them. And now
was an incurable disease *to be* an incurable disease? Certainly
not! Disease was only a part of me—not all of me!

From then on, everything was all right. I got up and
walked about the streets; the very power of putting one foot
in front of the other, of swinging with the earth-swing, of
feeling the wind blowing in my hair, brought about calm
and finally exhilaration.

Peace flowed back to me and, with it, acceptance of what
had come to me in all its implications. So far from misery I
had cause for pride—pride because it was my destiny to be a

fighter: a fighter, moreover, who would never know defeat, for I should die in the last ditch.

I straightened my back, I lifted my head. And there, right in front of me, was the magic talisman, "Aerated Bread Company." On this autumn day, when I heard of my certain death, these homely words, from every hint of autumn I had ever stored up in them began to unfold for me the essence of what would be a perfect autumn day in town—to remember *somewhere else*:-

A vehement wind is pouring over Hyde Park, hurtling the leaves across the lawns where the red-coats are walking. This same wind is lifting the breath of cart-horses like veils round their noses.

The thin lemon-coloured light of the sun falls suavely over the teeming streets and the squares where, in a hush, the great trees are gathering themselves together to act as hosts for winter.

The wind-whipped nerves of London, so tenuously strung between the red buses and the bleached white spires, are sharpened and shrill, a metamorphosis that livens leaf and limb.

Celery and big apples are odorously piled on street-stalls, and at many a corner cluster the exuberant polls of chrysanthemums and dahlias, a combination of vulgarity and princeliness.

Hoarse cries of coalmen presage dramatic yellow fogs and blazing brands, while sniggering urchins with tin cans are begging alms betimes for Gunpowder Plot Night celebrations.

High heels are knocking down the arcades, teetering about from display to display of blue fur gloves, gay Persian scarves and jumpers by Schiaparelli.

Box-office windows are besieged for the riches of autumn entertainment, and alert announcements flourish of evening-classes for everything from shorthand and shirt-making to lessons in counterpoint and Chinese.

The foliage of many trees is still untouched by the Chinese fireworks blaze of decay, and in Bloomsbury Square the lime trees waterfalls of fire, and the pinkly-ringed chestnut leaves stand out in beautiful contrast to the sombre green of unravaged plantations.

Outside a public house with creaking bay trees at the door (bay-trees are to keep witches away!), an "ex-Soldier Trying To Exist," pulls a dashing tune from a barrel-organ, and a prisoner in a passing police-van, through the grating glares enviously at the fallen hero.

In the city, the scarlet coats of Chelsea Pensioners animate the drab clothes of office workers scurrying into lunch-time restaurants, where the gothic fantasies of summer delectations are crumbling before the solid Norman pillars of fare calculated to make blood and bones withstand the vigorous attacks of approaching winter.

From the tops of buses it is possible to see rows of fiery little trees standing arm-in-arm along the walls of town gardens, and Michaelmas daisies and the frozen faces of asters mopping and mowing over tiled paths. A masterly wind relentlessly shakes the elm trees whose small sparse leaves lie along the branches like brilliant beetles.

But in the afternoon the sunlight is one rich marigold and brassily winks on the waves of the Thames. The gardens by the Parliament Houses are disturbed by a mad maypole dance of the winds that raise crimson tides of fallen Virginia creeper leaves under the lavender plumes of smoke from burning weeds.

On the Lambeth shore a russet haze transfigures the chimneys and kilns of the potteries there, and above the moaning tugs drift the vigorous oaths of old Elizabethan watermen whose ghosts, in creaking aprons, still solicit passengers at the river stairs from the Savoy to Wapping.

Pilfering pigeons stalk over the pavements and squabble throatily with the newly-arrived gentlemen of St. James's—the seagulls—who have come to take up town residence for the winter.

In shop windows stand the unabashed little hounds of the publishers' autumn packs!

But the warbles and shrieks do not silence the nether melancholy chords struck from the heart of the troubled earth, disturbing the flow of the days, having an affinity with the uneasy potencies of bowling leaf and scuttling stone, and with strange occult Presences lingering beside wind-defeated trees, haunting streets steeped in the silver snail light of waning afternoon; distraught Presences, agitating over summer's fallen day, passionately attacking minds unaffected by fact and those who watch beside a beauty that is not obvious to the world of common forms.

In the evening, electric signs, red, blue, bronze, and limegreen leap promiscuously in the streets—snow and silver shine in the cafes.

This keen sweet wind that has blown over leagues and leagues of lonely moor and mountain to the knowing lights of the town, with its derelicts and diamonds, cabmen and queens: the smoky rose-rubbed west and sky glowing green, beginning to be scattered with thick yellow stars: these pears with their beautiful distinctiveness in the light-drenched window; the fallen leaves curled like vermilion fishes under the Ritz arcade; and scurry of ghostly notes issuing from Dover Street where Chopin once stayed—all these things seem to possess the whole character of autumn, and there is power in this beauty to console for the harshness of approaching winter ...

When I finally turned for home the twilight was down. As I turned in at our gate it began to rain. The night was all a windy nothingness. The boughs were full of murmurs, and the air was sweet and damp and held the same kind of thrilling nuttiness as on that rainy afternoon when Bernard and I stood clasped close in the emerald alley and he said he loved me. Tensed and bewitched as I was by this day's news, I was then so overwhelmingly aware of life I saw that death was *impossible*. I could only die of life into life. And I had a sudden violent delight in the feel of my own impaired body, in the vibrating consciousness of being alive at all, though maimed.

Even decay has its own strange harmonies, and as I tasted then a surge of blood coming up nonchalant and salty from my sundering lungs, I saw some analogy between these ruined lungs of mine and the torn and sodden foxgloves, following a storm in the woodland; the completeness of the pattern of corruption rose and transcended its bitterness. I thought: better to die now when I have committed *some* sins, than later when I shall probably have committed *all* sins!

Happily, I let myself into the house. It would have been ungrateful in me to have made whimpering demands on the future when the present was giving me so much. And to my gods I breathed then: Let me be what you want me to be; let me do what *you* want me to do.

Quietly I went up to my room to make myself attractive for Bernard. There on the window-sill was the single bloom of geranium in the flower-pot. It stretched its smooth glossy crimson poll against the gull-grey evening light, it glowed fiery and still. In its solitary pride and exclusiveness, overriding its certain decay within the next few days, the geranium was another fount of courage to me: it signalled "Hold on." This one geranium was another emblem of faith in the final defeat of what might have been a most faithless day.

Bernard and I had a gay supper together. While I drank soup, snatched at the table-napkin slipping off my knees, and reached for bread and salt, I made two resolves. The first was that I would keep the news of my illness as long as possible, and to the end if possible, from the one who, beyond all, would receive it the most desperately—my brother Steve.

He would look upon the event as the closing down of a company that used to pay him good dividends and now would not do so any more. Were I to tell him he would study my face looking for fear at the prospect of non-being: this would help him to fight not to weep before me as he listened. Well, I knew how to die by now, the machinery would not creak, but, just the same, I had no intention of enlightening him.

The other resolution was—to tell Bernard soon. At first I had thought to go away without telling him the true reason—that I was sick and done for; to lie to him—say I no longer loved him—make him release me by an untruth. But I saw at once how cowardly that would have been, and how I dishonoured him by even thinking of such a course for a second. I reasoned like this: suppose it had been Bernard who had heard that he must die, and suppose he had felt that I could not bear the parting; suppose that he had decided I was such a shabby person as not to be able to face the truth and he had lied to me, brought down our love, used that

as the lever to get away from a girl *he had decided* was a fit
companion only for pleasure and joy, a girl who would be
found wanting when it came to sharing sorrow. How should
I have felt in that event? So I could not do that to him—or to
myself. Bernard must know the truth; after he had accepted
it, then it was for him to decide whether I should leave him.
He, not I, must declare whether his love was enough to bear
my dying self as it had so warmly embraced my living self.

One morning he made the opportunity for the disclosure
by telling me, as he went through his mail, that soon he
would have to return to America and, of course, I should
be going, too.

"You'll love it there, Laura," he said. "Your life obsession
will flourish even more exuberantly in America, and the
change will do you good! Come to think of it, you haven't
seemed very well just lately. You're so thin and pale, my
darling. Do you feel really well, Laura?"

"Yes, yes. I feel fine," I answered.

"Even so, a sea voyage will do you good," he continued.
"I'm taking a lot for granted, of course. I'm taking it for
granted that you will ... Laura, you will come to America,
won't you?"

I took up a piece of bread from the plate. I felt its own
special *bread feel*, and this gave me the courage for what I
had to tell.

"No," I said," I will not go to America with you, Bernard."

"You mean ... you wish me to go alone, and you to
remain here?"

"Yes," I replied, "that's it!"

"Have you ... dear, have you any particular reason for
not wishing to go to America. You see, I must go back
some time, being still an American citizen. Of course, if

you'd rather, I'll become a British subject. It is just as you wish, Laura."

"Then, I wish you to go back to America."

"For good?"

"Yes."

"But, Laura ... all at once, I am afraid. Laura, excuse me, tell me one thing ... have you ... do you ... love me?"

I had been looking into his face all this time, but now I transferred my gaze to the window and the garden beyond.

"Laura? Tell me."

I looked at him. As always, my eyes betrayed the violence of my love for him. He hurried round to my side of the table and, dropping on his knees held me tightly to him.

"You fool—you little fool! What are you saying? What are you trying to do to me? We loving like this and going about the world alone—apart! You're mad to say it! Laura, is there anything troubling you? Tell me, for I love you so. Is there anything I can do? You know that the least concern of yours is of compelling interest to me."

"I'll tell you a thing," I said, finding out his bare shoulders through the open neck of his shirt. "Without mentioning it to you, I was in Harley Street a week or two ago, for I kept haemorrhaging from my lungs till I didn't know what to do. And *he* said, the specialist said ... well, that I'm done for. I've got about a year ... And I thought that since you're going to America it would be a good idea to part now."

His face had gone very white.

"You thought it was a good idea, did you, Laura? But listen to me—I've got a far better one. You are going to America with me, just the same, just the same—as though nothing has happened. Nothing *has* happened. Are you, of all in this world, are *you* going to let a little matter like *death* have power over an unconquerable thing like our love? You love me, I saw it in your tell-tale eyes; I know! And I love you. It's the only thing that matters. We shall be together till ... Oh, Laura ... darling ... darling ... till the last beat of your wild little heart. And then—what then? For a time things will be a little changed from what they used to be. I shall say things to my girl as I always did, and though she will not reply she *will* answer. I shall hold my girl not against my heart but *in my heart*. Wherever you are, you will hold me. What has death to do with people like us? There is no death; there is no parting. The only thing that twists my heart is the thought ... the thought that you have pain to bear, and I am so helpless to take it from you. But I swear, by God I swear it, I'll do everything in my power to make it easier for you. Do you tell me now to go to America—alone?"

But I huddled into him and could not answer for crying down tears of joy and gratitude for his words that had shattered me. He cried himself, till we laughed at our queer, broken-up faces, and hugged one another.

"Oh," I gasped, "aren't we two idiots?"

"Uproarious idiots," he agreed, dashing the back of his hand across his eyes. Then he said, quietly:

"America or England—which is it to be? Does Laura turn me off—now?"

"She doesn't," I said, "she can't, she won't." I slipped down on to the floor beside him; I put my arms round his neck. "And I think," I said, "I'd rather go to America with you, my dearest. I often wanted to go and live in America; it'll be rather a stunt to go and die there!"

"Well, we haven't said the last word yet on that doctor's diagnosis. Who knows, Laura—he may be wrong!"

But here, my lungs, feeling that they had been called

upon to endure more than enough for one morning, suddenly and importantly asserted themselves. The bright red stream came up. I turned away from him but he had seen. He picked me up in his arms and carried me to the sofa.

"There's my brave one!" said Bernard, smoothing back my hair from my eyes.

The haemorrhage soon stopped, leaving me to expostulate with the intolerable weariness creeping over all my bones.

"It looks as though ... eminent chest-man has the last word," I said. "But, Bernard, isn't it a lovely bright red! It's just the colour I was thinking of for my winter jumper."

He had been holding my wrist. He buried his face in my hair.

"Oh ... my girl ...my girl!" said Bernard.

Chapter VIII

"Life being more than all else to me ..."
W.H. HUDSON

TO fend off my brother's hungry questions, Bernard and I decided to keep secret the date of our going to America. No one knew of our intent and the house, not being ours, showed no signs of disturbance for departure.

One evening, a few days before we were due to sail, Bernard being gone to a theatre-world banquet, I was sitting alone by the fire reading.

It was a wild night with spirits of rain dashing out from the tail of the wind of the autumn equinox. It was fourteen minutes past eight o'clock when, through the silent house, the door-bell startlingly shrilled. Wondering who on earth was calling, and with that faint apprehension which often comes to a person alone in a house when an unexpected visitor gives evidence of his presence on the doorstep, I went to see who had come.

I opened the big front door. A gust of wind blew in an arid leaf or two, and also seemed to throw my brother Steve through the door.

"Oh! It's you, is it?" I said, with some relief.

"Why," he said, "who did you fear to meet?"

"An assassin, maybe!" I laughed, shakily.

"Good God!" he exclaimed, following me to the sitting-room fire; "and perhaps an assassin has come, too!"

He was hatless and wearing an old oat-coloured raincoat with the collar turned up. Throwing off this coat, he sat him down at the fireside, his hands hanging straight down at his sides, his eyes on my face.

He looked as though he had been going the pace lately. His face was white lead. I sighed and went to pour him a drink, for he looked as though he needed one; as I did so, I noticed the time again—soon it would be half-past eight: he ought to have been at the theatre long ago.

"Why aren't you at the theatre?" I asked, giving him his drink, and sitting down at the opposite side of the hearth.

Between gulps he said rapidly, brightly:

"I've given myself a holiday! Why not? I have served my public long and faithfully since the time I was fourteen years old. I've had little rest and no peace. The time has come for a holiday!"

I shrugged.

"No reason at all why you should not have a rest. Only, it is so very odd of you to decide on a holiday right in the middle of the week, right in the middle of a run of Shakespeare!"

"Well," he said, smiling," don't mind it, as you always used to say. Give me another drink, Laura. If you have any brandy I should like some of it." He drank so seldom, it was strange to hear him ask for it.

I gave him the drink, and sat down again.

"I suppose," I said, "you have quarrelled with Oriel?"

"Oh, yes," he replied. "We quarrelled, all right. I seem to have lost the capacity for humanizing things—if ever I had it! Without this a person gets so stony! Do you know something—a week ago I dreamt I had killed Oriel, quite, quite calmly—no heat, no passion!"

"Did you? But one often dreams that one has committed a murder; it doesn't make a person a murderer! Your only iniquity tonight is a row, and coming to me when you should be in the theatre."

"I have come to you," he agreed, "and I have come to tell you something that is altogether out of the usual in the way of news."

He paused, then he said, still keeping his eyes on me:

"I have just killed Oriel: this is no dream."

I stretched my eyes as though to make more clear the wonder of the thing.

"You mean," I said, after a few seconds of silence, "that you ... you had an accident?"

"No, no," he answered. "I murdered her!"

I bent and began to poke the fire in a kind of desperation as if this everyday action might restore the normal and the unaffrighted again. I turned to him:

"You must be off your head, Steve! You are not playing a rather terrible joke on me, are you?"

"No, I'm not."

Suddenly he put his arm across his eyes.

"Would that it were a joke—only the recurring dream!"

"But ... but," I said, and could not go on.

Steve sat up very straight and began to speak quietly, looking all the time into my face:

"You get down to it, you get right down to the mud on such a day as this! What happened was—Oriel and I were having our daily row, or one of our many daily rows; I was thinking of getting ready for the theatre—it really was not so very long ago—and she said to me that she had had enough. She said she was going to return to Bernard who, being a man with peculiar notions of honour and pity (so she declared) would be compelled to take her back, and send you away—send you back to me.

'No,' I said to Oriel. 'Oh, no. You are not going to interfere with them. You will stay with me, whether you like it or not. To leave your husband for me was your choice, not his, and certainly not mine. Laura and Bernard have arranged their lives as a direct result of your choice, and you are not going to upset their happiness now. They are the only happy people I ever knew, and I will never allow *you* to wreck what they have.'

But Oriel replied that I had dictated to her for the last time, that nothing would give her greater pleasure than to wreck you and, by so doing, finish me. She declared she was going back to Bernard there and then. She made a move to the door: I prevented her from reaching it.

'You shall not go,' I said.

But she kept on shouting that she would go. It got on my nerves, always strung to breaking point, and I put my hand over her mouth. She bit me. I had no thought, even then, of murdering her: I was only nervous and exasperated; she had also deeply shocked me by her intention.

She bit me again, and I suddenly moved my hands to her throat. It reminded me of when I was Othello in America. I did not like my Desdemona. Every night as my hands went round her neck in the death scene, I used to wonder what it would be like if I squeezed harder, *harder*. And, while I was thinking this, I was pressing Oriel's throat—harder.

Her hands were making little struggles in the air. This annoyed me, though, for none of the time was I furiously angry, not even *angry* at all! I had stopped being myself, you understand? Stopped being Steve Valley the man, and Steve Valley the actor; if I was anything, I was Steve Valley the analyst. For I felt, as much as to say—here is a human being in thus and thus a situation. What is going to happen, what will this person do? *This person*, mark you, not Oriel McCann! And the person, well, she died, of course.

From the time my hands went to her throat till ... till the end, it seemed as though they were directed by a will other than mine. A will that was full of the cold strength of a loathing for her and for all: and there came with it some far-fetched need to get my own back, not so much on her as on *life*, and so—I slew her!

The ... the manifestations of her death recalled me to myself. My own will flew to my hands. I dropped them from her poor neck. For two or three seconds she stood, and I wanted to ask her to remember herself, for she looked so ... so deranged with her eyes bolting at me, and ... well, then she crashed down, fetching her head a cruel knock on the fender. I felt glad, yes, I did, I felt glad, that at any rate, she would not be able to feel *that*—which must sound strange when I had just murdered her! But to me it isn't strange at all considering that during the time I was ... killing her, I wasn't myself!

Well, when I was myself, I saw how things stood. I wished I had someone there, then, someone who knew all about murders and could tell me what to do next."

He stopped speaking. He had not taken his eyes away from me once, and I had listened to what he had to say with a feeling of imminently bursting into a blaze of madness.

I could picture it all. The murder springing up suddenly from nowhere: the insulting word dying in a low laugh, the laugh choked down for ever.

"But, Steve" I cried, galvanized, "you may not have killed her. You can't be sure—not yet. Oh, how can you tell? She may only be unconscious. We'll go at once to the cottage and perhaps we can revive her."

"No, no," he cried. "She ... I ... I, of course, tried, ugh! I tried to bring her round. She's dead!"

"But," I said, "you have ... you have killed her for something that you yourself were most ardently trying to bring about—my return to you! Every time we met, you tormented and besought me to come back to you. What, then, were you trying to do all along?"

"I was trying to make you come back to me, all the time. I wanted nothing better. I should have done anything to bring you back. I would have ... I would have *killed* Oriel to bring you back; as it is, I murdered her so that you should *not* return—so that nothing should be messed up for you. Because it was only when Oriel spoke of what she meant to do, I saw that really the only important thing to me was your safety—above all, your happiness, your not being wrecked in a world where most everything *is* wrecked!"

The irony of this—when Bernard and I would soon be parting for ever as far as our earthly union was concerned. I drew a great sigh, and though terror was addressing me in long lunges I had a single gleam of relief in that now Steve would never know about my own approaching end, need never say, as undoubtedly he would have said so querulously: "But what about me? Where do I come in? What will I do?"

These questions now had an answer. Steve continued:

"Well," he said, "this is what it comes to! You live a long

time and you think something steady has come about. Then, out of the blue, an occasion whips up and, before you know where you are, you have committed murder! It comes as a shock to see how horribly shabby one really is! I used to wonder why I was born, and probably you wondered, too often. We see now. It was to be a murderer, and that is not a little role! There have to be some murderers! People like me are needed! It is necessary to have some wickedness in the social scheme! What is the use of goodness if there's *only* good? Engines can't run without grit! A murderer is an example, and, by his fate, some improvement is achieved. Murderers and martyrs benefit the whole community.

"It does not become me to make such a speech at such a time, not even an Empedoclean soliloquy, but, Laura ... listen: the purpose of such a life as mine, though seemingly useless and bad, is *real*, designed, and of *good intent!* I *had* to do what I was destined to do. For a *purpose* even Judas was created. There have to be, there must be those whom Fate sends down into the dark so that others can rise to the light. And if I have achieved nothing else, at least I have prevented your separation from Bernard whom you love. As for me—do you remember Homer's noble words, spoken by Zeus, Our Father Kronides, or Our Father Who Art In Heaven—they're both the same: 'And now he has atoned for all at once.' Well, perhaps I shall, Laura, perhaps I shall, too. Before I left the cottage to come here to you, I telephoned Scotland Yard. I told them to come up to the Hampstead address; I told them what they would find. Then I asked them to call here and ... and pick me up. I have left the light burning and the door ajar to facilitate the discovery."

I stared at him. It was the worst time of my life. I suppose it was his worst time, too. No, it could not have been worse than the night our mother told him he must leave school and he burnt his beloved Greek books, changing all in an hour from a little boy to an appalling grown man. Immediately I thought:

If there had not been *that* night there would not be *this* night.

I sat, enislanded by disaster, feeling that I had stepped for good and all off the plane of normal contact and was jolting about in some dangerous unknown territory.

I thought of the serious-faced, silent police now on their way to the Hampstead cottage. The Rowlandson faces in the hall would be leering softly in the subdued light he had left on. The fire would by dying down. The air would be rushing still with emanations from that violent death.

What beggared words was the atrocious strangeness of the thing. I had to recognize with diamond-etched lunatic clarity that this man, this self-confessed murderer whom the police were already on their way.to arrest, who would stand his trial and surely hang—this man was my own brother Steve: Steve the haunted, so subtly fanciful, so abrupt and ruthless, so touchingly dear.

He would hang all right. They would fix the date. He had killed Oriel, but she'd had no rumour of what was coming; now, to requite this, he must wait and *know*. As he might once have said—on the 15th I am going to tea at the Countess Irene's—so, with the same stunning casualness soon he would be able to say—on the 15th or the 16th, whatever they would decide, I am going to die by strangulation.

The beauty, the genius, the fame, and the end—a heap of bones in a pit of quicklime.

Shut up the door and quench the light. Here, indeed, is atonement for all in one!

Memories began to hurry into my head. I saw my brother standing on the stage when he was fourteen singing his poor little song, "Everything is Peaches Down in Georgia," having neither the verve nor the vulgarity to carry off a music-hall turn, yet carrying it off simply by magnetizing his audiences with the incredible beauty of his face. Then his going to the repertory theatre, acting his life because he could not live it, going from his first big part as Ralph, the apprentice in the "Knight of the Burning Pestle," to an unpredictable flowering as one of the greatest actors of his time—a success that was nothing more to him than an accidental in earning money. From the first hand-clap it had been too late to give him grovelling veneration, to find in him glamorous interest. All his savage peculiarities, his sparkling malevolence, he had worn as a cloak to help him as best they might in his way through the world with the smiling grief of a heart crushed and broken by the shambling cruelties of his childhood.

Never forgetting this, I went and, kneeling beside him where he was sitting, I put my arms round him.

The white teeth between his parted red lips seemed to be demanding of me very intensely:

"Must we lose our sharp bites on food, our snarls, our smiling? Must charm be laid? Must we be still in the grave everlasting?"

I drew him to me in close desperation, as if by so doing I could absorb him into myself, catch him away for ever from his trial and certain death.

He was returning my gaze; even in this catastrophe his old tender recognition of me was burning steadily, blandly, unaffectedly, in his eyes.

And then, it was *then* I saw the light gleam on his cool

gold hair, I saw his parted mouth, the skin laid so flawlessly upon the delicate bones of his face; I felt his strong tender livingness under his clothes, and suddenly I was back in harmony with things, just as I always returned, no matter what happened, and I had been wrong to fear that I should fail tonight.

The fact of anguish and disaster faded before the brilliant, the dramatic, the dynamic fact of *life*, of having the *power* to experience even this horror because we, Steve and I, were alive. The famous thrill of this—the aliveness of living! You live your life from day to day, and it's a charnel underneath— but, you're alive!

And even as I thrilled to his livingness, he rose on the crest of mine: clenching his hands in my hair, he said breathlessly:

"Do you suppose I don't know what you're thinking now? Even now? Do you think I don't know how you got through school and life and everything? I tell you, I understand how you did not even notice the poverty and sordid misery of our childhood. For the success was that you *began again every day*. You discarded everything that had gone before, and took every day as though it were the first dawning for you, blurred by no familiarity.

I've seen you going about with quiet crazy joy because you could *breathe*. I've seen you proud and surprised at the curious power of your own unaided locomotion. Singing birds were never heard in our street, but you listened to the dust rustling by in the gutter as raptly as Blake listened to his angels at Peckham Rye.

You gaped at things! You *drank* the milk, you *tasted* the bread. You were amused at the utility of cups and chairs. You took nothing for granted. Endlessly you speculated and you didn't try to solve anything—what would there have been for you if you *knew*?

You were always too busy with your feelings, too engrossed with the timeless values of the humble incidents of daily life to be bored or wretched or afraid! Oh, the happiness of every hour you've passed, the riches of every day, the wonder of your lifetime!

I have seen you looking at your hands, thrilling over them because they were your hands, *your* hands—alive! And the reason I knew was because a few minutes earlier I had been looking at my hands, understanding them for my hands but, in my gloomy cowardly way, unable to reconcile being alive with living. Nothing was changed for me because I recognized life! Why was it changed for you? Because you, Laura, had the courage, you had the *inhuman humanity* to be faithful to life. Ah, there was always something special about you.

And it's only now, *now*, Laura, that I know and understand your secret. Everything is speaking of it to me— this fire making its little sounds on the hearth, these hands of mine in your warm hair. It has taken me the whole of my life to learn it; if I'd understood it an hour ago I should not have killed Oriel.

I ... I must go on telling you: we never said these things together before; we shall never say them again, we shan't need to.

When I saw that Oriel was dead, I was going to do something to myself, too. Then I thought of you. I thought:

If I go to my little sister and ... and tell her, if she gets over it, if I see that secret light at the back of her eyes as I have seen it her life long, if she can overcome this, I shall understand, I'll believe. At the last hour I shall see there was something, after all, in her singleness of purpose.

That's why I telephoned the police to come here for me.

When I was telling you, I watched you, Christ, how I watched you! I saw your shock and fear. I saw you seeing the hangman. I saw your misery for Oriel. And then, when you came and knelt beside me, I saw your *recognition*. I saw the light begin in your eyes, and I understood the spell. I understood that the *sweetness of life itself need never be lessened.*

This feeling of life, your mania for life, overcomes *everything!* What is for you is now for me. All the hordes of life run one.

You're not shocked or reluctant or afraid: No more will you be on the very morning when they ... when I ... At eight o'clock you'll look out of your window, you'll see some little cloud sailing by and, in the rapporte between its being and your own, you'll lose the grisliness of what is happening to you through me.

You're concerned with nothing at all but *living*. You are living these very minutes, as I am, Laura, as I am, at last.

It's only because I knew you had got hold of something that I went on existing at all. If ever a wisp of happiness came to me, as it did so rarely, I'd think: I must be on the fringe of that secret wayfaring of Laura's! And, trying to get to the heart of it, not accepting it for its own sake, I'd analyse and analyse till I had ruined it, instead of giving myself up without question to what had come to me.

But I always hoped to come into my own some day, through you, as I have, as I have this night. For the first time I see life as life-size!

I've never cared about anything but you in all my life. Oh, how you always· did charm away my hushed hates!

Your lovers, mine, our friends, no one, no one has been as close to us as we are now to one another.

Do you suppose it will be good-bye for us when they hang me? By God, it will not. I shall go on—in you, my darling; in you—and beside you. For people who know life as we do can't die. The force of our perception—*that's* the BeyondLife! *That's* what immortality means. It's what those absurd old men of letters are always fumbling after, it's what they never find!"

Steve was smiling now, swift little pleasure smiles: he was decked to the last with some undefinable distinction.

"I shall always be with you now," he said," to remind you in case you forget—as though you would ever forget! Oh, how will you be able to bear it, Laura, when you can hardly bear your radiant life alone? How will you support this double acceptance of things, this *double aliveness,* this joyful me-in-you?

How now does it seem that my life has been a staggering failure—a well choked with leaves! To have muddled through my miserable self-cheated days, to have wrought nothing but catastrophe everywhere, and the end—the brutal conclusion of the gallows—it must seem a fearful destiny. Ah no, it is only failure to those who do not understand real success. But *we* understand, *we* know where the bright water springs eternal; we know, my dearest girl, in what *splendour of triumph I shall go to the hangman.*

I've got my hands in your hair, and I'm kissing you right through to your life—with my life. I am a criminal. I am also somebody splendid and new, and very very strange!"

The door-bell rang. We let it ring twice more, then together we went to open it as though we were not expecting those who had come and, indeed, they had lost their horror for us. Everything had lost its horror—the parting, the prison for one whom nothing now could bind, the trial for one who had already been tried and emerged triumphant, the deaths we were soon to die by hanging and by disease.

In that moment we carried to its ultimate conclusion the triumph of life over every obstacle, even the grave. Death would not be death for us. Changed we might be, it would not matter, for we were "ready to be anything in the ecstasy of being ever!"